HAUNTED MOON

/ / / /

J.R. RAIN
&
MATTHEW S. COX

SAMANTHA MOON ORIGINS

New Moon Rising
Moon Mourning
Haunted Moon

Published by
Crop Circle Books
212 Third Crater, Moon

Printed in the United States of America.

ISBN- 9781080807727

Chapter One
Off With Her Head

Deeper and deeper down the rabbit hole, I go. Is there a bottom? Nobody knows.

In the midst of reading a Disney children's book of *Alice in Wonderland* to Tammy and Anthony before bedtime, I find myself pausing and staring at an illustration of the little blonde girl in the blue dress tumbling down a dirt shaft. Her 'oh dear what have I done' expression is way understated for a plummet into a bottomless pit.

I know how you feel, kid.

Much like Alice, it sure seems as though my life is hurtling toward a vast, scary unknown and the walls are too smooth to grab on and stop my fall. As unbelievable as it sounds, I've apparently become a vampire. My reflection no longer shows up in mirrors and whenever the kids finish a bottle of milk, the empty winds up in a second refrigerator in our detached garage filled with blood. Danny represented a guy named Jaroslaw, a butcher originally from Poland, in a case awhile back. Evidently, they won big enough that he's indebted to my husband and has agreed to provide a steady supply of cow and pig blood. He thinks we're using it for some weird gardening project. Or at least that's the surface story. Most likely, the butcher thinks we're doing something really strange, but people from the Old Country are masters at minding their own business.

Danny suggested we put the blood in small packets, like the ones they use at blood banks. Not sure why since it seems like it would be a lot of work to transfer blood into them out of the huge jugs of it the butcher gives us. I suppose it might make it easier to ration it out in portions, but wouldn't someone somewhere start noticing it if we're buying medical supplies like that routinely? That's not exactly normal. Anyway, I'll worry about that later. For now, the milk bottles do the trick.

I'd been almost certain my days as a federal agent working for HUD would've ended when I got suspended-with-pay pending an investigation into my going full Rambo to bring down a group of small-time arms dealers who put my partner Chad in the hospital with a gunshot wound. Apparently, Fate has a weird sense of humor. Or irony. Or cruelty. Exactly which one it is, I'm not sure yet. A week shy of two months after I walked out of Nico Fortunato's office for what I'd thought would be the last time, he called to tell me the investigation cleared me and he wanted me to return to duty

ASAP.

My brain had been too numb in response to hearing that to think properly. I surrendered to emotion and told him yes. Within an hour of being off the phone, the feeling of elation crashed and burned. The best way I can think of to describe it is being obligated to be the maid of honor at the wedding of a distant relative who is a complete bridezilla nightmare... only to find out that her mother demanded someone else be the maid of honor and let me off the hook. And right as I start to feel the relief of escaping a horrible situation, another call comes in and tells me I'm the maid of honor after all.

Right. Aargh.

Don't get me wrong. I love—perhaps *loved* would be more accurate—my job. Becoming a federal agent had been my dream ever since the summer between high school and college. Frustratingly enough, exactly *why* that became my obsession eludes me. But still, working as a government agent had been my ultimate goal. Granted, joining HUD had been unexpected—as opposed to like the FBI or something—but it worked out. However, despite busting my backside for so long to achieve my dream, my present circumstances make it dangerous. Not really for me as much as for my partner Chad and any civilians who happen to be too close to a bad situation.

See, the problem is entirely that damn vampire thing. My body does *not* like functioning during the day. The earlier it is, the more sluggish and disoriented my head is. My response time is in the toilet. If it's too bright, I can barely see a thing, and if it's too early, frequent blackouts hit me. All of that would be plenty annoying for an ordinary office job, but it's another whole level of bad when my job involves dangerous situations with guns and people breaking the law.

Oh, and there's also that whole spontaneous combustion when exposed to sunlight deal. Massive amounts of strong sunblock and modest clothes actually help with that to a point, but a constant burning like I'm being microwaved is another nail in the coffin of my ability to concentrate on anything but wanting to run to the nearest shade.

If any chance existed for an entirely after-dark shift, that would have been absolutely perfect for me. At night, things are the exact opposite. My senses are ridiculously keen and I'm stronger than a pro—male—weightlifter. Not to mention even a bullet to the heart doesn't slow me down. Pinches a little, but the worst thing about it is ruining a top.

So, yeah, at night? I'm like supercop or something. Problem being, HUD's kind of a nine-to-five sort of deal. Well, more like an eight-to-four. People don't appreciate random property inspections at two in the morning. I know right? The nerve. Lots of agents think of HUD as some kind of ideal paradise: day hours, mostly boring office work, and infrequent situations that can kill you.

What they don't tell you is that we get tapped all

the time by the FBI or other agencies as extra bodies, usually on raids. Sometimes they'll throw us some grunt work that none of the other agents want to do. Despite that—and despite my husband Danny's constant worry about me getting hurt—I *loved* my job. Even an eight-hour day crunching Excel spreadsheets felt like paradise.

Wow, maybe I am crazy after all.

Alas, I've mostly abandoned any hope that the vampire stuff is just a product of my imagination while I lay semi-comatose in the hospital after a brutal mugging.

(Or in a padded cell somewhere, which is still a distinct possibility.)

I *should* have resigned, but the unexpectedly "good news" caught me off guard. As soon as Nico's voice came over the phone, my heart braced for him to drop the bomb about me having to choose between resignation or termination. Figure he'd have at least given me that option because he liked me, and he knows why I went after that compound: they'd hurt Chad. He *doesn't* know that the risk to my life had been almost nothing. No way in hell would a bunch of moonshine-blind rubes trafficking in unregistered military-grade weapons just happen to have silver daggers... let alone silver bullets.

However, to anyone sane who doesn't believe in vampires, my going alone into a heavily armed compound like that had to call into question my judgement and/or sanity. The agency psychologist started our interview assuming my partner died and I'd gone in there expecting to go down in a hail of bullets. I managed to change his mind about my being suicidal, and he kinda bought my reasoning that my training and caution was more than a match for a bunch of guys who'd ordinarily be hanging out at a mechanic's garage drinking beer. My intent going there hadn't been to kick off a small war, just arrest one suspect... but things happened.

How I managed to convince the psychologist of this, I still didn't know, but he seemed almost... giddy to go along with me. Did vamps have some sort of power of persuasion or something? I mean, could I change minds? I didn't know. Truthfully, I didn't want to know. Who wants that kind of control? Anyway, as a result of that interview, they apparently gave Nico the green light to reinstate me.

Yeah, I'm weak—still haven't called him back to say no. My hope is that I can talk him into giving me mostly desk duty due to my 'xeroderma pigmentosum.' Danny found that online. It's a disease that causes extreme sunlight sensitivity. Perhaps as good an excuse as possible. Had the existence of *actual* vampires not been revealed to me via becoming one, I'd have assumed the legends and myths got started because of someone suffering that disease—or porphyria. I'd be happy enough to still be officially an agent even if my job became little more than an armed office clerk. It was never about glory at all.

"What's wrong, Mommy?" asks Tammy. Despite my arm being cold to the touch, she clings tightly to it.

"Nothing, sweetie. Sorry. My thoughts ran off."

She grins. "Did you catch them?"

"Yes." I wink at her, and resume reading to her.

My daughter likes this crazy story. Admittedly, it's unnerving to hear her yell 'off with her head' when the Red Queen shows up.

Anthony, on my right side, has already fallen asleep. Rather than accuse me of being boring, it reassures me that he feels safe in my presence. The kids both seem aware that Mommy has changed somehow. It's doubtful they understand exactly *what* happened, but they've both looked at me in odd ways several times since *that night*. Tammy decided within minutes that it didn't bother her, but Anthony had been standoffish for a while, looking at me like he didn't quite trust me. Eventually, he got over it. Having him fall asleep leaning on me gives me hope that my family might just make this work.

No sooner do I say the words 'the end,' than Danny whisks in and scoops Anthony up to carry him across the hall to his bedroom. More and more lately, my hubby's been failing to hide his nervousness around me. It's almost as if he's afraid to leave the kids alone with me. So far, I've let it go since neither of us really know all that much about vampires or how possible it is that I might lose control. My gut tells me that unless I'm starving for blood, there's little chance of me losing control.

And, if we *did* run out of blood, I would absolutely resort to biting total—adult—strangers before touching my family. Though, breaking into a hospital or some such place and stealing donated blood is far more preferable an option. And yes, the thought of biting people makes my skin crawl the way most people would react to the idea of putting escargot on pizza. Or eating escargot at all.

Then again, the instant I think for a half second my presence here endangers my children, it's 'fling myself into the sun' time. There is *something* inside me, some other presence taking up space in my head that doesn't belong there. What—or whoever —it is, I'm not entirely certain yet. It could be a demon, a malign spirit, even a dark reflection of my own personality given awareness due to vampirism. Numerous people have accused me of being 'too sweet' over the course of my life. (Don't tell anyone, but as a child, I believed in faeries. Around nine or so, one of them might've even appeared to me—but in the hindsight of age, it was probably the product of an overactive imagination.) Anyway, could be that whatever darkness is associated with this unbelievable circumstance that's befallen me has created an anti-Sam inside my head made up of all the cruelty and avarice missing from my soul.

Sometimes, when it's completely silent, it's almost like a voice is trying to whisper to me. In a bid not to admit to myself that I may have also cracked and gone legit insane in addition to becoming a vampire, I've been ignoring that voice as much as humanly (or inhumanly) possible. The stuff it says scares me, so it gets the mute button.

After tucking Tammy in and kissing her on the head, I sneak out of her room and pull the door nearly closed. Danny's scent and heartbeat fill the air behind me, so it doesn't make me startle-jump when I turn and find him almost close enough to kiss me.

"So you're really going back?" asks Danny. He already knows why I blurted yes to my boss. He's merely surprised I haven't changed my mind in the week since the call.

I look down. "Yeah. And yes, I know it's not a wonderful idea."

He chuckles. "'Not wonderful'… maybe you're the one who should've been a lawyer."

"Right?" A smile nearly forms on my lips, but something in the way he's looking at me prevents any mirth.

For most of the time I've worked for HUD, Danny has been unhappy about it. Mostly, he doesn't want me to get hurt. He'd nearly come unglued when I took a bullet in a drug raid. But neither one of us ever expected my untimely death would've happened so close to home—and completely unconnected to my work for the government. Hell, I could've worked the bunny rabbit exhibit for the local zoo and *still* gotten attacked that night.

But now? He's almost amused at the idea of me going back. It feels as though he's looking at his too-drunk-to-drive ex-wife getting behind the wheel and saying 'try not to kill too many people on your way home.' Like he's hoping the next screw up gets rid of me for good.

That can't be Danny, not the man to whom I gave my heart. He should be afraid of me hurting other people. Hell, *I* should be worried about me hurting other people. For me, this is such a classic example of hubris. All those marathon study sessions, late nights, grueling physical courses, tests, qualifications… when it all came down to that three-second moment on the phone with the boss, I chickened out and couldn't walk away from everything. I'd put too much into this, wanted it for too long. I had to find a way to make the day job work.

I had to.

"I'd say you should probably go to bed early so you can get up on time, but…" He wags his eyebrows at me.

"Funny," I mutter. No amount of wanting or exhaustion could possibly let me fall asleep before sunrise. "I wish."

"Me, too." He regards me with a mixture of fear, contempt, and longing. "I'm not giving up yet. If there's any way to fix this, I'll find it."

"Thanks," I whisper.

Except his actions say otherwise. We don't touch each other. No hand holding, no face caress. None of that happens anymore. We act more like platonic roommates who share the same bed. Since my change, the few times we'd attempted to get romantic, Danny invariably lost interest as soon as he touched my cold skin. Suppose all those vampire movies and novels are wrong about the whole 'vampires are a sex symbol' thing. How can any guy get it up when the girl's ice cold? Though to be fair, if it had happened to Danny instead, my reaction to his parts being chilly would probably have been about the same.

As we've done more often than not lately after the kids go to bed, we relocate to the living room and sorta-watch television. He's taken to picking the show or movie without asking me what I think. If I complain about whatever he puts on, he'll usually change it, but it's hardly worth the five minutes of going back and forth to convince him why I don't want to watch it. So, whenever he puts on something I can't stand, it's Danielle Steel time. Sadly, we aren't *together* as much as we both happen to be in the same room.

And yeah, that's killing me inside.

Maybe I should be more assertive, call him out on this BS he's pulling. Mostly, I think it's my fault for being an idiot and going jogging at night. Nothing that happened to me is Danny's doing. He's not the one who ended up dead and changed into something that shouldn't exist. He's the one who has to share a house with what I've become. Maybe by sitting back and playing the part of the demure wife, I'm secretly hoping he'll be reason-able and not grab the kids in the day and run off somewhere when I'm helpless to do anything about it. Then again, he hasn't said or done anything to imply a deliberate intent to use the kids as a weapon to control me, but it still feels that way even if it's entirely a creation of my brain.

His constant digs about keeping the kids safe aren't as thinly veiled as he thinks they are.

Eventually, Danny decides it's time for bed. He tosses the remote to me, spends all of ten minutes rambling about how much he hates the case he's working on—defending a guy accused of running an illegal brothel out of a dance club—then heads off down the hall. I'm not sure if it's sad or humorous to hear him call the place a 'dance' club. The only ones doing any dancing there are women without much clothing on. Before the attack, my Danny would never have gotten involved with a client that filthy.

What's going on? Why the change in him too? It's as if the darkness in me is bringing the darkness out of him, too.

I spend the remaining hours while awake alone at night staring into space, trying to figure out what the heck is wrong with me.

No, not the undead part—the not saying no to Nico part.

When I am done beating myself up, I remind myself that I never asked for this, that I'm doing the best I can in a difficult situation, and that maybe, just maybe, I will finally wake up from this nightmare.

Chapter Two
Short Notice

Alarm clocks are the work of the Devil himself.

Well, at least the tools of a demon working for him. The Devil does grander things than make horrible appliances. The whole nine-to-five day job deal is probably his work. I'm only half kidding about that anymore. Religion didn't register to me for much of my life. My mother believes in 'vibes' or spiritual energy, nature stuff or some such thing like that. Dad believes in weed, LSD, and beer. If he has feelings on religion one way or the other, he's never mentioned them around me.

Danny's parents are pretty into it. In fact, they're *so* into it they managed to turn him against religion of any kind. Being an analytical sort of person myself, I never took it seriously since some things didn't make sense.

But... vampires don't make sense either.

A year ago, if I met someone who honestly believed vampires to be real, I'd have politely chuckled and backed away slowly, thinking them nuts. After learning the hard way what I thought to be myths were real, it's made me question all sorts of things about the universe. There probably is some sort of divinity out there or up there depending on how one wants to look at it. I'd ask why such a god would allow vampires to exist, but maybe this is what I get for doubting.

Apparently, he's not too forgiving. At least, visiting two churches, a mosque, synagogue, and even a Buddhist temple failed to change me back to normal. Guess he didn't find my 'message received, please put me back to normal and I'll go to church every Sunday' offer sincere enough.

Or maybe none of us 'down here' really understand what's going on 'out there.'

They say he's 'got a plan.' I suppose that plan includes *moi* as a vampire. Anyway, if He exists, the Devil must, too. That whole equal and opposite reaction thing, right? And come to think of it, the Devil definitely made alarm clocks—or at least set in motion a chain of events that required their creation. I've never been a morning person, but the grumpy little girl that Mary Lou used to have to literally drag out of bed in the mornings has nothing on 'Vampire Sam.' My body does *not* like being conscious during the day. Even with an epic amount of sunscreen or staying indoors, I'm sluggish and groggy. It's honestly amazing that Nico hasn't called me into his office to have a chat about me seeming drunk or sleep deprived.

I'd been back at work now for two weeks since coming back from the suspension. Two weeks of hell, if you want to know the truth.

So far, the earliest I've been able to wake up has been a little after 9:30 a.m. Somehow, the boss hasn't made any issue of that yet. It could be my subconscious trying to save me from causing other people to get hurt by doing things to get me fired—such as being late every day since starting work again. Danny managed to get a doctor he defended in a lawsuit to give me some documentation about that xeroderma pigmentosum condition I 'have,' claiming it affects my circadian rhythm and makes it impossible for me to wake up earlier than a certain time. That gets me wondering exactly what sort of dirt my husband has on the guy that he signed paperwork without even seeing me once. Stuff like that can cost a doctor their medical license. Then again, it seems the only time anyone cares about doctors doing shady things is if an insurance company is losing money. Giving me permission to be chronically late for work, not so much.

So, at least until some government doctor wants to examine me to verify that diagnosis, I won't get fired for being late. Fortunately, the two weeks since I've been reinstated have been highly tame, almost all paperwork and uneventful inspections. The most exciting thing to happen thus far was my walking in the door of a property and scaring a shih tzu so bad it literally crapped the rug where it stood. Yeah, I have that effect on some pets. Awesome. Predictably, Chad calls it a 'shit-zoo' now. Speaking of my partner, he's recovered from a bullet perforating his left lung, and is only coughing a little these days. It's going to be sore for months yet, but it doesn't appear to have slowed him down. Tough guy.

We used to be Nico's youngest, 'readiest' team, but now we're kinda the gimp squad. He's hurt and I'm stuck in a perpetual state of grogginess. Maybe that explains the easy two weeks. Of course the guys and gals in the department—in particular, Ernie, Michelle, and Bryce—gave me a whole heap of back-pats for my raid on those arms dealers. Officially, they're not allowed to condone my 'avenging Chad,' but… they had cake to welcome me back. Cake I couldn't eat, but faking it worked.

Another thing that surprises me is how he doesn't blame me at all for his being shot. He thought he saw me take a bullet to the heart, but I've convinced him the guy missed. It hadn't been a difficult bit of convincing. Obviously, had he shot me in the chest, I'd be dead.

The third Tuesday after going back to work starts with Nico calling us to his office.

My initial reaction is to expect the hammer to drop—being fired. That's my new most hated thing in the world, the feeling that every day I go to work is going to be the last day. It's honestly sucking all the joy out of the job that once meant everything to me. Every time eye contact with Nico happens, I flinch, expecting bad news. It's gotten to the point of me trying to avoid him.

Only one explanation makes sense for how they've put up with me stumbling around the office for two weeks: pity. Though, maybe I'm exaggerating how bad my being awake early affects me. While I *feel* like a damned zombie, maybe my body is merely 'normal,' as opposed to being superhuman at night... which I've kinda gotten used to.

I mean, Nico wouldn't keep someone around who appeared to be staggering drunk all the time, right? So, hmm. Maybe I look and act more normal than I think?

Maybe.

Without a word, we get up from our desks and head down the aisle to the boss' office. I go in bracing for bad news, but the look on his face shifts dread to a combination of relief and worry. That's not the 'you're fired' expression, it's the 'you're being loaned out' expression.

"Helling, Moon," says Nico, gesturing at the chairs facing his desk. "Got a call from the Marshals Service looking for an assist. I realize this is short notice, but... you two are currently the proud owners of the quietest case log in the office. That puts you at the top of the list for side projects."

Chad laughs. "No problem. Please tell me it's in Hawaii? I need some sun."

I fidget. If anything like that happens, there

won't be any choice for me but to step down. California's bad enough, but Hawaii or Miami? I'd go up in flames.

Nico smiles. "Will you take a rain check? Literally, rain. As in London."

"Umm, what?" I ask, filled with a sudden irrational aversion to having an entire ocean separating me from my kids. "London? Are you serious?"

"Quite. But not for very long." He leans back in his chair, lacing his fingers together in his lap. "The Marshals Service needs to extradite a foreign national to London to face trial related to suspected activities with the IRA. Apparently, the Brits want the guy yesterday and the USM doesn't have anyone available. Plan is for you two to pick the prisoner up at the US Marshals Office in L.A., drive him to LAX, and fly with him to Heathrow. There will be a delegation from the Metropolitan Police Force there to meet you and take custody."

Chad whistles. "That's going to be a long ride. When is it?"

"Thursday," says Nico. "Sorry to only give you two days' notice, but this kinda cropped up at the last minute. It's a ten-hour flight one way. You'll be dropping the suspect off and re-boarding another flight within a few hours to come back."

"Ouch," I mutter.

"Yeah, still less painful than dealing with the METRO Police to secure your firearms after the drop off. Which is why you won't be leaving the airport or getting a hotel room for the night." Nico chuckles. "Brits are a little funny about us running around London armed."

"Most of their cops don't even carry weapons." Chad snickers.

"Right, so we go right back on another plane." I shrug. "Okay, that doesn't sound too bad. At least we can sleep on the return flight."

Chad rubs his forehead. "My bio clock is going to explode. What time are we flying out?"

"You'll be picking the suspect up at 10:00 a.m." Nico looks at his computer screen. "Plane leaves at 11:00 a.m. Thursday, but you'll arrive in Heathrow at 5:00 a.m. Friday, their time. Your return flight is departing Heathrow at 8:00 a.m., landing at LAX at 10:00 a.m., Friday—ten hours later."

Chad shrugs, wincing slightly. "No issues here. I'd rather go back and forth right away than deal with a hotel anyway."

"Moon?" asks Nico.

My rational brain wants to say this is an awful idea and look for a way out... but my mouth has other plans. It's listening to my stupid heart and how much I want this job. "Yeah, sure. Sounds doable. My sister will help with the kids."

"Great. I'll let them know we're good to go then." Nico nods at us. "Any questions?"

"How bad a dude is this?" asks Chad.

"The suspect, Callum MacLeod, is believed to have connections with the Irish Republican Army." Nico gives us a flat look. "Yes, I know his name sounds Scottish, but I hear they're not too fond of

England either. According to what the Marshals Service sent over, he'd come to the US to solicit financial and other material support… weapons, explosives, that sort of thing for his people over there."

About what I expected. We nod.

The whole walk back to my desk, my mental voice is dropping F-bombs. Not exactly sure why, but this sounds like a fabulously bad idea. Upon reaching my desk, I grasp the cubicle wall and peer back down the aisle at Nico's door. My daydream self walks back into the boss' office, sits down, and resigns before I get someone hurt.

Stop being a chicken, Sam. It's only a taxi ride. Just going to be sitting bored for twenty hours in a plane as opposed to staring at spreadsheets in the office.

I sigh at the scattered scraps of my confidence lying on the rug around me. Head spinning, I gather them up, flop in my chair and try knitting them back together into something resembling the person I used to be.

Chapter Three
Power Nap

Danny took word of my assignment in stride.

If he harbored any secret hope that I'd walk out the door Thursday morning, fly to London, and never come back, it didn't show on his face. Meanwhile, a building sense of dread shadowed me all day Wednesday, even though nothing happened more dangerous than a two-hour refresher certification training for carrying weapons on aircraft.

We'd taken it once already soon after being assigned to HUD, but that had been a few years ago. As a federal agent flying in an official capacity—in this case, a prisoner escort—we're allowed to carry a weapon onto the plane. If we were flying to London on vacation, we couldn't be armed.

After work on Wednesday, I spent as much time as possible with the kids since I'll basically be gone for an entire day. Danny's up to his eyebrows in work at the moment, so we arranged with Mary Lou for the kids to sleep over at her house Thursday night. She's going to pick them up from school, keep them overnight, and bring them to school Friday morning. I'll be home in plenty of time to pick them up Friday afternoon—though whether or not I'm in any shape to drive is another question.

The real thing worrying me is the sun. This flight is going to completely screw with me. On the way *to* London, time will be passing faster than normal due to our flying east across time zones. What will be nine at night here in Fullerton will be five in the morning the next day over there, pretty much inches away from sunrise. A real chance exists that I might turn into a mannequin in front of British police. For a brief moment, the idea of telling Chad the truth about my 'condition' seems reasonable, but nah. There's no telling how he'd react to that. Theoretically, he could completely freak out and run away screaming. Though as close as we've become—almost like siblings—that reaction feels like a highly remote chance, but it's still a chance.

Besides, I just couldn't do that to him. After all, once my brain accepted that supernatural crap really existed, the world changed—nothing feels sane or normal. It's almost like maturing out of a second childhood and finding the world you'd grown comfortable with is a *lot* scarier than you thought. No amount of wanting to go back to my prior ignorance will change that, but the least I can do is spare Chad and protect his security of thinking he knows how the world works.

So, to explain my anxiety, I concoct some cockamamie story about a mental block I've had from childhood that makes it difficult for me to stay awake when the sun comes up. On our lunch break, Wednesday, I make sure Chad knows that my 'disease' has made this situation worse and there's a strong possibility of me involuntarily blacking out at sunrise while we're in London and he shouldn't panic. Just stick me in a seat and wait with me for our boarding call.

The sun is going to be a constant pain in my backside on the return flight. We'll be leaving at eight in the morning as far as London is concerned, landing two hours later due to the miracle of time zones after spending ten hours in the sky. I warn Chad that my butt will most likely spend the entire return flight asleep, and he can totally have the window seat.

All in all, the worst part of the plan is going to be Thursday morning, trying to force myself awake early enough to even make it to the US Marshals Service facility for the prisoner pickup at 10:00 a.m. Granted, if we're a couple minutes late, it won't matter *too* much. Not like they're going to call the whole transfer off if we arrive at 10:01 a.m.

In the wee hours of Thursday morning, I lay down on my bed only due to knowing the sun *will* knock me out when it rises. Better to be lying down than standing, as I'd learned once or twice during all of this. Danny, as usual, is scooched all the way over on his side. It should probably please me that I've got most of the bed to myself, but it feels like he's turning his back on me more than literally.

Before the sun takes me into the non-space of vampiric sleep, I chant over and over again to myself about the need to wake up early. Mind over matter, and all that. At least some parts of the vampire myth are just that: myth. We're not *forced* to stay asleep until the sun is all the way down, my body merely *wants to* the way Anthony wants cookies. Nor do we flash-burn to ashes in an instant when exposed to sun. That's more of a several-minute-long agonizing process. At least, if nearly losing my fingers a few times demonstrated a consistent burn rate.

It really is kinda funny in a way that sunblock works. Feels wrong somehow, like mixing science and magic.

And as soon as the sun appears, I'm out like a light...

***

With an extreme amount of effort, I force my butt out of bed when the alarm goes off at two minutes past nine after only a few hours of sleep, the earliest I've been awake in months.

It remains unclear to me how much my new vampire self *needs* sleep or if it's merely some sort of daylight-imposed off switch for 'reasons.' My job has resulted in me breaking the 'sleep during the day' rule so often it's become more of a 'suggested best practice' than a rule. Thus far, I haven't experienced any symptoms commonly associated with sleep deprivation despite spending only three-to-four hours a weekday 'sleeping.' Any normal person going on three weeks of such little sleep would be exhibiting a whole slew of strange mental effects.

I've found this aerosol sunblock stuff that's a lot easier to apply than cream, even if it leaves me smelling like coconuts. Danny's in the kitchen with the kids. It no longer weirds me out that I can smell their cereal from down the hall in the bedroom. I didn't even know cereal had a smell, but I guess it does. Anyway, for extra protection, I spray myself thoroughly with the sunblock stuff while nude, apply foundation makeup to my face and hands so I show up on cameras, then hurry into one of my official looking pantsuits with a white blouse, shoulder holster and matching blazer.

After a painfully quick goodbye hug with the kids, Danny and I exchange a 'be careful' nod... and I hurry out to the Momvan with a tiny meta-phorical stake stuck in my heart over my husband not even attempting to hug me farewell. If Mary Lou ever told me Rick acted like Danny is acting, I'd be telling her to get ready for a divorce.

But I have a powerful weapon in my arsenal: denial.

Nope. Not me. Danny's not going to divorce

me. He's just freaked out over this vampire business and trying to deal with it as best he can. How should I expect a man to react to something like this? Hell, it happened to me and even *I'm* freaked out. What appears to be glaring evidence of a disintegrating marriage is really the side effects of discovering that paranormal stuff like vampires exists for real.

So, yeah. My marriage is in decent shape all things considered? Right?

Crap. Can't start crying on the way to the office.

Instead of crying, I end up singing the jingle from *Barney & Friends*. Some people may say that becoming a vampire is a curse, but they'd be wrong. The *real* curse was having a toddler and a four-year-old who *both* adore that stupid purple dinosaur. We'd been trying to shield them from it, but they caught an episode at my sister's place and... doomed.

I'm sure Chad won't question my sanity if I stroll into the office singing that demonically infectious song. No, like a lame horse, he'll just solemnly walk me out back and put a bullet in my head. Or send me to a special care home for parents of kids who like *Barney*. There has to be a recovery facility for that, right?

My luck holds out this morning. I only have three near-miss traffic situations on the drive to the office and not one of them is seen by a cop. And sure, any other rational person who realizes they are having trouble staying awake to the point that they nearly crash three times driving to work would probably also think it a *severely* bad idea to run around with a loaded gun escorting prisoners on airplanes, right?

Hello, my name is Samantha Moon and I'm in denial.

Fortunately, the sluggishness keeps me from looking as nervous and rattled as I am. I mean, all of this is a bad idea, right? Surely, I should resign... like right now. At this very moment. Ugh.

Guilt mounts and mounts as I wait for Chad to finish sending off an email. When he stands, my drowsiness causes me to fail to speak up about this being a really bad idea. Like some kind of simple robot, I autopilot after him outside to the car. One second, I'm walking across the parking lot, the next thing I know, we're in the department sedan on the road. At least Chad's driving.

He hasn't commented about anything so far, so I must not *look* delirious. Unfortunately, it's not even ten yet and the sun is seriously angry today. Thankfully, this assignment is almost entirely indoors— either in a building or on a plane. The problem being... this is definitely the sort of sunny day that will make me literally smoke even with high-strength sunblock.

Like smoke... as in, cooking.

Right in front of people's faces.

Gah. No wonder my guts are in a ball of nerves.

We arrive at the US Marshals Service office in Los Angeles a few minutes early. Fortunately, we're picking Callum up at a secure entrance that's in an underground parking area behind a security checkpoint. As soon as Chad drives us out of direct sunlight, my grogginess fades somewhat. I no longer feel like I've stayed awake for thirty-six hours straight after a crazy sorority party where everyone got too stoned to stand up.

A handful of Marshals meet us by a door standing on either side of a man in his later-thirties or early forties wearing a cheap blue suit, handcuffs, and leg irons. His black hair's short and combed neat, though he doesn't seem thrilled to see us. Thankfully, he's also at least an inch shorter than Chad and noticeably less muscular. My partner's hobby of amateur MMA fighting has had a predictable effect on the size of his chest, arms, and legs. Chad's replaced his shirts at least three times over the past year.

We spend a few minutes on the transfer paperwork, shake the hands of the marshals, and approach Callum.

Rick handles the 'we know you don't want to be here either, so let's just deal with this and get it over with' speech. He and Callum waver before my eyes... then disappear. Before my surprise shows on my face, I realize they're already in the car and I was left standing alone. At least I didn't fall. Damn... a small blackout got me again.

Oh, boy. This is going to be a long, crappy day.

I hurry to the car and get in. As tempting as it is to catch a power nap on the drive to LAX, it's not going to take that long and it would absolutely not look professional on my part. The usual tricks to stay awake while tired won't help me as the heaviness pulling me down has nothing to do with literal fatigue. It's purely my body's reaction to daytime. Blasting the AC, keeping up a conversation about something interesting, or bouncing in the chair aren't going to matter. Only mental focus on remaining conscious works.

We arrive at the airport at 10:21 a.m. and take advantage of a parking area for official vehicles that's reasonably close to the terminal. Once we're inside, people end up staring at us, mostly Callum since he's in shackles. We've both got our IDs out clipped to our belts to display our badges. It's fairly obvious to anyone looking at us that we're cops of some sort escorting a prisoner. Everyone's probably trying to figure out who he is, what he did, and so on. Callum appears to be a charmer type. He reacts to the attention like a celebrity, waving, grinning, and winking at any woman he catches looking, even though they're not checking him out in that way. At least, I don't think they are.

A brief conversation with TSA and some badge waving gets us around the security checkpoint. Of course, they call in a supervisor who sucks up a few more minutes of our time before deciding we're legit. By the time we reach the terminal from which we'll board the flight to London, Chad's looking around like he's expecting snipers.

Within two minutes of us taking seats in the waiting area, he bounces up to his feet. "Be right back. Two large coffees want out, if you catch my drift."

"Oh brother," I say, trying to cling to my tattered consciousness. "Just hurry."

At least the giant window looking out over the tarmac is facing west. The sun isn't punching me in the face. Chad dashes off to the nearest men's room.

"How's your husband feel about you working with a man?" asks Callum in a deep brogue accent.

"Doesn't bother him."

"Nice. I hear some men can get jealous." He reclines in the chair as much as he can, smiling as if merely on a casual trip. "Been a marshal long?"

I glance sideways at him. "Long enough."

He stares deep into my eyes, then smiles. "This is all political, you know. The Crown's never been very keen on the notion of national sovereignty, nor the will of the people in Ireland and Scotland."

Okay, wow, I love how he pronounces 'Ireland' and 'Scotland.' *Ayre*land and *Scoot*land.

That said, I do my best to focus on him. "Can't say I've followed UK politics much, I'm afraid."

Callum proceeds to ramble about the political unrest, mostly of Northern Ireland. Despite his accent, the subject matter is dreadfully dry and he's got the same sort of toneless voice as a history teacher I had in high school. Between that and the weight of my eyelids, I know I am in trouble...

"Sam!" shouts Chad.

I snap awake.

Shit. Callum's gone.

The handcuffs he'd been wearing are presently tethering my left wrist to the metal bar supporting the row of seats I'm sitting in, themselves bolted to the floor. Empty leg irons lay on the cushion in the adjacent seat. Fortunately, the weight of my service weapon is still under my arm. Guess he didn't want to risk waking me up. Bad enough he got the handcuff key off me.

"I see him! Wait here!" Chad sprints off to my right, chasing Callum down the concourse.

"Well, duh," I say, rattling the chain at my wrist.

And like everyone's looking at us.

"I tried to wake you, miss," says an old lady to my right. "But you wouldn't move, and the man— he was terrible, threatening me..."

Dread that I've just screwed up fatally shocks me into full awareness. Fatal in the sense that my career probably just went down the toilet. Dammit! I never should've accepted reinstatement. I grab the steel around my wrist, snap it like a plastic toy, and leap up to chase the slippery son of a bitch.

At least I wore flats today.

Chapter Four
This Girl is On Fire

In a remarkably short time, the surge of wakefulness fades.

You know what's a really awful place to fall asleep? On my feet while running full speed down an airport concourse. One second I'm sprinting, then I'm sliding face first into someone's luggage. The alarmed traveler who belongs to said luggage, a fiftyish guy with a few extra pounds and a pear-shaped face, reaches to help me up.

"Are you all right, miss?" he asks, taking my hand.

"I've had better days." I flash the briefest of smiles and force myself to keep going.

Seriously, whoever designed vampires did *not* intend for us to operate during the day. Like, at all. My muscles are stiff and uncooperative, my vision oversaturated with too-intense light. Almost everywhere I look is painfully bright and washed out courtesy of the massive windows on both sides of the concourse. Still, I manage to spot my partner chasing Callum up ahead and try my damndest to stay focused.

"Federal agent, stop him!" shouts Chad while running past a trio of TSA employees who just stare at him like he's got blue skin.

Fortunately, while the sun makes consciousness miserable, I'm still a vampire even in daylight. Superhumanly strong muscles propel me up to a run beyond trained Olympic sprinters. Scary thing is, without the stiffness and disorientation of the sun affecting me, I'd be even faster. But, it's probably good that my speed's not maxed out right now. Someone watching me wouldn't realize I'm exceeding the limits of human physiology.

In six seconds, I've overtaken Chad. In ten, I'm closing in on Callum.

He shoves an airport employee out of his way and rams open the door behind where she'd been standing. The blast of direct sunlight in my face forces me to involuntarily slam on the brakes, hissing. Despite how much I loathe my fangs, they extend on their own in response to the blistering pain of sun on my face, but I get my arm up to hide my mouth before anyone can see.

Whatever's outside appears to surprise Callum as well, since he hesitates at the door. However, Chad barreling closer motivates him to jump. He vanishes into the blinding glow, and a soft *whump* echoes back a second or two later. Chad catches himself on the doorjamb, peering out. I get a brief glance before he, too, decides to jump. The shoved woman climbs back to her feet and dashes over to a podium, paging security.

The initial shock of daylight over, I power my way to the open door. Heat blows over me in waves. Moving toward the opening makes me feel like the witch in *Hansel & Gretel* going headfirst into a raging oven. Upon reaching the doorway, the featureless white glow of the outside world grad- ually resolves to a sun-beaten tarmac littered with baggage trucks, carts, other unfamiliar vehicles, and airplanes. Callum's hesitation makes sense now. It's about a fifteen-foot drop to the ground level from this doorway, which is clearly intended to be used with a boarding tunnel that's been shifted over to the adjacent terminal.

Below me, Chad rolls off a cart full of luggage. Callum's a fast-distancing dark spot on the other- wise blurry-white field of concrete. My vampiric nature pulls back, fighting my very real desire to chase our prisoner. I clench my jaw with the resolve of a virgin sacrifice duty-bound to throw herself into a volcano out of fear her entire village will be destroyed otherwise.

Somehow, I overpower the thing I've become.

No idea if sleep got me again for a second or if this blackout came from panic, since I go from standing in the doorway to flat on my back atop a luggage cart in an instant. Now, I feel like a piece of bacon in a frying pan. Smoke peels off my front, even places covered by clothing.

Panic has a similar effect on vampire muscles as it does to human ones. My attempt to shove myself upright launches me into the air. For one tiny second, I'm awestruck at my ability to fly until realization hits me that I'm not flying—my body threw itself. My landing isn't *too* clumsy, though the hazy overly bright blur of the tarmac everywhere around me is disorienting as hell. Still, I'm on my feet and that's saying something.

Meanwhile, Chad and Callum are engaged in a wrestling match a good distance ahead of me near another baggage transport. They spill over a cart in an avalanche of luggage, rolling to the ground on the other side. Callum scrambles to his feet and tries to run, but my partner's on him fast, grabbing him from behind in a bear hug. There's no way in hell the smaller guy is going to get away from Chad… or so I think. Right as I start to allow myself to slow from a sprint to a jog, thinking we got him, Callum steps up on the cart like one of those 'walking up the wall' tricks, shoving them both over backward to the ground. He somersaults over Chad's face and avoids a grab for the ankle before dashing off over the tarmac.

Son of a…

Ignoring the searing pain all over me—worse on my face and hands—I run after him, leaning down to drag Chad to his feet with one arm on my way past him. We weave around other baggage carts, a few small tractors, a truck with a stairway on the back end, and several large cargo boxes before going straight under an idling jetliner.

Withering daylight has me in so much pain my speed isn't much faster than a normal person. Maybe I should stop concentrating on *not* screaming... and just let it out. The mental effort to remain stoic on the outside could be costing me a few MPH.

Callum runs down a taxiway straight onto a runway, crossing it mere seconds before a giant FedEx plane touches down not even a hundred yards away. Chad and I eat the jetwash, but it's not strong enough to sweep us off our feet. Paving, dirt, and more paving goes by. Heedless of the danger, Callum runs out under a taxiing 747, dodging the nose wheel and narrowly avoiding being run over by one set of rear tires.

Not trusting my navigation skills, I let the plane and its huge tires go by before continuing the chase.

At least, after that runway, only open concrete separates us from a giant chain-link fence topped with coils of razor wire. Callum jumps at it and starts climbing, but Chad—who's pulled a little ahead of me due to the stupid sun—crashes into him and drags him back down.

The guy whirls and slugs Chad right in the jaw, though the hit doesn't appear to faze my partner. Chad simultaneously shakes it off and punches Callum in the gut, lifting the Scotsman off his feet and forcing a wheezy breath out of him. Upon landing, Callum attempts to run to the right along the fence, but I zip in front of him to block.

He crashes into me like a football linebacker, trying to slam me off my feet... and emits a bark like a punted goose when I stop him cold. Well, mostly cold. A little sliding happened since I don't weigh that much. My dangerous mixture of agony and anger lashes out in the form of me hauling him around and shoving him face first into the fence with all the finesse of a beat cop throwing a suspect at a wall for frisking. His head bounces off a steel pole, making a hollow bell-like *clang*, and he crumples to the concrete, mostly unconscious.

Oops.

Chad pounces on the stunned man, securing him in handcuffs. I stand there shaking from pain, clenching my hands in fists and releasing them over and over in a repetitive de-stressing maneuver. Faint wisps of smoke coil around my arms. Lucky for me, the spray sunblock is in my pocket. While Chad's distracted with the prisoner, I re-coat my hands and face.

"Holy crap, Sam. What the hell was that?" asks Chad, dragging Callum upright.

The guy's still out of it, wobbling on his feet. Damn. That lump on his forehead is pretty big. Someone's going to ask about that.

"You mean throwing him? I dunno. Adrenaline? Not really sure how I tossed him like that."

Chad gives me side eye. "That, too, but I meant how the heck did he get away from you?"

I grab Callum's left arm at the elbow, helping drag the guy back toward the terminal. Two LAPD cars race toward us across the tarmac. "It's complicated. I'm sorry. Never should've let Nico reinstate me. Whatever's going on with my health is kinda like narcolepsy, but only early in the day. After like three or four, it stops."

"Sam…" He looks at me like I'd just told him I have terminal cancer. "Narcolepsy? That's a disqualifying condition."

"It's not exactly that. Just kinda like it."

He sniffs. "Is something burning?"

Other than my lifelong dream? "Smells like tires from the runways. They briefly catch fire at the moment of touchdown."

"Umm. Yeah." He peers around the still-dazed Callum and looks at me. Fairly obvious he doesn't quite believe me. "Wow. You weren't kidding when you told Fortunato about having a sun allergy."

The stink of burning flesh hangs in the air on the smoke still leaking out of my pant legs. Fair bet my face and hands are at least sunburn red if not worse. Probably looks like I went to the Chernobyl tanning salon.

"I'll be okay once we're inside. It usually clears up in a few minutes."

With that, we get moving.

And yeah, I keep a fast pace.

Damn sun.

Chapter Five
Aisle Seat

Once the cops realize we are federal agents escorting a prisoner and not crazy people, they help us bring Callum inside and back to the terminal.

One cop who moonlights as an EMT checks the guy's forehead over and says he's probably got a mild concussion but doesn't think it's anything that can't wait for London. I must look like hell because he makes to check me out too, but I wave him away. Last thing I need is a once-over by a para-medic.

With four minutes to spare until our flight boards, we again arrive in the waiting area for the terminal. By some miracle, no one stole or messed with the leg irons, so Chad puts them back on Callum and drops the guy a little ungently into a seat. Almost everyone in the terminal area stares at us like minor celebrities. The traumatized older lady has moved to another seat. I don't blame her.

I stare down at my shoes, beating myself up mentally for putting Chad's life at risk, as well as anyone else around me who Callum might have hurt. My body shut down to sleep against my will. He could've easily taken my gun and done who-knows-what with it. We lucked out that it had only been a dash across the tarmac. Well, lucky for the rest of the airport. For me, it might as well have been a dash through the streets of Hell. That said, we could've had a hostage standoff, dead civilians, or even a hijacked plane.

All because of little ol' me.

And the thing I'd become.

So, yeah. These next twenty hours of flying to London and back are going to be my last twenty hours as a federal agent. I'd say 'better enjoy it while it lasts,' but enjoying anything at the moment is out of the question. This is going to be the first and only time in my life I can bring a gun onto an airplane. Once Nico gets wind of us nearly losing this guy, mostly the specifics of *how* it happened, I'll have better chances of pulling a magical sword out of thin air than ever walking onto a 747 armed again.

"So, what do you want to do here?" asks Chad. "Drag this guy back to the Marshals and add on some charges for attempted escape, or just keep going like it didn't happen?"

"It happened. I'm not going to ask you to lie about that. But, we're already here. Plane's boarding in a minute or two. Personally, I'd just as soon get this guy out of the country and let him be the Brits' problem."

Chad nods... but still looks unsettled. I don't blame him. How I know this, I don't know, but I suspect he's seriously questioning whether or not he can continue being my partner. I mean, all the guy did was go to the john, and the next thing he knows he's jumping fifteen feet out of a doorway and wrestling with a known criminal across the tarmac. "Yeah. I'd rather not deal with the paperwork either."

We remain quiet for the short time it takes the airline to announce boarding. Callum's still shaky on his feet, though I'm not entirely sure if he's faking it. He evidently noticed me having trouble keeping my eyes open before and hit me with an exceedingly boring story, trying to lull me to sleep. Wouldn't put it past him to overact being delirious so we let our guard down again and give him another chance to make a run for it.

Our seats are all the way in the back near the bathrooms. We stick Callum in the window seat with Chad next to him and me on the aisle. Grogginess hits me within minutes of sitting down, despite the airplane shielding me from direct sunlight. The people in the rows ahead of us whisper amongst themselves, asking what's burning. One man with a British accent suggests it's the in-flight meal and then proceeds to complain about American food.

I nearly chuckle. Something American burned,

but it wasn't food.

Chuckling, of course, would take too much energy.

Chad keeps looking at me, specifically the backs of my hands which are somewhere between pizza and spam. I hate the visual—and painful—reminder of becoming a monster. Only lacking the energy to move keeps me from tucking my hands away. I'm vaguely aware of the aircraft lurching forward before the sickly smell of crummy airplane lasagna coming out of nowhere makes me realize I'd passed out again.

Crap!

I sit up abruptly enough to make Chad jump, but my initial panic fades upon seeing Callum where he belongs, a small ice pack pressed to his forehead. All three tray tables are down, my plate's the only one with anything left on it. At least my hands are back to normal.

"You okay, Sam?" Chad looks me over. "You zonked pretty hard there for a while."

The sky visible in the window past Callum isn't quite dark yet, but it's well on the way, enough that my body is no longer protesting being awake at all. It's so damn nice to *not* feel like I'm roasting alive.

"Fine now, yeah." I eye the faux lasagna. This is a ten-hour one-way flight. If I don't eat this, Chad's going to *know* there's something very wrong with me. It bothers me on a deep level to lie to my partner, but how can I admit to being something that isn't supposed to exist. Sure, I could show him the fangs, and he probably already suspects something weird went on with my unusual display of strength throwing Callum around like a rag doll. But, for one thing, *I* hate having fangs and don't want to acknowledge them. And for another thing, inflicting the truth about vampires and other crap on him isn't fair. What right do I have to completely break someone's worldview?

This is going to suck. Or, should I say, blow. As in blow chunks.

Can't do the spit into a cup thing here, so my only option is to pull a Lyle. This guy in my training class at Quantico, Lyle Kilgore, had come straight from the US Army. The dude could eat a full plate meal in a little over forty seconds. Apparently, the Army didn't give the new recruits a whole lot of time for chow during basic training, so he'd developed the habit of eating like a starved wolverine gene-spliced with a wood chipper.

After a moment of mentally preparing myself, I tear into the meal in front of me in an effort to scarf it down as fast as possible while not turning completely into a cavewoman. Based on my initial experimentation at home, the longest I've been able to hold onto actual food while concentrating on keeping it down is approximately ninety seconds. Spicy stuff tends to rebel faster. Also, focusing on the idea that I fully intend to allow my body to purge said unwanted food as soon as I get to a toilet or something can occasionally buy me another minute or two. Plus, I don't have to eat *all* of it. I am a lady, after all. Well, that's what I tell myself at least.

As soon as I've eaten half the stuff in a few generous bites, I slither out of my seat to stand in the aisle. "Be right back."

Chad nods, eyeing my food. He looks up at me with eyebrows raised, hopeful.

"All yours, buddy."

He grins and I hear him going to town on it as I turn away.

The bathrooms are barely four steps from our row. I dart into the nearest one, lock the door and lean over the tiny toilet. Speaking of people from my past like Lyle, I knew this woman named Roberta in college. That girl loved to party. She got drunk—and high—so often, vomiting for her became as casual as mild indigestion. Roberta once got sick during a study session and simply picked up an empty paper cup to puke, filling it like a human soda fountain. Not a trace of discomfort or alarm on her face whatsoever.

While I'm not quite the master she was at blasé vomiting, I've found that expecting and wanting to let my body get rid of food it doesn't want makes the process less awful and much quieter. Since his seat is about seven feet away from the door, Chad would've definitely heard me barfing had I not managed to control that aspect of it. The last thing I'd need is him grilling me over bulimia on top of everything else. In a minute or two, I'm staring at a mess that pretty much looks and smells like airplane lasagna after running it through a blender. Not that my guts would do anything to food anymore, but even if digestion were possible, the stuff hadn't been down long enough to change at all.

After flushing, a quick mirror check confirms no sauce spatter or cosmetics malfunctions. Satisfied nothing is out of place, I head out of the bathroom into air thick with a thousand smells. The aroma of the cheap lasagna lurks beneath perfume and cologne strong enough to water my eyes. So many 'person scents' collide in my sinuses they merge into a frankenstink. I still haven't gotten used to the ability to detect the smell of a person like a bloodhound. Someone sitting near us must have a cat, evidenced by a hint of cat litter. Their closet must be relatively close to a litterbox. My nose is *that* sensitive.

Chad looks up at me as I retake my seat. Something in his eyes tells me he has a lot to say or ask, but with Callum alert now, he doesn't want to talk much about what's happening with me. He does, however, keep making concerned faces in my direction. I'm sure it's entirely over his worries about my health and nothing at all about me screwing up so badly. And yes, I screwed up. Not so much in falling asleep at the airport. That happened to be out of my control. My error came in not resigning or trying to talk Nico out of sending me on this assignment.

For the remaining two-ish hours of the flight, I gorge myself on a high-calorie sundae of shame and guilt, with a little cherry of anger on top. The anger's directed at the son of a bitch who attacked me and inflicted this ridiculous, impossible nightmare on me and my family. Everything else is a giant pile of what-ifs, all the ways Callum's last-ditch effort for freedom could've been worse… because of me. How can I do this job if I can't even stay awake?

I can't.

In the stillness of a transatlantic flight where no one is talking, my brain leaps from one memory to another. College and Quantico mostly, various moments of disappointment, frustration, or triumph as I fought to be taken seriously. As a woman, I had to do twice the work and show half the emotion to make it, and despite that, wound up at HUD instead of the FBI. Still a federal agent though, even if I do feel like a fake now. Not sure which is worse, knowing I'm likely to be fired as soon as I'm back in California, or knowing the only responsible thing for me to do is resign. Chad not saying a word, carrying on like nearly losing the guy we're escorting didn't happen, only makes me feel even guiltier.

Right around the time the pilot's voice announces we're on final approach to Heathrow, my wandering daydream is treating me to a slideshow of Danny smiling at various points in our past. If my brain is trying to cheer me up by showing me all the best moments from the first few years of my marriage, it's having the opposite effect. It feels more like the video some funeral parlors put on to 'celebrate the life' of the guy in the box next to the television. This isn't a fond reminiscence of happier times—it's a requiem.

Much like my career, I suspect my marriage is dead on its feet... like me.

How apropos.

On a detached, intellectual level, I understand that neither losing my job as a federal agent nor my marriage to Danny is 'the end of my life.' Both events have only as much power over me as I give them. Also, both events are likely imminent regardless of anything within my power to change. My marriage, at least, is largely at the whim of emotion —chiefly Danny's. Saving it might be possible. The job... not so much. Not with serious risks to others and numerous witnesses to my ineptitude.

It's become obvious that my husband is afraid of me. I'm sure he's been thinking about leaving already to get away from the monster, but he's hesitating out of fear. That can only mean he wants to take Tammy and Anthony with him, away from me. He knows me well enough to understand how fiercely I'd protect my kids. Obviously, he's worried what I—or 'fake Sam'—would do to him for trying to separate them from me. That thought fills me with conflicted emotions. I mean, if I can't force myself to stay awake, *can* I force myself not to hurt the people I love the most? How much of me has become a creature of darkness?

There's also the chance that I'm allowing anxiety to run off its leash and he's planning nothing of the sort. His obsession with 'saving' me runs deep. Some men develop a drive to task that keeps them around dangerous things despite the risks. Like vulcanologists sitting 200 yards from a caldera about to explode or Louis Slotin handling a nuclear core by hand. Sometimes, the dangerous obsession kills them. Though, it's unlikely Danny has *cajones* that big. As soon as he truly fears for his life, he's probably going to run for the proverbial hills.

"Attention passengers, this is your pilot speaking. We should be on the ground in a few minutes, a little early. Expecting touchdown at 4:49 a.m. London Time. That's 8:49 p.m. California time."

I secure my seatbelt when the light comes on.

The landing happens without a hitch. It's not even slightly bumpy. Smoother than driving the freeway back home even. Better, it's dark outside. I'm wide awake, alert, and ready for anything. Chad gives me a slightly confused glance.

"What?" I ask.

"Guess that nap did you good. You look like you're ready to take out another entire camp of militant arms dealers by yourself."

"No. That only happened because they hurt you."

"More adrenaline?"

"Something like that. And Nico's right. I was way out of line doing what I did."

He chuckles. "Still, you're back to your old self now. Even more so. There's a... I dunno. 'Fierceness' in your eyes that didn't used to be there."

Yeah. Danny sees it too. Pretty sure that's what freaks him out. I'd be lying to say it didn't occur to me that my feelings have shifted a little darker than they should be. Disturbing thoughts, too. Like, how I used to sneak onto the farm down the road from home as a kid to steal vegetables so we didn't starve? The thought occurred to me a few weeks ago that it would've been easier to kill the farmer and take *all* the produce. No way would I ever act on such a thought, but that I even had it at all freaked me the eff out. Obviously, this new darker part of me is lacking in foresight. Killing the farmer would stop any future planting. The idea hadn't come from any logistical need for obtaining a large quantity of vegetables but, scarily enough, how fun it would be to kill the guy who had so much food. Needless to say, this has caused me to double think everything before speaking. Especially so nothing slips out of me to further make Danny come unglued.

Or freak out my HUD partner. Or kids. Or sister. Ugh.

Given how close we're cutting it to sunrise, I stand when a flight attendant goes by and catch her attention with my badge. "Excuse me. We're escorting a detainee. For security reasons, we need to disembark first."

"Oh, of course, Agent Moon." She nods at me then hurries to the little booth where she makes an announcement asking the passengers to remain seated until the plane comes to a complete stop at the terminal gate. Then, she waves me to follow her.

With the plane still rolling, Chad and I escort Callum up the aisle to the door, while admonishing a few passengers not to take photos. Of course, none of them pay any attention to our request. Luckily, those little flip phones take fairly blurry images. I hope my make-up holds up.

A two-year-old boy near the front end of the coach section makes eye contact with me before erupting in an ear-splitting scream. Sweet mama. Just what I needed to feel all warm and fuzzy: another reminder that I'm a monster. It's not worth it to stop and try reassuring the kid, so I push on to the space right behind the cockpit. Two flight crew, a man and a woman, stand by the outer door, both giving us wary smiles. Callum tries to flirt at the woman, though she refuses to look at him.

A moment or two after the plane stops rolling, mechanical whirring outside ends with a soft *thump* against the hull. The flight crew opens the door, revealing a boarding tunnel connecting to the terminal.

We're here. My God, what a surreal flight.

Now... to finish the job at hand.

"C'mon, asshole," I say, and lead him off the plane.

Chapter Six
Morning Person

At least Callum doesn't look too roughed up.

Fair bet he won't complain about me throwing him into a post or Chad slugging him. To do so would be to admit that he attempted to escape. He's most likely taking our lack of interest in charging him with escape as reciprocity for his not complaining about being roughed up.

Each of us hold Callum's arms above the elbows, walking him down the concourse toward the international arrivals area of Heathrow where the local police should be waiting to take custody. My inner alarm sense begins tingling, likely due to the imminent sunrise. Having an innate danger sense is kinda handy, even if it reminds me that I'm no longer human. Unfortunately, it's frustratingly imprecise. This little nagging noise just inside my ear could mean the sun's about to ambush me as easily as someone's lining me up in the scope of a sniper rifle to take a shot at me. Other than 'danger incoming,' the only information it provides is an abstract notion of relative risk. The more the threat, the louder the ringing noise in my ears gets.

Presently, it's kinda quiet. So, it's probably a warning that I'm soon to face-plant when the sun comes up.

However, after the epic screw up at LAX, it's not a good idea to make assumptions or take chances. A line of people, passengers from other flights, extends out of the arrivals area into the right side of the concourse, all queued up for customs processing. We walk past the line and continue on toward the wider atrium up ahead. Two men in green jumpsuits with mop buckets by a bathroom door on our left interrupt their conversation to stare at us. It's not an unusual reaction to the sight of someone being walked around in chains, but these two don't have any trace of curiosity about them, more a sense of mission.

I narrow my eyes in suspicion. "Chad, watch those two—"

The janitors pull their hands from their jumpsuit pockets, revealing pistols. My supernatural reflexes stretch time into almost slow motion, enough for me to realize they're armed with Tasers instead of guns. Chad shoves Callum protectively toward the floor, likely assuming the men intend to assassinate him.

Both janitors fire, barbed darts exploding out the front end of their weapons.

Before our prisoner is halfway to landing on his chin, I yank him up into the path of the taser darts heading my way. Don't need him getting any ideas about running off and I'm not too keen on the idea of being zapped. Better him than me. And yeah, I thought all of this while the barbs were in mid-flight. I'm kinda freaky like that. They hit him and Chad at the same time, followed by the electrical clicking of 50,000 some odd volts. Despite his size, my poor partner emits a shrill high-pitched tone and collapses to the carpet like a sack of wheat.

Callum, as well, crashes toward the floor, convulsing.

I jump over him as he goes down, taking two steps into a right hook that connects with the jaw of the man who tried to shoot me. The force of my punch throws him six feet back into the wall. His accomplice tosses the spent Taser aside and comes at me, flicking a collapsible baton out to length, arm raised high to crack me over the head. I spin toward him, catching his elbow in one hand to stop his strike from coming down, trapping his wrist in my other. He shrieks in pain when I lift him off his feet by that arm and fling him straight to the floor on his chest, chicken-winging the arm up behind his back. The baton goes rolling off out of his grip.

Janitor One bounces off the wall and falls into an unconscious heap, blood trickling from his lips.

"Bloody hell," rasps Callum, launching spittle from his lip.

Four London cops plus a man in a dark raincoat

rush out of the international arrivals atrium and hurry over to us. Chad picks at the Taser barbs stuck in his shirt, gradually working them out. While the cops gather up the fake janitors, the man in the raincoat, an Inspector Hollister I soon learn, approaches us.

"Rather sorry about that," he says. "Didn't think MacLeod had the stones to try such a brazen stunt. Bloke's got some friends in the IRA who are rather keen on getting him back into the fold."

"Thought they were trying to silence him," says Chad, holding up a barb. "Wasn't expecting this."

Sunrise is coming soon. I *really* want to get this over with as soon as possible. My need to hurry things along is due in part to what feels like a physical energy leaking out of my brain.

Inspector Hollister's attention shifts to me... and his eyes sort of glaze over. As they do, his conversation trails off and he hands over some paperwork. His movements, if anything, are robotic. What the hell?

"That's Callum MacLeod all right," he says listlessly. "I'll just need you two to sign here for the custody transfer. You've got some paperwork for me as well?"

Chad pulls out the folder and offers it to him. Or tries to. He gets his shaking hand under control by the second attempt. Poor guy.

We sign each other's paperwork while even more cops show up to secure the area, remove Callum into custody, and drag the two janitors off.

Hollister takes a brief statement from us regarding the ambush.

"Right. That should do it then. Doubt we'll need much from you about that. Whole thing's on vid, plus the five of us saw it all with our own eyes." Hollister glances at me. "Nice moves there. You could teach us a thing or two."

"Thank you."

He nods. "I've been told you'll not need to surrender your firearms as you're intending to fly right back out?"

"Basically." Chad sets his still-shaking hands on his hips. "Bit of a layover, but you're correct. We're not planning on leaving the airport."

"Ahh. Nuisance that. How long?" asks Hollister.

"Departing flight's leaving at eight," I say. "We'll be waiting here at the terminal. Probably catching a quick nap."

Hollister hands us both a business card. "Sounds good. Ring me if you need anything or something else happens."

"Will do." Chad shakes his hand.

I shake as well. "Thanks."

The British police inspector and officers leave.

"That was… faster than I expected." Chad folds his arms. "Nice of them to trust us not to sneak out into London."

"Yeah." I check my ticket, look at the signs, and start hurrying toward the terminal area.

"What's the rush?" asks Chad after catching up.

"My condition. I didn't have a chance to tell you

this yet." Shaking my head, I power-walk faster. "No one's been able to explain it to me, but that whole narcolepsy-like thing? It hits me hard at sunrise."

"Strange."

As we hurry to the terminal, I cook up this weird story about my parents waking up at the butt crack of dawn and Dad smoking pot before he'd even gotten out of bed. So much weed, in fact, that a giant cloud of smoke would roll into mine and Mary Lou's bedroom. This resulted in some kind of mental block around sunrise. Of course, it's a total fabrication. Sure, Dad *did* smoke a joint as soon as he woke up—when he hadn't been playing minor league ball anyway—but not to the chain-smoking point of flooding the house with a cloud.

Once we get to the appropriate terminal, I look around for the most secluded spot to sit away from windows and head for that chair. Chad sits next to me.

He raises an eyebrow. "So what you're saying is… what?"

"I'm saying that I might have like a narcoleptic attack or something real soon." I stare into his eyes. "It's going to be difficult to impossible to wake me up for a while. Please don't freak out or panic. It's normal and I'm not in any danger. Also, you might need to carry me onto the plane."

"Oh. Okay." He smiles as casually as if I'd asked him to grab milk on his way home from work.

This is starting to get weird. First Inspector Hollister seems to rush through process as soon as I think about wanting him to. Now Chad's totally cool with me telling him I'm going to pass out due to a kind of narcolepsy. When the whole vampire thing first happened, Danny found it amusing at first… to the point he rented or bought every possible vampire movie he could find. Most of them depicted vampires as having powers of mental influence or mind control.

The creepy notion that I've just *done something* to two men makes me shrink in on myself, overcome by instant revulsion. I try to rationalize my guilt away as not having a choice due to being stuck in a bad situation, backed into the corner.

"So, um, when we tell this story back home, is there any chance you could maybe *not* mention the part where I squealed like a little girl when the taser hit me?" asks Chad.

"I'll try not to, but I can make no promises."

Chad's laughter fades to silence as sunrise wallops me over the head.

Chapter Seven
Darkness

To make up for the slog of two back-to-back international flights, we have Friday off.

Apparently, despite spending ten hours in the air flying west, my vampire body reacted as if time froze for only two or three hours. One moment, I'm sitting at Heathrow Airport, the next, I'm at home in bed.

Except for my shoes, I'm still fully dressed in my pantsuit that smells like grill-charred meat. That is a likely sign that Chad's the one who put me in bed. Danny might have undressed me a little more or changed me into a nightgown. Or, maybe not. He *has* been avoiding contact lately. With a sigh, I sit up and take in my surroundings. It's dim out. The clock on the nightstand reads 6:19 p.m.

The voice of Barney the dinosaur coming from the living room almost sends me flying out of bed wanting to smash the television. However, I settle for clenching my fist and wishing that the fleas of ten thousand dogs infest the nether regions of whoever designed that show—and that music. It wouldn't surprise me if the CIA developed it as a way to torture information out of foreign agents without leaving marks on their bodies.

In addition to the stink of 'roasted Sam,' the air's full of breaded chicken. Danny probably microwaved chicken fingers or something for the kids. He used to love cooking, especially spaghetti, but he's been relying on shortcuts more and more lately, blaming his law practice for consuming all his time. I'm ninety-nine percent sure he's not cheating on me, but he's definitely up to something that isn't law-related.

Since the kids are eating, I get out of bed and head to the bathroom for a shower. Normal people probably wouldn't be able to smell it at all, but the odor of burned vampire is making me feel like a walking corpse. That, and I'm covered in makeup and sunscreen that's been on me for over twenty-four hours.

So, yeah. Kinda sucks to be me right about now.

But the shower is so amazing, I actually manage to spend about twenty minutes *not* thinking at all about the disastrous prisoner escort or even my worries about what my husband is up to. Once I'm thoroughly saturated in the scent of 'rainforest botanical' shampoo, I cut the water and stand there dripping for a few minutes, enjoying the warmth.

One of the odder things about what's happened to me is that I can tolerate extremes of temperature, such as showering in all-hot water. Doing so for sufficient time actually heats me up enough to pass for human by touch—for a little while. Cooling off happens way too fast. And yeah, I tried doing that once or twice to help Danny not be so freaked out during an attempt at intimacy... and it didn't work too well. I was ice cold before the foreplay really got started. Yeah, I know... TMI. Anyway, at least I can still enjoy the awesomeness of a hot shower.

By the time I walk down the hall, the kids are done with dinner and back in the living room. Danny eyes me from the kitchen where he's doing dishes, more like the way he'd acknowledge the return of a roommate he didn't fully trust to leave alone with expensive new dishes. Whatever. Couples fight. We're just having a... phase or something. He'll eventually realize we need to reach some new normal and everything will be fine. I shouldn't jump to conclusions and expect the worst from the man I'd fallen so deeply in love with.

I click the remote and Barney goes bye-bye— and not a moment too soon. The kids don't seem to mind me suggesting *Finding Nemo*, which only came out last year. Sure they've already seen it a bunch of times, but we're talking about a two- and four-year-old. They could watch the same movie every day for a month and still not get sick of it. Tammy's that way with *The Little Mermaid*, too. Wait, every day for a month? Try three times in one day.

They both cuddle with me on the couch while the movie plays, chattering about their sleepover at Aunt Mary Lou's. My kids seem to sense how much I need to be with them. Anthony's not usually a clinger. He'll stay close to me when he's nervous or frightened, but leaning directly against me is out of the norm... until now.

Not that I'm particularly concerned with them being around me or worried about anything happening... but right now, they're the most solid thing in my life. Jobs come and go. Even a husband can go. My connection to Danny is strong, but it's pure emotion. Tammy and Anthony are my literal blood. No matter what else happens in my weird, new life, they'll always be there.

I'll make damn sure of that... or die trying.

Danny sets up shop at the dining room table with his laptop. I can feel his eyes on the back of my head as he works on whatever. The unspoken mood between us is more like a lion handler biting his fingernails while some idiot decided to use one of the big cats for a petting zoo and let small children near it. He's watching me, but isn't at all confident in his ability to do a damn thing to stop me should the monster emerge. The palpable sense that he would try to put himself between me and the kids if, for some impossible reason, I flipped out offers a small glimpse of the man I remember. Whatever his feelings for me have become, he loves the kids enough to risk his life for them.

My daughter invariably asks about London. She's disappointed to learn I didn't really *see* much but the airport. Anthony shouts, "Big-end" a few times—he better be trying to say Big Ben and not commenting on Mommy's posterior. As far as Tammy knows, her mother spent twenty hours bored out of her mind on an airplane. Danny makes a few noises that tells me he's not buying my story.

Had the near-escape at either LAX or Heathrow made the news? I didn't know, and truth be told, I didn't want to know. If not, then I'd underestimated Danny's sixth sense. No way he should know anything had been off.

I've come to hate quite a bit about what happened to me. Every inhuman reminder makes my skin crawl. No longer being able to go to the beach, a once-favorite pastime, hurts, too. By far though, the worst thing is the time it steals with my kids. They both go to bed around eight. Only having two hours—or so—to be with them some days is a dagger right to my heart. How many milestones am I going to miss due to the daylight forcing me to sleep? The kids first time riding a bike, tying their own shoes, all those little precious moments... my children aren't going to rearrange themselves to a nocturnal existence. I can't ask them to do that, nor would I try. It's also probably against the law. No, they deserve as normal a life as possible.

I can't let what I've become interfere with them. As far as my kids are concerned, they're going to grow up, go to school, and get on with their lives like vampires don't really exist. None of this weird crap is going to taint their future. Sure, they'll think they've got a weird mom with some funky disease that makes her sleep during the day. Maybe I'll even jokingly refer to myself as a vampire as a form of misdirection.

That might work.

Though... it's going to become a bit obvious when they're in their later twenties and people mistake me for their sibling rather than their mother. At least, it will if it's true that I'm not aging anymore. Heck, I'm thirty-one but look five-ish years younger. I don't, however, recommend un-death as a beauty regimen. The startup costs are a tad expensive. Wish I could return it.

No, I'm not going to be able to keep this completely from my kids for their entire lives. The best I can hope for is to preserve their childhood in as normal a state as possible. Once they're adults, possibly married, living on their own, then we'll have *the talk*. Best laid plans, right? While I'm hoping for early thirties, something tells me they'll both notice my lack of aging earlier than I could ever prepare myself for.

Fingers crossed they're at least in college by then.

"Bit late, isn't it?" asks Danny.

I eye the clock on the wall. Twenty after eight. "Yeah. C'mon you two. Bedtime."

Soon, the nighttime routine of teeth brushing, changing to pajamas, and a too-short bedtime story is finished. Danny kisses Tammy goodnight, then carries Anthony to his bed.

"Night, Tam Tam." I kiss her on the forehead.

She grins. "Night, Mommy."

I cross the hall to kiss Anthony goodnight. When I lean down to do so, he stares at me with a fascinated look, as if mesmerized by something in my eyes.

"Night, my sweet little prince." I kiss him on the top of the head.

He babbles in toddler-speak, saying good night back to me.

Danny shuts the light off and practically pulls me out of the room with his expectant stare, then follows me down the hall, not speaking until we're in the living room. He sits in the closest dining room chair, folds his arms. "Something happened in London."

"Yeah," I say, turning my back to him.

"How bad?"

"You're going to get your wish."

The dining room chair creaks from him getting back up. Squishing footsteps in the carpet, nothing any normal human could hear, comes up from behind and to my left. "Which wish?"

"Monday, I'm either going to get fired or resign."

He moves around almost in front of me. "That bad? I honestly hadn't been asking about that…"

"What did you ask about then?" I peel my gaze off the floor and look at him, more vulnerability than I like in my expression.

"Mostly why Chad carried you in." Danny takes half a step closer, picking up on my lowered defenses. A note of regret, perhaps guilt shows in the curve of his lips. "And me having to go get your van from the office."

"You were home?"

He nods. "Had the house to myself all day. Decided to work from here to save the gas. Is the cat out of the bag or does the big guy somehow not understand why he had to carry your inert body back here?"

I sit-lean on the couch back, grasping the fabric on either side of me, unable to figure out if I want to keep looking at Danny or stare down at the floor. "Not sure exactly. I blamed the Xeroderma thing and made up some crap about my Dad smoking so much weed early in the morning that it made me phobic of sunrise."

He chuckles. "If he bought that, you have powers of mind control."

"Ugh. Don't remind me."

"You should practice doing that. Maybe help me out with clients… or juries."

I gasp. Okay, that's definitely *not* Danny talking. "Umm. I'm not convinced I have any powers like that at all. And even if I do, how could you suggest using them for something *that* unethical?"

He offers a blasé one-armed shrug. "Just saying it would be nice to defend some actually innocent people for a change, and maybe make sure those who really are innocent don't go to jail. That's not unethical. But, never mind that for now. What happened that's got you ready to quit?"

I sigh at the floor and explain about Callum taking advantage of me when I lost the battle to force myself awake during the day, the chase, fight, and so on, even the attempt his buddies pulled in Heathrow to bust him loose. Chances are, the date and time of his transport leaked from the British side, but Nico's still going to launch an internal review. Well, more to the point, the US Marshals Service is going to investigate. No doubt they already know and are already investigating.

Danny listens to my story, showing little emotion to anything except when I bring up Callum having people waiting to help him escape at Heathrow. That gets raised eyebrows and a whistle. A leak of confidential police information triggers more of a reaction than me being in a dangerous situation or screwing up. I'd like to think he's simply not worried about me as much anymore since I've become quite a bit harder to kill.

"So, yeah. That's what happened." I end up looking down again. "I'm expecting Monday to be my last day. But, even if I'm not fired, I'm going to resign before blacking out again gets someone hurt."

"Probably a good idea," says Danny with no more emotion than if I'd announced we were having Hamburger Helper for dinner. "Guess it's harder to pretend to be a federal agent than simply impersonating Sam."

I snap my head up, glaring at his back as he returns to his seat at the dining room table. Glow from the laptop screen tints his face whiter. His words hurt more than the gunshot I'd suffered weeks before the change. "Danny... I'm still me. When we first met in college, you had a cramped little Celica that smelled like hot soft pretzels inside." I walk over to stand next to him at the table. "Your mother obsessed over the flowers at our wedding, insisting the girls carry purple ones. It's me. No one else. Me."

He studies me for a moment until finally, his face softens. "I'm sorry. That just slipped out. I've got a lot on my mind." He runs a hand over his face, nods to himself. "Look, I'm happy you're going to be safer—I really am—but now I'm worried the law practice won't be enough to keep us going."

"I'm not planning to just sit around, you know."

Danny finally makes eye contact. "I'm going to find a way to help. Help Sam, that is."

"Help Sam? Like you're not even talking to me? Dammit, Danny! I'm still me! I'm still the same person I've always been... just with some challenges."

My almost-shout takes even more color out of his cheeks. He's clearly afraid of me, or afraid of the creature he thinks looks like me.

I stop looming over him, half turn away, eyes downcast, voice quiet... already ashamed at my outburst. "Maybe I can't stay up during the day very well anymore, but I'm still myself."

"I can see it in your eyes." He stands, moves in close like he's going to kiss me, but hesitates, one hand on my cheek. "It's visible like a tiny flame burning somewhere deep inside the black of your pupils. Whenever I look at it, I *know* it's not my wife I'm seeing. Something else is looking out at me."

Wanting to wrap my arms around him, but being afraid he'd run off if I tried, crushes me. What happened to my pillar of security, the husband who would always be there for me in times of need? "I'm me."

He takes a step back, fidgeting in discomfort at being close. It doesn't escape me that he wipes the hand that touched my cheek on his jeans. Maybe it's the sunblock and not me he's trying to wipe away... until I realized I went from the bed, to the shower, to here. No sunblock applied.

"I've been doing some research," he says.

"Oh?" I back off to the end of the table, pull out the chair and sit facing sideways. "What about?"

"Vampires being real. Apparently, there are sightings of werewolves, too. Can you believe that?"

"If not for what's happened to me, I wouldn't. But... maybe a lot of things we didn't used to believe in are real. Why not werewolves?" I almost say mermaids, but stop myself. I mean... c'mon.

Danny sinks into his chair, gaze locked on the laptop screen as a long, slow sigh leaks out of his mouth. "It's not easy for me to say this, but I've accepted that my wife is dead. You might look like her, but something else got into her body."

I drum my pointed fingernails on the table... and decide to come clean. Maybe brute honestly will help. No other reasoning seems to. "Okay, look. I'll admit, sometimes, it does almost feel like I'm not alone in here. As though there's someone else in my head with me. Maybe there is. But, I'm still in here, too. I'm not *pretending* to be your wife, Danny. No one stole this body... at least, not completely. You have to still be able to see that. Some random *thing* jumping into this body wouldn't remember everything."

"Sure it could. It's got access to Sam's brain. How do we know it can't simply read whatever it needs to in order to manipulate people?"

I clench my hands into fists to stop them from shaking. It's more difficult to hold back my tears than it had been to force myself out onto the airport tarmac in broad daylight—but I do it. "You know that's not true. If I wasn't me, the kids would know. They'd be afraid of me."

"They're kids. Maybe they're easier to fool. I don't know." He refuses to look over at me. "It's almost kinder to think Sam's free somewhere. If..." His lip quivers. "If I accept that you're still somehow Sam, I'd have to accept your soul's been twisted."

"I didn't think you believed in souls."

"Didn't used to believe in vampires, either. Like

I said, I've been doing some research. If it's possible to fix you, I'm going to find a way."

We sit for a moment in silence.

Eventually, I look him straight in the eye. "What if it's not possible? Is this really that bad? I'm still around. I can't get sick anymore. We didn't exactly want more children. You get to have a wife who stays young and beautiful forever. The beautiful part is your word, not mine."

He squirms, glancing sideways at me.

What good is a perpetually young wife if he's disgusted at the thought of touching her? Is he wondering how long it will take before I descend into madness and feast on him? Or maybe he just thinks it's going to get kinda creepy when he's past fifty and I still look like this. I'm not sure why it would bother him to think we couldn't be intimate anymore. Not like he's touched me in weeks.

"It's late. I should go to sleep." Danny stands and walks down the hall to the bedroom without even looking at me.

I lower my head, burying my face in my hands, as distraught as if I'd lost my husband out of the blue in a reality where nothing weird happened to me. It's clear to me that my marriage is done. That man has no feelings for me beyond some obsession quest like Ponce de León seeking the Fountain of Youth, only Danny's chasing a 'cure' for what's happened to me. Something tells me he's going to have the same luck as the old conquistador.

Our bedroom door closing with a *thump* makes

me jump like a bang many times louder. Still, the message is unmistakable: stay out.

Overcome with a chaotic mess of sorrow, anger, indignation, and hopelessness, I leap from the chair and run to the kitchen. Old autopilot takes me to the fridge. An open bottle of red wine on the top shelf calls my name like it used to. Before I know it, I've chugged two glasses' worth straight from the bottle.

Normally, downing that much wine that fast would've knocked me on my ass.

I stand there by the open fridge, swaying on my feet, waiting for the alcohol to kick in and distract me from the disaster that my life is becoming. No one could ever have accused me of being an alcoholic, though high-stress moments often resulted in a glass or two of red wine and a bunch of 'alone time.' My thoughts drift to one such moment during the time when we'd been renovating this house. Months of working a day job then coming home to struggle with disastrous home repairs finally caused me to reach a breaking point.

I remember the evening clearly. One glass to calm down became three. Only, that time, Danny joined me and we both had a 'screw this, we need a night off' moment. As soon as I picture his semi-sober smile, the paint-smeared drop cloths in the living room, and how we'd gone from ready to choke each other to making love right there on the floor… nausea churns in my stomach.

It occurs to me I'm not drunk or even tipsy. Angry churning in my gut tells me what's about to happen. Not even my trusty liquid friend wants to be with me anymore. I hurriedly set the bottle on the counter and lean over the sink. Fury rages in my gut, growing stronger with each second. I try to shout 'God dammit,' but instead of my voice, a torrent of wine sprays into the sink, splattering all over the steel and splashing up onto the tiles beneath the window. Nothing burns quite like red wine streaming out the nostrils. Even a sun scorch is pleasant by comparison. The fire in my sinuses is like a cheap shot to the head from the Universe.

It's not bad enough that the job I worked so hard for is slipping away.

Not bad enough that my husband can't even bear to look at me.

Fate's gotta take away the wine, too.

The Universe has to kick me one more time when I'm down.

Eyes watering, I lean on the counter, gasping for breath I don't need, watching the traitorous liquid seep down the drain. The shrinking puddle makes me want to cry like a dear friend just told me off and stormed out over something trivial. It shouldn't bother me at all. I didn't even have wine all that often, but it had always been there for me during the worst times.

Like Danny should have been.

Defeated, I let gravity pull me down to sit on the floor, leaning my head back against the kitchen cabinets. The fridge hangs open, but I couldn't care less. I simply stare into space, no motivation at all to clean up that mess in the sink.

A few minutes of total silence pass before a droplet of wine runs down my chin like a curious spider. The tickling sensory input somehow jump-starts a neuron in my ears. I become aware of the whirring refrigerator motor, but it fades as my awareness hones in on the gossamer wisps of Tammy and Anthony breathing in their sleep—my two biggest reasons never to quit fighting.

I wipe my chin on the back of my hand and stare at the trail of dark purple liquid slipping over my wrist. Okay, Universe. You knocked me down pretty good, but this girl isn't done yet.

Not by a damn long shot.

Chapter Eight
Death of a Dream

Saturday and Sunday—except for a brief emotional unloading session with Mary Lou—I spend as much time as possible with my kids.

With my kids being two and four, options for 'going out and doing fun things' are somewhat limited. Pretty sure I'd get some really weird looks if I walked around a park at night with toddlers. So, we ended up at my sister's house. Her husband Rick barbequed on Saturday. Smelled awesome, but I had to fake eating it.

Danny watched me like a hawk the whole weekend, though something came up late Sunday afternoon and he left the house without telling me where he was going as soon as I appeared awake enough to look after the kids. Either he decided I'm not as dangerous as he fears or whatever pulled him away had been extremely important to him. He didn't come home until eleven. Don't tell him, but I let the kids stay up late... until nine, just to have another hour with them. Someday, Tammy and Anthony are going to wonder why most of their childhood photos with me appear to be taken after dark.

Sunday night after Danny went straight to bed with barely a goodnight nod in my direction, I sat on the couch with a plastic half-gallon milk bottle of blood watching crappy movies on cable. More accurately, I sat there with my eyes aimed at the screen. Watching implies comprehension. Mostly, my thoughts circled around how horrible a day I'd have on Monday. I also tried to figure out what would hit me like a gut punch more, being fired or quitting. Never did manage to answer that one before sunrise knocked me out.

I wouldn't have even bothered moving off the couch to go to bed, except for the giant living room window. Might as well let the alarm clock do its evil work for the last time, right?

And maybe someday I'll buy a heavy shade for that damn window.

Or wall it in with bricks.

***

Like an android, I mechanically drag myself out of bed when the alarm goes off and go through the motions of getting showered and dressed.

My dread for what's waiting for me at the office

makes it difficult to stay awake, but it's big girl time. No avoiding this. Gotta face it. While hovering in the kitchen watching the kids have cereal, I find myself focusing on gut-wrenching what-ifs... like what if Callum had taken my gun away from me and the subsequent running shootout had killed a handful of innocent bystanders, possibly children among them? Or what if Chad and I find ourselves in a bad HUD inspection where we catch the residents with drugs or some such thing and out come the guns—and my delayed reaction time or straight up blacking out gets Chad killed?

My attachment to this job is entirely based on pride.

I worked my tail off and caught my dream, and I've been damn proud of that.

Too proud lately.

Danny's parents would call pride one of the seven deadly sins, tell me I shouldn't be prideful of anything. I don't agree with much of their opinions on the world at large, but in this case, they might have a point.

The illusion that working for HUD was 'tame' compared to something like being an FBI agent or a CIA operative allowed me to accept Nico reinstating me after that suspension. Guess Danny had been right, too. Working as a federal agent puts me in dangerous situations. Granted, it would be highly unlikely for anything the mundane world could throw at me to be a serious threat to my life now. If it was only my life hanging on the line, maybe I'd fight to keep this job.

I can't allow my pride to kill innocent people.

A little trace of pre-Sam-becomes-a-monster Danny peeks out this morning. He keeps looking up at me with a little bit of a smile. I'm guessing whatever he did Sunday had to be related to his Fountain of Youth quest—that is, his quest to cure me—and he's fooled himself into thinking progress happened. Acting like he hasn't spent the past couple of weeks treating me like a stranger could only mean he believes a cure is almost within reach and I'll be back to normal soon. Yeah right. That's as likely as me inheriting millions of dollars from a mysterious relative I didn't know existed.

Hey, not that I object to his efforts at finding a cure. Normal sounds really damn good right about now. But... the reality that becoming a vampire requires death makes any sort of 'take backsies' seem farfetched. Something twists at the back of my consciousness at the thought, reinforcing the notion that this change is a one-way street. For an instant, a strange vision fills my head of an ascending series of landscapes stacked on top of each other... a colossal crystalline skyscraper cut open to reveal that each floor contains whole worlds rather than rooms, the tower stretching upward too far for me to see what's at the top except for blinding pure-white light.

The vision fades as fast as it came out of nowhere.

Whoa. I haven't seen anything that trippy since

Mom screwed up and put Dad's weed on our spaghetti after mistaking it for oregano. Only, he'd stashed a batch of what he called Khadafy Weed in the cabinets... basically, pot spiked with LSD. Yeah, I had a crazy night. Mostly, I thought my stuffed animals talked to me. Mary Lou went full space cadet and stared into the fourth dimension for an hour. My oldest brother, River, didn't show any reaction whatsoever. Dusk freaked out, thinking all the doors in the house were trying to eat him. My youngest brother, Clayton, had a blast. I don't really remember exactly what he did other than running around laughing a lot and trying to fly like Peter Pan. That's probably why he became such a fan of recreational chemicals. He'd been twelve then, which would've made me ten. Yeah, Mom and Dad definitely won the 'parents of the year' award a few times.

But still. Giant crystal building with moving landscapes on each level? Weird.

Did that come from my subconscious trying to tell me that what's about to happen today is insignificant in the grand scheme of things? Hell, I'm technically deceased. My brain could be doing anything.

Eventually, it's time to head out. I drop Anthony off with my sister and take Tammy to her preschool, then head to the HUD office downtown for what's probably going to be the last time.

Chad's already at his desk when I walk in at 9:38 a.m., earlier than I had been showing up since the suspension. Guess being on edge *does* let a vampire wake up early. Most people would consider Chad slightly fidgety today. Anyone—like me—who knows him would realize he's extremely nervous. The man's usually calm as can be, so his appearing visibly worried has me on edge. However, I've already accepted that this is going to be my last day, so I won't be going into Nico's office with any semblance of hope.

Sure enough, the boss walks over within a few minutes of me sitting at my desk. I didn't even bother trying to log into the computer, half expecting my username to already be locked out. Though, I didn't do anything actively criminal or deliberately wrong… so maybe not.

"Moon, Helling," says Nico. "Got a minute?"

Chad gives me this odd sort of 'we got this' look, then stands. "Sure."

"Yeah." I stand and follow the men down the cube row to the end, and into Nico's office.

"Heard from an Inspector Hollister that you had a little bit of excitement at Heathrow," says Nico. "I realize you're going to be documenting things, but I'd like to hear it from you in person."

"Yeah, MacLeod had a couple friends waiting for him." Chad gives an accurate rundown of everything that happened after we landed in London, not mentioning anything about us almost losing him at LAX.

Nico looks at me.

"Yes, that's pretty much how I remember it, too.

A pair of men dressed like maintenance workers stood by the mens' room. When we came close enough, they drew weapons—Tasers—and tried to shoot us. The man going for me missed and hit MacLeod instead. Since neither man had a deadly weapon, I engaged with non-lethal means and neutralized both threats."

"Inspector Hollister's email said you rendered one man unconscious, breaking his jaw in the process, and had the other on the floor before the constables could run across the international arrivals area to your position," says Nico.

"Yes." I nod. "The area was pretty big. Those cops had to run all the way across the atrium to the hall, maybe sixty or seventy yards. I had plenty of time to deal with the attackers before the cops came close. It didn't happen all that fast."

"What about MacLeod? How'd he end up with a cracked skull?" Nico raises an eyebrow.

"Might've sustained that injury when he got zapped." Chad makes a shoving motion. "I didn't realize at first the men had stunners. Thinking they pulled guns to assassinate our prisoner, I shoved the man to the floor... perhaps too hard."

Nico leans back, his head tilted slightly to the left. "How'd it go at LAX?"

It's obvious to me he knows something happened. Or at least suspects. His tone of voice tells me he already knows the answer to what he's asking and wants to see if we're going to lie about it.

"Nothing we couldn't handle," says Chad, fidgeting his hands. "MacLeod attempted to escape, but he didn't get too far."

Now I know why he's nervous. He's trying to walk a tightrope between not lying and covering my ass. If he pushes too far in one direction, I'm toast. Too far in the other, he's toast—or we both are. He's probably going to resort to claiming Callum broke the handcuffs.

"Sir," I say, "My medical condition gave MacLeod an opportunity to run for it. Chad needed to use the bathroom, and while alone with the suspect, I had a blackout beyond my control. When I regained consciousness, MacLeod was halfway down the concourse, having pickpocketed the key to his restraints from me."

Chad cringes, practically yelling 'why did you say that?' with his stare.

"I see." Nico looks down at his lap. That disappointment is a sign he suspected something of that sort happened, but not exactly what. At least he seems to appreciate me being honest.

"Ever since my attack, I've been having... health issues. I just can't stay alert and sharp in the morning anymore no matter how hard I try, and no doctor can explain it. We were extremely lucky at LAX in how that ended. You don't need to tell me how much worse it could've been. That's all I've been thinking about since it happened." With every scrap of composure possible to summon, I hold my chin up. "My body is doing its own thing now and I can't stop it. I don't want to be responsible for something like that happening again, someone innocent bystander or Chad being hurt again. It's not fair to him or anyone else. I don't *want* to resign, but the events at LAX last Thursday have made it abundantly clear to me that I'm in no physical condition to properly carry out the duties required of me here. This job has been a dream come true for me, but…" I let out a long breath. My voice shakes and I don't entirely trust myself not to break down and cry.

Nico sits up out of the slouch he'd fallen into. At that moment, I know for a fact he was going to cut me loose and felt like complete shit for it. My resigning lifts a weight off his conscience.

Chad puts a hand on my arm. "Sam, we can figure something out."

I smile at him, though it's more sad than happy. "I already have figured this out, Chad. Really, I appreciate your loyalty. It's beyond infuriating that the guy who attacked me did so much damage he killed my dream job. But, I can't let him hurt you or any civilians who might get caught in whatever situation escalates out of control because I can't function at a hundred percent in bright/early conditions."

"I hope they find that mother…" Nico swallows the rest of the word, sips his coffee, then runs a hand up over his head into his white hair. "It pisses me off, but I have to agree with her here, Chad. Look, Sam… I'll put it into the system as a medical retirement."

"Thanks." I look him in the eye. "It's not your fault. You fought hard to reinstate me, and your trust means more than I can express in words. It's my fault. I never should've accepted reinstatement in my condition. And because I value your trust, I can't put you in a position to catch the fallout for me."

"You'll get some benefits on the medical retirement, but those won't last forever. Might qualify for SSD, but that'll be a gauntlet of doctors. If you need me to go to bat for you with them, just call."

Chad leans toward me. "Sam, come on. You can beat this." He looks at Nico. "What about putting her on desk duty until her medical situation resolves?"

Before our boss can speak, I jump in. "What if it never resolves, Chad? And if the FBI or the Marshals Service comes knocking for warm bodies, I'd still be technically an active agent. Nico's 'inside policy' of leaving me on a desk won't matter to them. I'm sorry, Chad, but it's not fair to you, to Nico, or anyone here. My body's out of control. Sometimes, I feel like it's not even listening to me anymore. I may never be able to control it." I let out a somber chuckle, thinking of one of the weirder Chinese vampire movies Danny found. "The way things have been going lately, it wouldn't surprise me if I turned into a dragon."

The guys laugh.

"That's any woman once a month." Chad winks.

Nico wags a finger at him. "Someone needs another sensitivity training session. I can't hear crap like that."

We all chuckle.

"Chad had nothing to do with the issues at LAX. It's all because I couldn't stay awake. And it's not like I screwed off and decided to catch a nap on a whim. I literally *couldn't* make myself stay awake. Like narcolepsy."

"Ugh." Nico grimaces. "That's rough. I hope it isn't actual narcolepsy."

"The doctor's tentative diagnosis is xeroderma pigmentosum. God, I feel like such a cop drama cliché." I stand, remove my blazer, and shrug off my shoulder holster, depositing it on Nico's desk, then surrender my agency badge/ID wallet. "There it is. Guess I need to say I officially tender my resignation, effective immediately."

Nico bows his head like a relative died. Maybe a distant one like a cousin he saw once or twice. "Dammit, Sam. It's a shame to lose you, but it's the right thing for everyone concerned."

"Not me, but…" Chad stands and pulls me into a hug. "If you're sure."

"The only thing I'm sure of anymore is that I don't want to get anyone hurt."

Chapter Nine
Nocturnal Sunshine

As if that meeting hadn't been awkward enough, Nico asks me to stay a little longer to fill out paperwork and go through an exit interview with the Personnel Office.

He brings the whole squad into a conference room: Bryce Anders, Michelle Rivera, and Ernie Montoya, the agent who mentored me over my first few months here. The mood is instantly somber. It's likely that they all suspect what happened given my recent suspension, a sudden meeting with Nico, and Chad and I looking like we're ready for a funeral.

"I'll be brief," says Nico. "Agent Moon is resigning as of today for medical reasons. I wanted to take a minute and thank her for the years she's put in here, and wish her luck with her recovery and wherever the future brings her."

Michelle gasps in shock. Bryce makes a sad

face at me.

Ernie shakes his head and pulls me into a hug. "Dammit, Moon. All that time I spent training you and you're gonna leave us?"

I chuckle, returning his back pat. "Not exactly my choice. That guy who jumped me really messed something up inside."

Nico, Chad, and the others all stand around wishing me well, offering condolences, apologies, and suggestions on what I should do with myself now that I'll have 'all this free time.' The whole scene becomes surreal, like my mind is floating outside my body, watching everything happen to some other dark-haired woman in a movie. When the meeting reaches painful levels of awkward, the others reluctantly head back to their desks.

I watch the Samantha Moon lookalike walk back to her desk and pack up her personal effects. Chad brings her a cardboard file box and stands there talking about the funnier moments we've had and a few 'holy crap' ones as well, like that guy unloading six shots out of a revolver at me and missing every one.

Consciously, I realize that this is a resignation, not a firing, but it feels no different. Probably due to the lack of actual choice in the matter. My new physiology is incompatible with early mornings and dangerous situations before sunset. I didn't have a choice because staying here *will* get someone killed. Also, Nico sure seemed like he planned to let me go. 'Quit or be fired' is sad either way you look at it.

A lump like I'd tried to swallow a jelly donut whole lodges in my throat as I collect the small picture frames from my desk with photos of Danny and the kids, a couple of stupid little figurines I've had since college, and a handful of minor awards and some certificates—nothing impressive, merely proof I'd completed various training courses.

Nico watches from a distance due to regs. I'm sure by now my access to the computer system has been disabled, but they can't exactly leave a former employee—even one leaving on ostensibly good terms—unsupervised in the office. Still, he's not giving off any sense of distrust. More that he *has* to be there. I give him a weak smile and a 'yeah, I know' nod.

Once I've gathered all my stuff, I stand clutching the box, feeling way too much like a rebellious teenager being kicked out of her home. Everything around me triggers one memory or the other, usually of random little funny things that broke up the long, boring days here at work. Even though I can't eat donuts anymore, the sight of the small brown table by the coffee machine makes me acutely aware that I'll never again stand around with these guys for a few minutes in the morning. Looking at the wastebasket makes me think of Flora, the cleaning woman who came through every day about twenty minutes before I'd go home. The old mechanical government-issue clock on the wall reminds me of how often I'd stared at that thing wanting time to move faster so I could go home—except now I don't want to leave.

It feels like the son of a bitch who attacked me in the park has stolen yet another piece of my life away from me. Sure, this job had its flaws—what job doesn't—but it was mine. *Was* being the operative word. Maybe I'd accepted the reinstatement knowing it would lead to a situation like this where choice got taken away from me. Though it *is* better for everyone that I resign, the tenacity with which I fought for this job wouldn't have let me walk away easily.

Bryce, Michelle, and Ernie come over. We go through another round of something that's part condolence, part well-wishing, part goofing around like we always used to. Numb to it all, I stand there like an idiot clinging to my box of stuff. Nico doesn't seem to mind everyone idling around me, even joins in the conversation for a little while.

"I can't believe this," says Ernie, shaking his head. "I thought for sure you'd have ended up in Nico's chair twenty years from now."

Everyone chuckles.

Oddly, that might've even worked. Blacking out at the boss' desk wouldn't typically get anyone killed. But even if LAX didn't happen, my Rambo-style raid on the militia compound probably would've kept me from getting any real promotions. The brass hadn't been *too* upset, mostly because it'd been a direct response to another agent being hurt—we're protective of our own—plus it spared the FBI from having to deal with it. I managed to do for basically free what the agency would've spent fifty or sixty grand in time and personnel costs on. It all kinda came down to a 'nice job, but don't do anything like that ever again' deal.

It's difficult enough to rise through the ranks as a woman with a spotless record. Something like that, they'd have used to keep me on the wayside. Though, Nico's not *that* high up the food chain. Commander of a squad might have been within reach, but… yeah. At this point, that's about as likely as me going sunbathing ever again.

Eventually, everyone offers one final handshake or shoulder pat and returns to their desks. Unlike yours truly, *they* still have a job to do.

Chad walks with me out to the Momvan, both of us funeral quiet as I open the passenger door and set the box of stuff on the seat.

"We might have been able to save that in there," says Chad, barely over a whisper.

Chuckling, I shove the door closed and turn to face him. "You didn't see the way Nico slouched. He'd already made up his mind that he had to let me go before he ever called us into that office. Want to bet how many times he watched and re-watched video surveillance from the airport over the weekend?"

Chad sighs. "I'd rather take another bullet with you than get stuck with a new guy. How am I supposed to do this without you, kiddo?"

"I'd stay if I could, Chad. You know that."

He nods, then looks at the ground. "It's not gonna be the same without you, Sunshine."

His nickname for me has taken on a rather painful unintended irony, but I'm too sad to react much to it. "Am I leaving a job or are we getting a divorce?"

"Painful either way." He glances off to the side at the distant street outside the parking area. "So what are you going to do with yourself now?"

"Try to figure out what's going on with my health."

He whistles. "Sometimes, our whole system kinda sucks. Whatever you've got makes it difficult to work, but without a job, you can't get health coverage."

"Yeah, well..." I pull my hair off my face, tucking it behind my ear. "It's not that I can't work at all. I just shouldn't be running around with a gun and putting people at risk. If I blank out for a few minutes in an office, no one's going to die. And, the XP—that's what I call the disease now—is pretty rough early in the day. Doesn't seem to affect me at night. Should be okay with a graveyard shift somewhere."

"What about overnight air traffic control?"

I shiver. "I'd rather bag groceries."

He laughs.

"Seriously though... the training is all daytime stuff. I'd never get past that. Besides, I suspect my paperwork now states I have 'narcolepsy-like symptoms.' Without a solid diagnosis, it's going to make getting another federal job a pain, especially one like ATC."

"Ahh." Chad hooks his thumbs in his pockets, giving me a 'yeah, that's a problem' nod. "Hey, if there's anything I can ever do for you, let me know."

"Thanks. I really appreciate that. I'd make the same offer, but... yeah."

He winks. "You'll eventually claw your way back up to somewhere I might need a favor from."

At the word 'claw,' I become uncomfortably aware of my pointy fingernails and fidget, trying to hide them. "Yeah. Thanks for the vote of confidence."

We stare at each other for a few minutes.

"You should probably head back inside before Nico accuses you of goofing off." I playfully punch him on the shoulder. "I'll be okay."

"You sure?"

"Sure? No. Hopeful, maybe. Things will work themselves out. Never did like big changes in my life. Growing up was so chaotic and random most of the time, I need things to be stable. My biggest fear is not being able to give my kids that sense of stability they deserve."

"Hey, if things get tight, don't hesitate to ask for a little help, okay?" He glances back toward the doors. Nico's not looming there like an annoyed owl, so he's not in trouble yet.

"Sure. Thanks,"

Chad and I shake hands one last time. I stand

there beside the Momvan watching him walk back into the office that's no longer my place of work. Wind throwing my hair in my face gets annoying after a minute or two, so I trudge around to the driver's side of the van and get in, but can't bring myself to start the engine.

The idea of asking my ex-partner for charity is basically a slap. It took me too damn long to feel like I didn't depend on someone—my parents, Mary Lou, even Danny—to survive. I might be unemployed, but I can't let myself slide back into being that hanger-on sponging off other people's kindness anymore. No, this girl had a taste of self-sufficiency, and it's addictive. Still, if it comes down to my kids needing food or clothes I can't provide, what choice is there? Can't let it get to that point. I've lived that as a kid, and my children aren't going to go through it. My kids aren't going to have to steal food from a nearby farm, shoplift from the grocery store, run around in clothes ready to fall off them at any moment, or go two years without owning a pair of shoes that fit.

I stare despondently into the speedometer dial, my mind drifting back to memories of all the school and training it took for me to become a federal agent. So much time and work wasted. This had been more than a job. Carrying papers around an office or fixing cars is a *job*. Being a federal agent was something higher. A calling perhaps? Maybe I'm simply being prideful again, mourning the status of having authority over others. I never wielded that status over those who hadn't broken the law, only wanted to use it to help those in need, stop those who'd exploit the system.

My father never liked the idea of me working for 'the man.' A near-feral hippie child turning into a federal agent sounds like the sort of life story they make movies about, only I need a new ending. Something like 'breaks up a massive housing scam and rides off into the sunset with her husband and two happy children'—not 'gets turned into a vampire and lives in shadows.' I hate movies that turn weird like that. Dammit, this is supposed to be a buddy cop film, not a supernatural horror.

The mirror under the sun visor confirms I'm not dreaming. Invisible spaces where my eyes should be, an empty mouth. My reflection, or lack thereof, is merely a shell of foundation makeup, a hollow head-shaped balloon with holes in it. It's so surreal, I almost want to laugh—at least until the sight of what I've become enrages me.

I slam the sun visor up, grab my head in both hands, and scream an F-bomb.

The reality of what just happened, that I've given up being an agent after all that work, surrounds me like a cloak of cold darkness, dragging me toward a pit of depression. Tears well in the corners of my eyes. They nearly fall, but I somehow hold them back. I'm no longer the dirt-covered half-dressed woodland waif who always ran to her big sister to fix every little problem. No, I gotta deal with this myself.

Not giving up.

I might not be a federal agent anymore, but that doesn't mean all that training and experience stops existing. But it's not like I can leverage it much. Trying to get on a local police force, even for a night shift, comes with the same set of issues that ultimately forced me out of HUD. I don't need to be in law enforcement, just find something to do that brings in money. Preferably in the dark.

And no, not stripping.

Somehow, I'm going to beat this... circumstance.

First things first, stop hanging out in the parking lot of my old job like a stalker girlfriend who can't let go after a breakup. I need to go home. It's almost two in the afternoon, so Mary Lou's probably on the way to pick Tammy up from preschool already. Might as well go to my sister's place. No, I'm not running to her like I used to do whenever stuff got scary or too difficult. My kids are there, and I'd rather not be alone now.

Just a job right? I can get another one.

Right?

I start the engine and cast one final look at my old office. Gonna miss this place, but it's time to move on. The Universe wants my life to go somewhere else, apparently. My mom's a big believer in fate or destiny, thinks nature guides us to where we need to be. Not sure 'nature' has anything to do with whatever sort of monster I've become, but the message that I don't belong working a dangerous day job has finally come through loud and clear.

"Take care, guys," I whisper at the building while dropping the Momvan in gear.

Time to move on.

Chapter Ten
Trust

Sunset brings consciousness.

I'm alone in my bed at home. It's Wednesday, two days after my dream died. The alarm clock shines its meaningless numbers at me from the nightstand. Doesn't matter what time it is when I get moving. Not like I have anywhere specific to be. Waking up when the sun goes down is how I'm *supposed* to work, but why does it feel so damn wrong? Like I've wasted the entire day.

My ex-partner Chad would be home by now after having worked a whole shift. I spend entirely too much time dwelling on wondering what he did all day—no doubt going through the motions of home inspections and audits with his new partner. HUD has dozens of different forms that I could fill out in my sleep for every conceivable situation. The knowledge of how to do that has become as helpful to me as the recipe for making dodo soup.

Barney the dinosaur's annoying guffaw comes down the hall from the living room television courtesy of DVDs Mary Lou got for the kids. Gee, thanks ML. It feels like he's laughing at me personally, and I want to punch his lights out. Like the red wine from the other day, my kids adoring such a brainless thing feels like another middle finger from Fate. And not just a casual flip off, either. It's shoving that finger right into my face, half an inch from my nose.

That sorrowful look Nico gave me haunts my memory. His expression changed from 'dammit, I don't want to do this' to 'I agree it's the right thing to do,' then he seemed to be wondering what hap-pened to me that I went from one of his better agents to someone he had to terminate. After a minute or two of oscillating between feeling like a total failure or a helpless victim, I catch myself crying. It's okay here in the privacy of my room where no one can see me, but I can't show that in public. That's what everyone says. Women can't handle things. They always cry. Dammit, emotions are real. Why do people always say it means weak-ness to show them? Sometimes, I feel sorry for men. If a woman cries in public, it's 'oh, typical.' But if a man shows the same emotion, he becomes a laughingstock. Unless, of course, a close relative just died. Then he's the right amount of sensitive.

Is it weird of me to feel like something dear to me died? My career hadn't even gotten off the ground. Only a couple years as a full-fledged agent, only two years making more than Danny. Not that I ever bragged about it, but that did make me feel like a valid adult. Never did figure out if he stank as a litigator or if it's a question of putting in the grunt years before a practice takes off. Nah, he's not a bad litigator. Maybe he's simply got bad instincts for choosing clients... keeps representing people who don't have a lot of money.

Well, congratulations, Danny. You earn more than me, now.

Not that he ever said anything (though I always suspected it might have bugged him a little).

I don't have the heart to tell him my medical retirement benefits—technically short-term disability—are still roughly even with what he earns. But, that won't last long. Surrendering to sorrow and apathy and laying around the house all night isn't going to accomplish anything except making a bad situation into an awful situation. Unfortunately, depression is real and it's not exactly something I can just decide to ignore.

Mary Lou doesn't think I'm 'depressed.' At least, not in a clinical sense. She called it mourning. Since I hadn't been depressed before being made into a monster and losing my job, she thinks it'll pass once I've had a chance to cope.

Maybe she's right. Danny's not going to be able to afford this house—modest as it is—on his own. I don't want to give up on it either. My kids need a stable home. I might not have had much growing up, but the one thing my parents *did* manage to provide was a permanent home. The place might've looked like something from a post-apocalyptic movie set in the deep woods where banjo music strikes terror into the hearts of men, but I always knew where home was.

I start to get up, but pause at the unusual sight of a myriad of small figurines set up on the two nightstands flanking the bed. There are seven on mine, five on Danny's side. All made of wood or stone, crude human shapes that resemble Anthony's superhero action figures if they'd been handmade by a tribe deep in a jungle somewhere. One or two have an almost Aztec design. Stranger than their sudden appearance, they're giving off a weird energy.

It's not quite the same as having a live person watching me, but the little men feel like more than simple inanimate objects, as though a fragmentary sentience lurks within their empty wooden heads. Nothing appears to have happened, and that odd 'alarm' sense I have is completely silent, so whatever. They're likely part of Danny's continuing quest to 'fix' me.

Wonder if Nico would take me back if I ended up human again?

An odd sense of laughter drifts across the back of my mind, as if the dark hitchhiker inside my head finds that idea hilarious. Can't tell if it's more amused at my pathetic hope of going back to HUD or the notion of 'curing' me. Probably both. Yeah, I get it. Clinging to any hope of getting my old job back is pretty pathetic. Then again, I could have imagined the laughter. God, I hope I'm not going nuts.

Tammy scurries in, jumps up onto the bed, and crawls into a hug.

"Hey, Tam Tam."

She squeezes me. "Is I s'posed to say g'morning or g'night?"

"That's a good question." I kiss her on the head. "Why don't we use 'good morning' for when some-one wakes up?"

"Okay." She smiles. "Are you still sad?"

Danny hovers in the doorway, arms folded. The way he's looking at me is like I've been given supervised visitation of the kids and he doesn't want to leave me alone with her. To avoid starting a fight, I decide to convince myself that it's the hitchhiker he doesn't trust, not me. Or, maybe he's watching me not out of fear of what I might do to Tammy, but out of wanting to see if his little tribal figurines have any effect.

"A little," I say. "But I'm not going to stay sad for much longer."

"Why are you sad?" Tammy peers up at me.

"Because I lost something that took a lot of work."

She tilts her head, not following.

"Remember when you made the macaroni paint-ing at school?" The painting hangs on our fridge in a place of honor.

She grins. "Yeah. That was fun!"

"If a mean kid at school took it away from you, you'd be sad."

Tammy nods, her smile wilting.

"That's kinda how I feel."

"Oh. I don't like mean kids. Are you gonna hit the mean kid in the nose?"

A brief, blurry flash of a vaguely human shape flits across my thoughts, emitting a bear-like growl. No amount of wanting to kill that son of a bitch is going to help me figure out what he looks like. "If I ever find him, yeah."

"Good." She nods. "If someone stole my macroni, I'd hit him in the nose."

Trying not to chuckle, I give her a squeeze, then stand. "Hitting someone in the nose is not the best way to solve a problem. You shouldn't do that unless they try to hit you first."

Tammy contemplates this as I pick her up and move around the bed. Danny sees us coming and retreats to his work area at the dining room table before I can walk past him or even get close. Speaking of punching things in the nose, the enormous purple nose of Barney the dinosaur fills the TV set. Breaking the television wouldn't give me any sense of satisfaction, so I merely convince the kids to switch gears to a Disney movie. Naturally, Tammy picks *Little Mermaid.* Anthony, who admittedly hadn't really been watching Barney either, continues to focus most of his attention on the toys littered around him.

One thing that's definitely going to change is my sleep schedule. I don't care if it is a fundamental law of the universe for me to stay asleep until sundown—the bastard who attacked me isn't going to rob me of time with my kids. If nothing else, my ass will be out of bed by two or three in the afternoon, enough time to pick them up from school... and maybe catch a few episodes of Judge Judy.

Anyway, they say anyone can get used to anything with enough repetition. I'm going to hold that true in defiance of supernatural phenomenon. If I can drag myself awake at 9:30 a.m. albeit barely functional, late afternoon should be a walk in the park. Doesn't matter at all if I'm a little bit drowsy in my own home.

Danny emits a chuckle despite nothing particularly humorous happening on the screen. I glance back at him. He gives me this smirk like I'd done something funny. It's not insulting or condescending, but he's laughing at me for some reason. I ask 'what?' with my eyes, but before he can say anything, the odd notion strikes me that he's amused at the irony of me being in the *living* room.

Ugh.

Wait. Did I just pick up his thoughts? Or am I assuming? Undead in the living room... does that qualify as a 'dad joke'? Maybe he's coming around to realize this crap isn't anything I asked for and we need to work together to get past it.

That said, I've got little hope that he's ever going to want a return to intimacy unless I somehow start generating body heat again, but it would be nice if the hostility that's been brewing goes away. No point starting a fight, so I look back to the screen and cling to Tammy like an oversized kid holding a squirmy teddy bear.

Pretty damn sure I'm upset now since my thoughts are going places like wondering if it would be possible for me to tolerate Danny having a side woman to give him what I can't. And yeah... no. As in, the answer there is a big, fat no. That I even thought about it kinda horrifies me. I don't want to lose my husband or the family we built. However, can I honestly expect him to be intimate with me when my body is as frigid as a dead person? There are so many vampire movies and books with sex as a major theme. I'm guessing that the fictional vampires aren't 'temperature challenged' like I am. Maybe I should stop using the V word. That legitimizes what happened to me as something that shouldn't exist, almost like accepting it. I've got a medical condition. Yeah, that's it. But, still, whatever I am, could there be a way to, like, redirect blood to 'certain places' for warmth?

The phrase 'preheating the oven' blindsides me and sets me off laughing.

If I don't laugh, I'd end up crying.

Tammy and Anthony laugh along with me, neither one of them having the first clue what struck me as funny.

Eventually, my all-too-short time with the kids ends at the approach of bedtime. Danny's completely engrossed in his laptop. Maybe because I'm technically a stay-at-home-mom at the moment, he makes no move to help deal with the nighttime ritual. Fine by me. Though, as soon as I tuck Tammy in, my husband appears in her room for a good night kiss. He follows me over to Anthony's bed, perhaps to 'protect' him from me. Whatever. Meanwhile, the boy gets a little cranky, not wanting to go to sleep, reaching for me.

Who am I to argue?

I stand near the edge of his crib and hold him, rocking until he drifts off maybe fifteen minutes later. With the precision of James Bond trying to remove the thingee from a nuclear warhead without touching the sides and setting off the bomb, I ease the boy down and cover him with the blankets. It's getting on about time to move him from crib to toddler bed. Maybe that'll be the first thing I buy with my next paycheck, wherever—and whenever —that comes from.

Danny trails after me down the hall to the front of the house. I stop in the space behind the couch that's neither dining room nor living room, staring ahead at the archway to the kitchen. Something's in the air between us, like he wants to say something but hasn't got the nerve. He's not giving off hostility or even snark, which intrigues me enough to turn and make eye contact.

"What's up with the little figurines?" I ask.

"Oh, just some stuff I thought looked cool."

I could ask why he's spending money on junk at

the moment, but they couldn't have cost that much. "They're strange. There's some kind of... energy to them. Are you trying to voodoo the vampire away or something?"

His innocent smile shifts to a guarded one, the same face he makes in court when his line of questioning isn't working. "Did they feel positive or negative?"

"Neither really. The best way I can think of to describe it is a feeling of not being alone. They didn't give me any particular sense of comfort or alarm."

"Hmm." He rubs his chin. "I'd been hoping they might help you. They're supposed to be guardians to ward off evil spirits. However, it's giving me a little hope that you noticed them as having power."

"Did it occur to you that they're not doing anything to me because I'm not an 'evil' spirit? Stuff we don't understand isn't automatically the work of the Devil." I fold my arms. "At least not always."

He blinks. "Did you just admit to believing in the Devil?"

"I don't know what to believe in anymore, but I believe in us, Danny. Our family. I'm a little concerned that you'd bring unknown stuff like that around the kids. What guarantee do you have that those figures aren't evil energy?"

"They're what's called a ward. Defensive things aren't usually bad."

I pace around, unable to believe we're having a

discussion like this seriously. Mostly, I'm unable to believe how it's affecting me. Truth is, I'm beginning to sound like my mother talking about healing crystals and putting dreamcatchers in the windows to stop bad spirits from coming in. "You can't assume that simply because something is defensive, it's not evil. Land mines are considered a defensive weapon, and they're evil."

He looks down, tapping his foot. "I have to protect the kids."

Anger rises inside me, but I hold it in. Becoming visibly upset will only give him more justification. "I will never hurt them. I can't believe you'd even think it possible."

"I know *Sam* would never hurt the children, but I don't trust that other thing."

"Other than sometimes not feeling like I'm alone in here, it hasn't done anything. Please stop pushing me out to arms' length. I'm still me. I'm still your wife."

"'Til death do us part," whispers Danny, not looking at me.

The phrase hits me like a knife. Not giving me time to think of anything to say to that, he turns away with a frustrated scowl, looking quite a bit like Dr. Frankenstein after a failed experiment. He almost sits again at the dining room table, but instead grabs his laptop, all the papers scattered around it, and carries everything down the hall to the mostly unused room at the back corner of the house, leaving me frowning at the rug.

Did we just have a fight? We certainly had a something.

The 'office' door closes with a *click*. At least he didn't slam it. Suppose he might be trying to do more research into whatever bizarre pseudoscience he thinks will fix me and doesn't want 'the thing' in my head to know what he's up to... but as fast as Danny walked off, he probably wants to be away from me.

I'd been using that room as kind of an office whenever work followed me home. We didn't really know what else to do with it. Danny wanted to make it into a 'man cave' or some juvenile thing like that, but didn't put up much of a fight when I pointed out that we could both use a home office space. We agreed to use it for that with the caveat that if we ever had kid number three, it would become a bedroom. But... yeah. That's not happening.

Despite Danny's job giving him a lot more homework, he'd taken to considering that office 'my' space, and did most of his work at the dining room table. Should I interpret his relocating to the home office as some kind of statement that he considers Samantha Moon dead and the room is his now?

No. Not going to bite—pardon the pun. I can't fall into a pointless argument over who gets to use an office room until I'm in a position to support myself. As distant as he's become, I'm afraid it wouldn't take much at all to push him away even more. The man in the other room doesn't feel like the same Danny Moon who I fell in love with. He accused me of becoming 'darker,' but look in the mirror, bud. Well, maybe he's not darker as much as colder.

It occurs to me that his weird little smile before might've been smug victory. Could watching me lose my job at HUD have somehow pleased him? He made that remark about me having a hard time 'impersonating' a federal agent. Is he gloating that the 'monster' is suffering?

Grr.

I look around, but there's nothing in easy reach I feel like smashing to burn off energy.

Energy.

That's it. I'll go for a jog. So what if it's dark outside? Not like I'll die *again*.

And if someone nefarious should cross my path tonight... yeah, I'm pretty sure I might just kill him.

Bad guys beware.

Chapter Eleven
Any Possible Way

Over the next week and a half, an increasing number of strange objects appear in the house, mostly the bedroom. Crystals, statuettes, bundles of sticks tied together, stone spheres… every time I wake up, there's something new hanging over me, standing near me, or glaring from a shelf. The figurines have grown to a small army.

Not everything gives off an aura, though.

Danny, at least, appears fascinated by my ability to sense that and has taken to straight up showing me things and asking if they have any 'energy.' At least twice, I'm sure he knew he had a fake item and used it to test me. Is going from 'monster in the house' to 'research project' a promotion or a demotion?

I've acclimated myself to waking up progressively earlier, reaching a begrudging equilibrium with getting out of bed around the time Tammy's due to leave preschool. The 'begrudging' part is my physical nature, not my desire. It seems that whatever my body's turned into, it lets me do the premature awakening thing in trade for one day a week where I can't budge until the sun is fully down. Guess even vampires need to catch up on sleep.

So, forcing myself vertical between two and three in the afternoon doesn't hit me with the same staggering zombie issue as waking up at 9:30 a.m. This is good. As long as I avoid exposure to strong sunlight, I can pass myself off as more or less functional. Still wouldn't want to get into a shootout or fight until the sun is down, but people looking at me wouldn't wonder what the hell is wrong.

Danny's futile optimism at finding a cure has become infectious. He's even warmed up enough to have reasonable conversations with me again, though how long that's going to last is anyone's guess. We've been trying to figure out what I might be able to do for a job. Security guard is an option, but ugh. And yeah, that's pride biting me again. It would almost be less humiliating to work at McDonald's. He suggested corporate security, roaming the corridors of a downtown high-rise at night. That's a little more prestigious than sitting in a tiny booth at the gates of a truck yard.

However, today, my focus is a little different. Ever since I started taking his quest to fix me seriously, his attitude changed for the better. Said quest still strikes me as an absolute exercise in futility, but on the off chance something good might happen...

I've arranged for Mary Lou to watch the kids today, a Friday, for a couple hours so I can consult with some 'paranormal experts' about my condition. Danny and I assembled a list of eight psychics, occultists, and one guy who claims to be a demonologist. Pretty sure that dude is a complete joke. I mean come on, the guy calls himself Dante Black. No way is that his birth name. The picture on his website kinda resembles a Goth Guy Fieri. Pudgy, spiky black hair, goatee, all black clothes. Yeah.

My first appointment is with a woman named Dolores Brandt. Early fifties and kinda reminds me of my mother. Over-the-hill hippie vibes. She's got a modest suburban house in Yorba Linda, which luckily isn't *too* far a drive; after all, Danny is at work and I'm going about this alone... and during the day. Ugh. He's lucky I love him. And yeah, I do love him. Lots.

She answers the door in a dress that looks like she crashed through the cart of a street vendor selling silks. Red, blue, orange, and yellow strips float around her as she moves. I'm sure they're actually sewn into a garment but it's tempting to pull on one and see if she unravels. A necklace of golf-ball-sized wooden beads hangs around her neck, a dozen bracelets of various type on each arm.

"Why hello. Ms. Moon, right?"

Not yet anyway, I think. Instead, I say, "Mrs.

And yes. Hi."

She flares her eyebrows as if to be ominous. "Please, come in. Tea?"

"Thank you, but I have to pass. Does strange things to my system. That's kind of why I'm here."

"Come in." She backs away so I can enter, then closes the door and leads me across the living room to a massive bead curtain hanging in an archway of dark-stained wood. The place is drowning in dream-catchers, crystals, bead curtains, and such. If I still had a normal metabolism, I'd probably experience a marijuana high merely from breathing in here, so much THC has saturated into the walls and carpet. "I do all my readings in here, my inner sanctum."

I thrust an arm into the beads, making an opening to a square room with the same polished wood on the walls, various symbols engraved all over. The aroma of weed gives way to several layers of incense and something herbal. An equally square table of thick hardwood stands in the middle of the room, surrounded by four gothic chairs that look like they belong in a church, made from the same wood as the table with blue velvet cushions on the seat and a narrow strip down the back. The decorative top of the seatback is as tall as me. Okay, Dolores gets some points for theatrics at least.

"Please, sit." She gestures at the seat on the right, catty-corner to the innermost one where she alights.

I take the indicated chair, already out from the table enough that there's no need to move it. Since it looks heavy, me man-handling it like a superhero might look weird.

"Tell me, Samantha, what brings you here?" Dolores sets her hands on the table, palms flat on either side of a deck of tarot cards. "Problems with your husband?"

That statement doesn't impress me too much since I'm sure ninety percent of her clients come here for marriage issues. While she may be technically correct, it's easily dismissed as a guess. "Health issues. Having some strange ones. I was hoping you might be able to help me figure out what, exactly, is going on with me and if there's any possibility of a cure."

"All right." She lights some incense in a bowl and begins shuffling the tarot deck while asking me some basic questions about my birthday, favorite color, and the last thing that I ate.

Not going to say pig blood. Hmm. Should I sidestep the question with 'pork,' or not technically lie by mentioning the last food I *attempted* to eat? Yeah, that last one feels right. "Spaghetti,"

She nods and goes to work. The first card she overturns is Death. Okay, that's a little too on point. And freaky.

"Don't be alarmed." Dolores smiles. "The card doesn't refer to literal death. It's a sign of an ending. Typically a relationship or even an interest, which can lead to a greater sense of self-awareness. Also, it represents change or metamorphosis."

"Is that referring to something that happened or

something that will happen?"

She eyes me for a moment, seemingly zoned out. "You've lost your job, I see. I'm sorry to hear that, Elizabeth."

"Elizabeth? I'm Samantha."

Dolores' eyes flutter and her cheeks take on a slight blush at messing up my name. "Curious. Do you have a close friend or family member with that name?"

"Umm." I scratch my head. "I think my mother had a roommate named Liz when she went to college. No one I can think of. Why?"

"It just seemed what I should call you for a moment there. Though, I'm not always accurate guessing people's names. Odd that you'd already told me your name was Samantha and Elizabeth still leapt off my tongue. Perhaps one day you'll give birth to a girl and name her that."

Heh. I highly doubt that. Still, the woman covered her error smoothly. Real smoothly in fact. She's either a highly trained actress—that is, professional liar—or honestly believes what she's coming up with. As far as losing my job goes, most employed people wouldn't show up at 4 p.m. on a Friday afternoon. I had also asked about it referring to a past event. Again, could be simple deduction. "That medical thing I mentioned forced me to resign from my last position."

"Ahh, yes. The metamorphosis aspect of the Death card could indicate a change of career."

I bite my lip. Or a change of species. Whatever

the hell I am now. "Could it mean anything else, something perhaps more literal?"

Again, Dolores stares at me for a long moment. "I sense you'll face challenges well in excess of anything you believe you are capable of handling. But, my senses tell me you are capable of handling them. Don't doubt your inner strength." She draws another card and sets it down face up. The illustration depicts a single castle tower with fire belching from the upper windows. "Interesting. The Tower is a herald of danger and destruction, also freedom. You are likely to experience an unexpected change that comes out of the blue, often a shattering of pride."

Being ambushed at night and turned into... whatever I am sure counts as an unexpected change, as well as destruction. Freedom? Not so much. Well, freedom from a day job. That's not exactly a good thing. Or is it? Broken pride? Wow. This is getting eerie. But, I still can't help but think these things are so open to interpretation that anyone could latch onto relevance.

"What about the..."

"Cure?" she finishes.

Okay, whoa. "Yes," I say.

"One moment."

Dolores draws the next card from the deck, revealing The Moon card. That *almost* makes me laugh. Talk about a fortune with my name on it. "This medical condition of yours. It is likely not what it appears to be. An illusion, or perhaps a truth you are afraid to admit to yourself."

Wow. The coincidences are stacking up to the point I'm starting to become a little freaked out. Xeroderma pigmentosum is indeed a lie, or illusion, I'm using to hide the truth from others. Then again, I've been in a bit of denial lately, too, referring to it as a 'medical condition.'

Maybe I'm in denial, but that's not the same as actually lying to myself. Is it?

"Is there a cure?"

She draws another card. This time, she fumbles it before setting it down. The card lands sideways on the table. Dolores stares at it for a while. "Five of cups. Upright, it often means a sense of self-pity or grief. Reversed, acceptance or a sense of finding peace." She traces her finger back and forth over the card, evidently accepting the fumble as 'how the card wanted to lay.' "It's inclined more to the reverse, indicating transition. You have, or perhaps still are feeling self-pity, but you will learn to accept this thing which you cannot change and find peace."

My eyes widen. Holy crap, am I starting to believe this woman's the real thing? "Does that mean there is no cure?"

Dolores sets the deck down and grasps my hand. Grr. These days, I seriously do not like to be touched, especially without permission. Hopefully she doesn't notice how cold I am, since lots of women have icy hands. So far, she pays it no mind, thank God. Anyway, rather than 'read my palm' as I expect, she seems to study my knuckles. "I see significant change for you. My gaze keeps drifting to The Tower. You will know freedom... but from what I am uncertain. The freedom you experience will be great and welcomed, perhaps coming about with a metamorphosis. However, it will come at a cost of great danger."

Crap. Does that mean I'm going to get a divorce and struggle to make ends meet? No, that can't be right. I don't see myself *welcoming* a divorce. Danny's been kinda crummy to me lately, but I still love him. Maybe she means freedom from undeath and a metamorphosis back to human? While welcome, my gut tells me I'm pretty much stuck like this.

"Is this going to happen soon?"

"That I am not sure. It could be years. Yes. I'm feeling it is many years from now. You carry a heavy burden, yet... you are unaware that you carry it. Great change is coming, too—perhaps that cure you seek, but not for some time."

I let all the air I don't need out of my lungs. Is it possible to believe this? Probably a stretch to hang all my hopes on this woman's words, but wow. Some of what she said hit close to home, especially the part about my metamorphosis.

"There will be rough patches, but I feel you will weather the trials." She offers a grandmotherly smile.

"Thank you. Anything else I need to know?"

Dolores closes her eyes, still holding my hands. Her pleasant expression contorts to a grimace of pain or extreme worry. She convulses as if about to vomit, bracing a hand on her chest below the neck. The spell passes in a moment. "Something dark stalks you. Be vigilant. Do not ever allow your guard to falter."

I nod… and catch myself under this woman's spell. I'm kinda starting to believe this stuff. She's good. Of course, it's equally possible that she's so adept at reading people she knows what to say to sound close enough to reality that my mind fills in the rest of the blanks.

We have a pleasant few minutes of 'after-reading' conversation, then the inevitable commercial part of the transaction. It's probably silly of me to spend sixty bucks on something like this, but that's still cheaper than a professional therapist. She wishes me well, and I head back outside to the Momvan.

As hokey as that session might've been, a lot of things lined up a little too close for me to laugh it off entirely as bogus. Even if she's pulling stuff out of thin air, hope that some great change awaits me years down the road is more than I had before. It would be foolish of me to expect to wake up a normal person someday, but she sounded so convinced something big is in my future. Maybe she simply didn't realize I've *already* become a monster. But that doesn't feel right either. No one would call vampirism a *good* change. It certainly didn't bring freedom in any sense of my interpretation, and definitely wasn't welcome.

Oh well. I guess I'll worry about being disappointed that a psychic's prediction didn't come true in a few years. For now, what's the harm in allowing myself a little hope?

And who the heck is Elizabeth?

Wait, am I sincerely thinking that psychic might've seen something real?

Yeah, guess so.

The sun can kill me, I don't show up in mirrors anymore, and I'm drinking blood. Who am I to say that psychics might not also be real?

Unfortunately, the next four people I visit, including Mr. Dante Black, are clearly all vaudeville acts. The first woman—who looks younger than I am—had been convinced my stepfather abused me when I was little and demons followed me around. She scrambled to recover when I informed her that I didn't have a stepfather and I'd managed to last thirty-one years without experiencing any unwanted assaults of a physical nature. The second woman, a decade or two older than Dolores, spoke in such sweeping generalities that the same exact 'reading' could've been given to a dozen different people and probably still been believable to anyone desperate enough to match what she said to what they'd lived.

Dante wanted me to use a Ouija board with him, which I declined, mostly because I didn't want his fingers near mine. Still, the black candles made for a nice touch, but his act was so... strange. For most of our session, he came off as fake as a sideshow huckster, but the last like ten minutes, he could've won an Emmy award. Finally, his performance grew so lame that I decided to cut things short and bail, but right before I got up, the candles started seeping blood, the flames turned black, and a woman's voice whispered from somewhere behind me, saying, "Sssimpleton. You know nothing of the powersss with which you toy."

The man screamed and ran out of the room. I couldn't help it and burst into laughter... but he didn't come back. Strange way to put on a show, but after ten minutes, I decided to leave. At least he didn't charge me.

I mean, I assume the woman's voice was part of the show...

Right?

Chapter Twelve
Degrees of Evil

A little after seven, I arrive at the last psychic I'd made an appointment with.

This woman, Indigo Murillo, lives in a smallish house in the hills north of Altacanyada. Strange fetishes hang from the branches of trees around the front yard, bundles of twigs and hair, some with beads. Guess she thought dreamcatchers too stereotypical. Much like Danny's little figurine army, the entire yard is giving off a palpable vibe of energy, stronger even than what I'd felt at Dolores' house. Having seen three or four wannabes, I'd started coming around to the idea that the first psychic might just be the real deal. I wonder if this woman could be legit, too?

After parking in the empty driveway by the garage, I walk over and ring the bell. A late-twenties woman with long black hair, dark complexion, and a rainbow-colored Gypsy skirt answers. The broad smile on her face fades fast to a look of guarded worry. Her bare toes peeking out from under her long skirt grip the floor.

"Hi. Indigo Murillo? I'm Sam Moon. We had an appointment?"

"Sorry, I'm not sure what you're saying," replies Indigo in Spanish, which I mostly pick up.

I repeat myself in Spanish—at least, as best as I can—ignoring that she spoke English when I called. *"¿Algo malo?"* I say, hoping I correctly asked her if something was wrong.

Her expression briefly indicates she's about to make an excuse, but instead, she shakes her head and takes a step back from the door, leaving it open. "There is an odd energy about you."

"So I've been told." I step inside.

This appears to surprise and worry her for some reason. She stares at the threshold for a moment in confusion, then backs up again, gesturing at the door. "Please, shut it and follow."

I oblige.

Indigo crosses her modest living room to what I imagine had been intended as a dining room, but it's more of a mystical shrine. Hundreds of talismans, some made of plant matter, others rock or metal, hang everywhere on the walls around small tapestries bearing patterns and writing in a language I can't even name much less read. Almost every-thing in here gives off a sense of *presence…* and my alarm bells start going off the loudest they've ever been.

Uh oh.

The woman glides around the small table to a shelf. She opens a wooden box, gathers a scoop of dark crimson dust, and rubs it into her hands before smearing it on both sides of her neck and over most of her bare shoulders like a Mayan priestess or some such thing. That done, she takes a seat facing me, gesturing at the opposite chair. My warning sense is too strong to trust sitting down, so I merely take one cautious step closer. We stare at each other and I get the distinct impression she understands exactly what I am.

"I didn't come here to harm you," I say.

Her pretense of civility drops to a hostile glare. "Then why did you come?"

"Answers."

"Why would one of you seek answers from me?"

"One of you?" I repeat.

"How long ago did your heart stop beating?" asks Indigo in a whisper.

"Couple months. But it hasn't stopped beating entirely." I point back over my shoulder with a thumb. "At the door, you were surprised because you didn't need to invite me in?"

Her narrowed eyes say I'm right.

"Maybe you don't have the answers I'm looking for. Otherwise, you would have known that 'invitation deal' is folklore." I am, of course, referring to the myth that vampires need to be invited into a home. I mean... who would monitor such a thing anyway?

She leans forward in her chair, both hands under the table. The alarm sense in my head rings louder. "What sort of answers are you looking for, *vampira*?"

"Is there a cure?"

"Yes." Indigo nods once. "Sunlight. Silver weapons."

I chuckle mirthlessly. "I was hoping for something a little less drastic. Maybe how do I go back to being normal?"

She tilts her head, clearly not expecting that. "I do not know that such a thing is possible. You are already dead. Death cannot be reversed."

"I didn't think it could be 'paused' either, but here I am. Mind if I ask how you knew?"

Indigo flares her dark eyebrows. "I'm psychic, remember?"

"Right. I walked into that." Training makes me stand in a way that leaves easy access to the gun that's no longer under my left arm. Dammit. "Are you being serious or was that a smartass reply?"

"I can feel the dark energy on you. You're pale as death, and your eyes have the flame."

"Even though I get the feeling you'd prefer to kill me instead of talking, it's kind of nice to finally meet a psychic who's the real deal. As in, the *real* real deal." Dolores was kinda almost the deal.

She nods again as if to thank me for the compliment.

"Do you know of any way I can, umm, 'manage' this? I want to live as normal as possible despite my 'condition.' Is there anything I can do to make friends with the sun somehow? Even a little?"

"Hah." Indigo takes her left hand out from under the table, grasps a purple pouch and dumps out a bunch of small stones, each marked with a rune. "Alchemists might have such abilities to shield one such as you from the daylight, but few would dare traffic with the undead."

"Wait... alchemists?" I raise an eyebrow. "Are you serious? They're real too?"

"They are as real as you and me, but their secrets are not mine to know. I have heard stories. Their powers are vast, including immortality." Indigo brushes her finger over the stones. "Interesting."

I step closer to the opposite side of the table from her. "How much do you know about what I've become?"

Indigo stares at the stones, almost in a trancelike state. "You have children."

"That's not what I asked," I say.

"Without my help, they will suffer because of you."

She flicks a runestone over. "What do you see here?"

I don't look at the runestone. "Suffer how?"

"You remain among them, not casting off your mortal life to embrace the darkness. Without my help, your children will both be forever changed. A lifetime of torment awaits them."

Annoyed, I lean forward, both hands on the table, despite the alarm screaming in my head. "What... what do you mean by torment?"

Indigo gestures at the runestones. "First, tell me what you see?"

Smelling a trap, I flick my gaze down for only an instant. Believing me distracted by the stones, Indigo springs out of her chair, diving over the table, a gleaming silver dagger in her right hand. Fortunately for me, this is not the first time someone's jumped at me with a knife. Though, usually, it's a junkie squatting in a house they don't belong in, not a crazed psychic witch... or whatever this woman is.

However, that silver blade coming toward my heart sets off some instinctual panic inside me. Before I realize it, my fangs are out and I'm hissing. Despite the not-Sam part of my brain trying to freak the hell out, I maintain control enough to catch the woman by the wrist and neck, stalling her attack and dragging her the rest of the way across the table. She regains her balance, then braces one foot against the table behind her, trying to shove herself forward.

Indigo's a skinny little thing, not much power in those leg muscles. I step back in time with her lunge, keeping the deadly knife a few inches above my breastbone. It gives off heat, nearly burning me from proximity alone. You know those lightsaber thingies in Star Wars? Yeah, feels as if I've got one of those pointed at my chest. Like a possessed zealot, she keeps trying to plunge the blade toward my heart.

Okay, not *toward*... try *into*.

"You should stop fighting," rasps Indigo. "This is the only way to spare your children. If you stay with them, they're both going to be lost. You want a cure? This is it."

"No!" I shout.

As I squeeze her wrist, her face contorts in pain, but she refuses to let go of the blade. I don't have the heart to crush her bones, since in her position, I'd probably react the same way to a vampire. We wrestle for a moment or two, scrambling back and forth across the room and bumping into walls. The reddish stuff she smeared on her neck stinks to hell and back, worse than the liquid that drips out of the back of a garbage truck. Nauseating. Oh, wait. That's pretty damn funny, actually. It's gotta be the vampire equivalent of the stuff dog owners put on furniture to stop Fido from chewing on table legs.

My snickering doesn't go over well with Indigo. She lets out a shriek, grabs the knife with both hands, and redoubles her effort to stab me. Still not wanting to break her arm, I lift her off her feet by a two-handed grip around her right wrist. She kicks, but her bare feet don't hurt too much.

Damn, this woman's around twenty-six, but she's so small I feel like I'm under attack from a twelve-year-old. A crazed, psychic tween with an incredibly dangerous weapon, but still. I can't bring myself to hurt her. Rather than inflict a compound fracture of her arm, I relocate our battle to the living room and hurl her away so she lands on the sofa.

Flat on her back, she points her left hand at me —and a freakin' bolt of yellowish light flies away from her fingertips. I'm too stunned at the sight to move. The damn thing hits me in the chest with the wrath of a whole nest's worth of stinging hornets and enough of an impact to throw me over backward off my feet. Electricity crackles along my nerves, a demonic case of pins and needles from the lowest level of Hell. It hurts too damn much to move.

This bitch just straight up threw a lightning bolt at me.

Shrieking, Indigo comes out of nowhere and lands on top of me, dagger poised over her head to ram down into my heart. A deep-seated survival instinct takes over, breaking through the jolting, paralytic pain. I catch her arm in mid-plunge and roll to the side. She's so light it's trivial to toss her aside, though I keep hold of her wrist, pinning her arms to the floor above her head while sitting on her chest.

She struggles for a moment, but lacks the strength to overcome my advantage in leverage. Once she realizes a vampire has her immobilized, she goes from wrathful to terrified, gasping and grunting while struggling to get away from me, her expression pleading—but that ringing alarm sense in my ears hasn't lessened. That means she's faking.

As soon as I let go, she's going to come after me again.

Worse, she knows who and what I am... and what I'm capable of doing.

The trouble, of course, is that I'm not even sure what I'm capable of doing.

My gaze falls on the blood vessels in her neck, swelling up from her effort to fight me. Despite the rancid-smelling stuff she'd rubbed into her skin, I could force myself to... No. The creature in the back of my mind whispers, *Drink, Sssamantha, drink...*

Its hunger for human blood is so powerful it almost becomes *my* hunger.

Oh, hell no. There has to be a better way. I'm not a monster. I can't murder an innocent young woman. Honestly, she's merely defending her home from a supernatural fiend. She doesn't know me. Hell, my own husband doesn't fully trust me. There has to be another way.

"Indigo," I say, half growling past my fangs. Damn having that silver so close is seriously unnerving. It takes all the self-control within me, but I manage to draw my damn fangs back in. If only I could get them surgically removed, they wouldn't keep reminding me how inhuman I am. "I don't want to kill you."

"So let go."

"If I let go of you, you're going to keep trying to stab me."

She bites her lip. *You're a monster, what do you*

expect?

I open my mouth to retort, but it hits me that she didn't speak. That voice happened in her head. Oh crap. This woman's right. Monster city. Oh, to hell with it. I'm already this deep in the moment. What's a little more monster-ness? Better than killing her.

You're weak, whispers a voice in the back of my mind.

Screw off.

I stare with purpose into the woman's eyes, not really sure what the heck I'm doing, but wanting her to forget entirely about ever seeing me. She keeps squirming in an effort to escape, though her fight loses some strength as if a mesmerizing effect has begun to infiltrate her consciousness.

A tremendous flare of pain scores across the back of my left wrist. It sets off an explosion inside my brain as surely as if a needle had been plunged into my eyeball. Nothing physically passes between us, but it feels like something flew out of my skull and into hers. All sense of fight leaves Indigo and she stares vacantly into nowhere.

The alarm that's been ringing in my ears since I stepped in the door finally goes quiet.

What the heck did I just do?

And ouch!

I examine my left arm. Looks like she scratched me with the silver knife. The cut's not too deep but it burned as much as a soldering iron raked across my skin. An urge nags at me to get out of here fast. For no reason that makes any sense, I'm sure she won't remember ever seeing me. It's probably best if she doesn't ask questions like 'why am I on the floor?' when she snaps out of whatever catatonic state she's in. So, I get up, carry her over to the sofa and position her like she'd decided to take a nap. Gingerly, I pick up the silver knife by the handle. Though it's tempting to destroy the damn thing, a significant change to her environment like that might make her start trying to remember what happened. Only a vampire would want to destroy a silver weapon, I'm guessing, so its absence would focus her train of thought somewhere I don't want it going.

Right…

Unfortunately, I have no idea if she had it stashed under the table or on her person. More likely, on her. Despite how wrong it feels to do, a quick search of her body turns up a scabbard concealed behind her back under the waistline of her skirt. Good. I replace the weapon where it came from and run to the kitchen for a paper towel to mop up the little bit of blood that dribbled on the floor from my cut. That done, I run out the door before she comes to, hop in the Momvan, and take off like the house is about to explode.

I drive without direction for maybe fifteen minutes before pulling into a shopping center parking lot by a Panera Bread and a Habit Burger grill. No, I'm not hungry… need to think. My head is spinning over everything that just happened. Calm down, Sam. Good, good.

First of all, it had been self-defense. She freaked out and attacked me. I didn't leave a mark on her except possibly some bruising around her wrist. Nothing's going to happen to her or to me. She doesn't remember me.

Knowing that I rewrote a woman's memory like that hits me with a crushing sense of guilt. It's a total violation of someone's person. Sure, she won't remember it but that doesn't make me feel any better for doing it. Danny's right... I *am* a monster. Sorrow and shame start building, but a sense of 'aww how cute' flickers in the deeper part of my consciousness. Feeling condescended to by my own brain is too much. My mood shifts in an instant to anger. Go to hell, brain. Or whatever you are. *Not* wanting to trample all over other people's sense of self is normal, and I'm not going to feel weak for trying to keep myself as human as possible.

However, it's hard to argue with my need to remove myself from Indigo's memory. As scummy as it makes me feel, that woman knowing my secret could hurt my children, threaten what little good that remains in my life. Heck, it might even blow back on Danny. I shouldn't feel *too* bad using such a power on her. It's got to be less evil than murdering her.

I look down at my chest. My shirt's got a two-inch hole in it where the blast hit me and the skin under it appears burned and charred. It also itches like a son of a bitch. That means it's healing. I should worry that the cut on my left arm feels like a cut should. No itching. Doesn't look any different than it did twenty minutes ago. Yeah, there's probably a good reason why having a silver weapon waved in my face set off a frenzied panic... it could legit kill me.

That's twice now that panic made my fangs come out. I'm going to need to get better control of myself. Can't go 'vamping out' like that every time something truly frightens me or my time on this earth is going to get real short real fast. Hopefully, like forcing myself awake, fang instinct is something possible to overcome.

Prodding a finger at the cut feels eerily normal. Reminds me of a nick I took from a meth head two months into being a HUD agent. Dude came after me with a knife during a property inspection of a supposedly empty house. He shouldn't have been there and didn't like being disturbed. All the antibiotic injections and crap I had to get after the attack hurt more than the slice. Probably don't need to worry about diseases now. Besides, that silver blade looked fairly clean.

Seriously, how often could she possibly use it?

I let my head fall back against the seat and stare at the beige fabric overhead. Crap. Visiting six psychics—well, two psychics and some con artists —is a fairly good sign that I've gone to extreme means to find any possible way to be normal... but normal ain't gonna happen. Dolores said some kind of good change is in my future, but years from now. No way possible for me to simply sit around and wait for that. We'll lose the house. What the hell am I going to do? My 'undead condition' is going to totally get in the way of any traditional job.

Hmm. Mary Lou sorta jokingly suggested working as a private investigator a while ago. The idea sounded silly at first, but thinking about it now… it actually sounds kinda close to what I'd been doing already for HUD. Plus, working for myself, I wouldn't have to worry about being to any office on time.

Suppose it's at least worth, umm… investigating.

Chapter Thirteen
Truth is Stranger

Once the kids are in bed that night, I stumble into a conversation with Danny.

Not that I'd been trying to avoid him or anything, but he hasn't exactly been too interested in being close to me—as in, doesn't like being in the same room. However, since I've started taking his 'quest to cure Sam' idea more seriously, he's lowered his guard somewhat. He asked about the psychic visits, so I filled him in on everything that happened.

Telling him about Dante makes him laugh—but only when I mention the candles turning black. Can you believe my husband thinks something *real* happened there and it hadn't been an act? Yeah, that's a little much for me. Then again, the dude didn't even stick around to collect payment...

So, hmm...

It can't be a good sign that my instinct tells me *not* to tell Danny about silver weapons—or that I successfully erased someone's memory. As far as my husband knows, Indigo turned out to be another 'people reader' psychic who tried to guess things based on cues she picked up. Apologies to the woman for calling her a charlatan, but the last thing I need is for my paranoid hubby to know about a legit psychic witch who can hurl lightning from her fingertips... especially if things between us worsen. Wouldn't want him, say, hiring her to destroy me.

Maybe he's right about me growing darker. I shouldn't be pessimistic about *us*.

At the end of that conversation, I bring up the whole private investigator thing again. Danny's expression lights up and he tells me about this guy he works with all the time named Sonny Hughes. He's a retired Sonoma County sheriff's deputy, now working as a PI for about eight years. Good sign there, means there's enough money to be made at it. Then again, if he retired from the sheriff's department, he probably has a pension.

I don't know what's more surreal between me sitting at home looking up information on how to become a PI or that Danny's right next to me like old times, helping. Once I get lost on a resource page, Danny moves over a bit to attack a bunch of paperwork for a case he's working on.

I'm still reading when Danny calls it a night and goes to sleep.

There's a lot more involved to this than I

imagined. Whole bunch of studying, mostly looks like a test about rules. Stuff like when is it legal for a PI to take pictures of someone and so on. Had to deal with plenty of that with HUD. This shouldn't be too bad... though it's something I'm clearly overqualified for. Still, it sounds kind of fun.

Samantha Moon, P.I.

Hey, it even has a nice ring to it.

I download a bunch of PDF documents and start studying.

***

The next day, I roll out of bed a touch after three in the afternoon.

It's Saturday, so no school for Tammy. Danny's also home all day, but overloaded with work. After a shower and a trip out to the detached garage for a blood meal, I collect the kids and swing by Mary Lou's for a while. My kids get to play with hers, and I get to hang out with my sister and talk about my plans to pursue work as a P.I.

She's thrilled to see I'm not letting my sorrow over losing my job at HUD devour me. If anyone knows how badly I wanted to become a fed, it's her. Neither of us have called or emailed Dad to mention it since we don't want to deal with the inevitable laughter. He doesn't much care for the government or anyone who works for it, so he'd be thoroughly amused that his daughter wasn't compatible with 'The Man.' Little does he know, I am compatible.

It's the stupid undeath that isn't.

Maybe if someday they decriminalized all drugs, he'd change his mind.

But that's neither here nor there.

Eventually, I head home with the kids. Going out in the daylight is still searing hot and wicked uncomfortable, but between sunblock and rapid dashes from Momvan to building, it's manageable.

I'm surprised and not surprised to find Danny gone. At least he left a 'back soon' Post-It note on the fridge. He might've gone out to do something for his case or, just as likely, he's off hunting for the Fountain of Youth. And by that I mean his 'make Sam mortal again' quest.

Since I am technically a housewife at the moment, I get started on dinner. Even if I can't have any, it keeps up the illusion of normalcy for the kids, and Danny has been working his butt off lately. With two small children, we've been sticking to stuff they'll eat... like chicken nuggets, hotdogs, or pasta. Might as well do mac and cheese tonight. If I attempt spaghetti sauce, Danny will invariably make a comment about me getting close but not quite doing it perfect like his mother's sauce. Or even his sauce, which he claims is a close second.

The kids settle in the living room, mesmerized by the television. No idea what the heck they're watching, something on Nick Kids. At least it's not that stupid purple dinosaur. Should I worry that my four-year-old daughter has figured out how to work the cable remote?

With the kids entertained and dinner on the way, I pull my flip phone out and try calling the number Danny gave me for Sonny.

"Hughes," says a gritty older man's voice that instantly fills my head with a mental image of a square-jawed cowboy sporting a greying beard. Sort of a Jack Palance type with a permanent squint like he's staring into a perpetual sunset.

"Hi, Sonny?"

"You got him. What can I do you for, ma'am?"

Gee, do I sound old enough to be a ma'am? Yikes. "My name is Samantha Moon, Danny Moon's wife."

"The attorney?"

"Yes."

"I know Danny. Go on."

"He mentioned you're a private investigator. I'm considering going into that line of work and was hoping you might be willing to talk about it? Danny thought you could give me some pointers."

"Aren't you the federal agent?"

"I was, yes."

He pauses, perhaps waiting for an explanation for why I quit. The explanation doesn't come, at least not yet. Finally, he chuckles. "Everyone wants to be a private eye. Sure, we can talk. How about we have a face to face. I'm old fashioned like that."

"Sounds good."

"Hmm. What's your schedule like tomorrow?"

I tell him I'm free in the afternoon, and we schedule a meeting at four at a nearby Starbucks.

He mentions that he hasn't heard from Danny and asks about him. I let him know my hubby has been particularly busy. I thank him again, perhaps too profusely, and we hang up.

"Mom!" shouts Tammy as I hang up. "Anf'nee asploded."

He's about eighty percent potty trained, but still wears a diaper for emergencies. I turn down the heat on the mac, plop the lid on the pot and run in to check the damage. Upon entering the living room, I'm hit with the smell of rotten egg sulfur so hard I practically get high from the sheer awfulness of the stink.

Considering Tammy isn't on the ground vomiting, I'm pretty sure the ghastliness is due to my enhanced vampire senses. Whoever designed the undead certainly didn't plan on them being around toddlers. Forget silver weapons… feed a two-year-old boy broccoli and his back end can incapacitate an entire legion of bloodsuckers.

Tammy giggles at the involuntary faces I must be making. Anthony seems proud of himself. Great. He's going to be one of those boys who thinks breaking wind bad enough that someone leaves the room is a point of pride.

"Did you potty?" I ask.

"No."

Tammy gives him her best 'stop lying' glare.

I scoop him up and do a pat check. Hmm. Diaper doesn't feel loaded. Possible he merely had a gaseous event.

"Do you have to go potty?"

He looks at me with all the seriousness of DaVinci working out the schematics of a flying machine for a moment before saying, "Yes."

"Okay." I carry him to the bathroom and remove the diaper—which is mostly dry except for something that looks suspiciously like a skid mark. Based on my experience growing up with three brothers, I'm certain that boys come in two distinct types: mostly clean underwear and 'put on a hazmat suit before handling' underwear. I wonder which category Anthony will fall into.

Anyway, my son uses the little seat like a pro. I'm so proud of him my eyes are watering. Wait. No. I'm proud of him *and* my eyes are watering. Good grief. Now I understand why they call vampirism a *curse.* It's due to the super senses, especially smell. I think I'm literally about to lose consciousness from how bad this reeks. Really, the room is blurry and it's burning my sinuses out.

Fortunately, I don't have to breathe anymore.

By the time I'm done cleaning the boy up, Danny's home. I've gotten really good at faking dinnertime, taking a small portion (don't want to waste *too* much) and either spitting it into a cup or not really putting every forkful into my mouth so it takes longer to 'eat.' Maybe we should get a dog so I can slip it food under the table?

Nah. We can't handle the additional expense of a major pet. As it is, we're going to be in the red as soon as the checks I'm getting for unused vacation time and medical severance stop coming. However, something unusual happens: I'm feeling excited about my meeting with Sonny tomorrow.

I fill Danny in on that over dinner, and he seems pleased to hear it.

"Sonny misses you, dear." I do a flirty little eye thing at him. "Says you haven't called him in a while."

He nearly chokes on his mac, then laughs. "I haven't needed him to go digging in accident reports or hunt down witnesses for a while, but that actually might change pretty soon. The case is getting weird."

"Hope it's not as weird as the swan guy." I smirk, trying to imagine what went through the heads of the cops who responded to the scene of *that* accident. A seventy-year-old guy had been driving around with a live swan under his arm, lost control of his car, and ran down a guy on a mountain bike. Yeah, live actual swan. Mean little sucker, too. Kept trying to bite the police whenever they got too close. Who would've thought carrying a swan in the car could impair a driver? The guy he put in the hospital hired Danny.

Danny chuckles. "Yeah, that guy had some issues."

It's comforting to know that there are people out there who make my life—such as it is—feel sane.

Chapter Fourteen
Fictional Creatures

Sunday afternoon, Danny zooms out the door within two minutes of me getting out of bed, with only a quick "I'm late, gotta run."

Back in the day, I would have asked where he was going—or he would have volunteered the info. Now, I get no such courtesies... or time to even ask the question. And, yeah, goodbye pecks on the cheek or lips have long since gone bye-bye.

I emerge from the bedroom to find the kids playing in the living room. The smell of PBJ sandwiches lingers in the air, and all seems normal except for Anthony pulling a Clayton, meaning no pants. As a kid, my brother hated clothes. My two sit on the rug in front of the couch, an abandoned diaper nearby. The instant I look at it, my senses pick up pee. It's unusual for him to wet his diaper these days. Usually, accidents involve the other stuff. However, given that it appears he's been enjoying 'freedom' for a while, I think Danny had been too absorbed in whatever he'd been doing to notice Anthony got tired of sitting in a wet diaper and peeled it off himself. Fortunately, the mess is minimal and I get the boy dressed without much fuss. While I'm changing him, Tammy fills me in that he'd been asking Daddy to take him to the bathroom but got 'in a minute' over and over until it became too late.

Grr. That doesn't sound like Danny. He's never brushed the kids off before.

It seems the kids are coming with me to meet Sonny Hughes. I douse myself with the spray-on sunblock, load the kids in the Momvan, and head out to the Starbucks off Gilbert Street.

My mental image of the grizzled old gunslinger turns out to be slightly off. Though he *does* have grey hair, he's closer to Wilford Brimley than Jack Palance. Figure he's a couple years into his fifties, little bit of a beer belly, but otherwise looks in decent shape. But hey, he's got a cowboy hat on. That counts as close, right?

Since he's the only guy in the place over thirty, I assume he's my guy and walk up to him. "Sonny?"

He's clearly not expecting to see me showing up with two small children, but recovers nicely. "You must be Samantha. And who are your assistants?"

Chuckling, I introduce Tammy and Anthony. My daughter waves and says hello. Anthony picks his nose.

One of the fundamental laws of reality is that a four-year-old is not brought into Starbucks without asking for a cake pop—or something sugary. Might as well bribe them for putting up with the outing. Anthony points at a cookie instead. So, Tammy gets her cake pop, the boy a chocolate chip cookie as big as his face. Two small hot chocolates seal the deal.

Sonny orders a black coffee. Damn, I miss coffee. The smell in here is driving me nuts. Not wanting to barf all over him and the kids is enough to keep me from caving in. We move over to one of the tables and sit.

"So, you finally decided to give up on the federal thing?" asks Sonny.

"Not entirely by choice," I say. "It's kind of a long story, but the short version is… I suffered an attack a few months ago while out jogging and it's set off some weird sort of health issue that's made it difficult for me to stay awake early in the day. Past late afternoon, I'm fine. Doctors haven't been able to explain it yet, but as I'm sure you can guess, randomly falling asleep isn't exactly conducive to working as a federal agent."

He whistles. "Yeah, I can see where that might get in the way. Sorry to hear about the attack."

"Thanks. Except for that sleep thing, I feel okay." I bite my lip, holding back mention of sunlight sensitivity. Indigo Murillo knows about the existence of vampires. If I drop too many puzzle pieces on the table in front of someone else, they'll figure it out. Especially if that someone happens to know about creatures like me. As they say, best to keep my cards close to my chest.

"That's good. Well, you were with the feds at least three years, right?"

"Yes. Just barely."

"Perfect. One of the requirements for obtaining a PI license is three years' of investigative experience. You've got that covered. Probably got a good jump on the other stuff, too, but there's a lot of information that's particular to being a PI that you wouldn't necessarily run into that you need to know for the test. Darn thing is pretty long."

I nod. "Yeah, I've been reading everything I can find related to it."

We talk for a while about being a PI, which feels mostly like he's prepping me for the test. I find myself taking a surprising amount of guesses based on assumptions of the law from my time at HUD. Alas, what an active duty federal agent can get away with is a bit more flexible than a private investigator. By the end of our conversation, he offers to let me tag along with him for a while as an unpaid assistant. Considering I'm still expecting two months' worth of income from the old job, I accept.

"I'll need to work mostly at night or at least later in the day. Anything earlier than three in the afternoon is pushing it. I'm guessing we're not going to be kicking down any doors or ending up having people shooting at us, so if we need to do something earlier than that it might not be a problem, especially if it's indoors."

He nods, scratching at his fluffy grey mustache. "We can work with that schedule. Up for starting tomorrow?"

"Sure. My sister should be able to watch the kids."

Sonny hands me a business card. "Swing on by as early as you care to. Most of the time, I knock off around six. Every so often, you'll get a case that requires working late into the night, such as tailing a suspected unfaithful spouse to their den of iniquity."

"Maybe you should write private eye novels."

He emits a dry, wheezy chuckle. "Been thinking about it. My office address is on the card."

I tuck the card in my front pocket and shake hands. "See you tomorrow."

***

Mary Lou pulls up behind me in my driveway as I'm unbuckling Anthony from his car seat.

She's brought her whole brood, Ruby Grace who turned three last month, Billy Joe who's a week short of five, and Ellie Mae who will turn seven next month at the end of November. Between her three and my two, it feels like we're trapped in a never ending cycle of birthday parties. In a few years, we're basically going to become part owners of Chuck-E-Cheese's. Assuming, of course, I don't end up a homeless divorcee living out of a hotel room.

Where did that thought come from?

As much as it would absolutely suck, if things got *that* bad, I could move back in with my parents... but I'd sooner crash at Mary Lou's. The parents' place is a bit remote, which would make my present dietary needs a bit of a challenge. Forest critters beware.

"Oh wow, talk about great timing!" calls Mary Lou while running over. "Figured I'd pop over to make sure you were okay. Been worried about you ever since you had to resign."

"Thanks." I throw an arm around her and hug her. "I'd be totally lost without you."

The kids rush through the house and straight to our backyard. They go nuts with Frisbees and rainbow-colored balls.

My sister and I stand in the shadow of the house out back, keeping an eye on them. Danny's idea to add a deck is on indefinite hold due to the money situation. I explain the trip to meet Sonny and that I'm starting to take the PI thing seriously.

"That's good. Sounds a lot less boring than most other night jobs I can think of."

I hang my head, not quite able to laugh. "What's the world coming to that a vampire needs a day job? Count Dracula didn't work. He just had this huge castle and all sorts of money."

"Hah!" She laughs. "True, but he's also a fictional character."

A weird sense of indignation comes out of nowhere as if my sister had just told me Danny only existed as a figment of my imagination. Odd. Why do I keep getting strange notions like that? I glance sideways at her. "Are you sure about that?"

"About what?" Mary Lou eyes the patio door. "Still have that wine in the fridge?"

"Yeah, all yours. And about Dracula being fictional."

"Wait. You don't think?" She stares at me.

I shrug. "Not a thinking thing. More a gut feeling. Vampires are supposed to be fictional and yet..."

"Wow. That's kinda freaky to imagine. Be right back. I can hear that bottle calling me." She ducks inside in search of wine.

Yeah. Kinda freaky. Welcome to my life.

Chapter Fifteen
Certified

Waking up at eleven in the morning is still unpleasant, but it's amazing how much of a difference an additional three hours of sleep makes compared to dragging myself upright at eight.

It's been about a month since I started working with Sonny to get a feel for being a PI. And yeah, it's nothing like the movies make it out to be. Ninety percent of it is staring at a computer screen and making phone calls. Then again, back when those movies were made, the internet didn't exist.

It's probably a good thing I've been 'working' and getting out of the house. That day four weeks ago when Anthony wet his diaper? Danny didn't get home until after midnight smelling like stripper perfume and beer. The instant he walked in the door, I questioned him about what had been so important that he couldn't spare a few minutes to take his son to the bathroom. He claimed to have been working on 'the cure' for me and thought he'd come close... and needed to run off and meet someone who could help him. Help *us*, he corrected.

My asking him if Bambi worked occult magic confused him until I pointed out he smelled like cheap perfume and broken dreams. His explanation for that involved meeting his present client at the 'gentleman's club' he owns in Buena Park before going to visit the occultist. Well, at least Danny answered fast enough while still making eye contact. That suggested to me that, yes, he might have been *to* a strip club, but he didn't do anything there that made him feel guilty.

Then again, if he thinks of me as a creature impersonating his wife, *would* he feel guilt?

I dunno, but I'm half-tempted to go to the bar and follow up with witnesses. Had my husband been there? Who had he met?

Damn, now I'm sounding a bit paranoid.

So, yeah... we haven't been talking much since that. Not from any deliberate spite on my part, but I couldn't say I've been going out of my way to interact with him. Maybe it's mercenary of me, but he's staying here, earning money, taking care of us. No point antagonizing him.

My time with Sonny has been roughly noon to around five or six in the afternoon depending on what we're doing. Lots of background checks, combing through various online resources available to private investigators. There's some old-fashioned legwork as well, like going to interview people who may have observed a subject's movements or seen a missing person. Once, we stayed out late to surveil a suspected cheater—a guy almost in his eighties. Turned out, he actually *was* cheating on his wife who hired Sonny... but when we went to the house to give her the photos, we found her with another guy.

People are weird.

Anyway, once I'm done for the day with him, my usual plans involved rushing home to spend as much time as possible with the kids before bedtime. Since Danny's about as interested in me as most sane people are interested in recreational root canals, they're all I've got left.

There is some good news, though. After a month with Sonny, I applied to take the test for my PI license. Amazingly, they had a late session—likely to accommodate people who still have day jobs. Much less nerve-wracking on me to go after dark when fully alert. The test felt like a mixture of easier than expected plus 'where the heck did this come from?' For those questions, I trusted my gut. In hindsight, it's possible the answers unwittingly came out of the proctor's head, but in the absence of intent to cheat, there is no guilt.

Considering I passed, my intuition is either spot on or some mind reading happened. Possibly feeling like a cheat dims my excitement a little, but that certification is—hopefully—the key to my being able to provide a stable home for my kids.

So, it's Saturday, two days after dealing with a state office to make everything official. My body no longer produces oil, but my fingers can still leave prints when helped along by ink. Whew. That would've been difficult to explain.

Mary Lou invites us over for a barbecue to celebrate. Initially, Danny doesn't seem to be interested in going, but he relents. We arrive at my sister's place a little after four. Her husband, Rick, heads out to the yard in a "BBQ King" apron to prepare the grill. I guess some people would consider it strange to have a barbecue in early November, but this *is* California. In deference to the time of year, the kids *aren't* going in my sister's aboveground pool, which is sealed up for the winter. Instead, they run around the yard on the massive playground-gym-swingset-climby thing that Rick built his kids. And Danny helped with.

Different times. Happier times.

Ordinarily, my sister and I would stretch out in swimsuits to absorb some sun… but yeah. Slight problem with me and sunlight now. So, we sit on the deck under a giant umbrella talking about—of all things—Dracula. Specifically, how the older folklore about vampires never mentions anything about sunlight being harmful to them. Heck, even in the fairly recent movie based on Dracula, they had him trotting around in broad daylight dressed like a dandy. He didn't seem the least bit sluggish for having a face full of sunlight.

And yeah, okay, I'm feeling annoyed that made up stories aren't fully in line with reality. Where *did* the whole sunlight burns vampires thing come from, anyway? Hearing that the old stories don't mention it makes me wonder what exactly I am, then. Because sunlight damn well affects me. Or... hmm. Maybe it affects the thing within me. Maybe it abhors the sun. Maybe it's *that* evil.

I shudder. Great, just great.

By all means, share my body then.

Danny stands over by Rick, the guys talking about whatever guys talk about. He keeps looking in my general direction with an almost annoyed expression that gets worse when Ellie Mae and Ruby Grace run over to show Aunt Sam their new dolls.

Soon after Rick tosses the meat on the grill, the smell becomes torturously good. Fortunately, I had a nice big meal of pig and cow blood before leaving the house, which left me as full as post-Thanksgiving dinner. When the food's ready, Mary Lou and I run a little con game. She takes a small portion and I take a small portion. Her chicken bones migrate to my plate with a little sleight of hand as she eats and I fake eating. Eventually, it looks like we both finished our food, even though everything ended up in my sister's belly.

Danny isn't much for conversation over the meal, fidgeting and giving me looks whenever Rick, Mary Lou, or one of their kids talks to me. It's almost like he's either resentful of them treating me like a normal person or fighting the urge to warn them to stay away from the dangerous creature. Even his responses to Rick are terse, begrudging. It's both painful and confusing since he's been trying to help me these past few months. Why would he sit here all afternoon and pout like a little boy forced to attend some family function he hated?

The next time he sends a dark look in my direction and we make eye contact, I get the distinct impression he's frustrated at his cure, or lack thereof. And, yes, I'm pretty sure I just read his mind. Anyway, he'd thought the cure had been close to working but something didn't go as planned. I glance away, ashamed of myself for being this *thing* with the ability to see into people's heads. Guess he expected I'd be back to normal by now.

Once everyone's finished with their food, the kids resume running around the yard while Mary Lou and Rick gather up the dirty dishes and carry them inside. I'm just about to collect the leftovers when a *thump* comes from my left.

I look over. Little Ellie Mae's flat on her face, having taken a spill. She rolls over into a seated position and starts wailing. Blood runs down her right arm from a cut on her hand. Danny and I both run over to check on her, but he slides in front of me, blocking my view.

"What are you doing?" I ask.

"She's bleeding." Danny turns his back to me and takes a knee to check on my niece.

I step around him, despite what might have been an actual hiss coming from him. Looks like my niece's hand found a small, pointy rock when she fell. Nothing too bad. I kneel down and say, "Shh. It's just a little boo boo."

Ellie Mae continues bawling. Her now-three-year-old sister Ruby Grace folds her arms, shaking her head at the drama. It's kinda mean of me to think, but I'm not sure how my sister and Rick produced a kid that smart. Not that Mary Lou or Rick are stupid, but Ruby's scary smart for her age. How many two-year-olds speak in complete sentences with real words... and recognize drama for what it is?

Danny pulls Ellie Mae's arm away from me, turning it to hide the blood. "I got this, Sam. Please go inside."

He thinks I'm going to flip out at the sight of a bleeding child. "Are you serious right now?"

"Yes. I got it." Danny glares at me.

Mary Lou runs over. "What happened?"

I'm not getting into a tug of war with Danny using a child, so I stand and fold my arms. "Ellie Mae wiped out and cut her hand."

Apparently, my sister noticed the way he 'shielded' her from me. She gives him a look, then collects her six-year-old daughter and takes her into the house. The other kids continue playing, leaving Danny and I standing there in each other's faces like a pair of boxers posing for the camera a week before a big match.

"I'm not going to lose my composure at the sight of blood," I say a hair over a whisper.

"Maybe, but I'd rather not take the chance."

I lean at him. "If you'd devoured an entire pizza by yourself, would you be tempted to eat the first piece of food you laid eyes on an hour later?"

He stares at me, confused.

"Before we left the house, I drank half a freakin' bottle. Even if the slightest chance existed of me feeding from a live person, I'm *still* stuffed. Besides, there's no way in hell I'd ever hurt a child. I thought you knew me."

"I knew *Sam*." He turns away, sighing. "Maybe there's some of her still inside you. I can't explain what it's like to look into your eyes and see someone else. You've changed."

"Duh. No kidding. Most normal people don't start smoking when they go outside on a bright day or can suck down a quart of animal blood without violently throwing it up all over the place."

I briefly consider telling him about that first day home after leaving the hospital when I'd been tempted to bite Tammy, how I'd sworn to that creature inside my head that I would dive into the sun and reduce myself to ashes if it dared hurt my kids. But, telling him that would be a bad idea. He'd ignore my mental triumph over the creature and see it only as 'almost bit Tammy.'

"I'm sorry it's not happening faster," he says finally. "The cure, I mean. I'm doing everything I can."

I put a hand on his arm. He tenses, but doesn't pull away. "Thank you for trying."

"You could at least try to sound sincere."

"That is sincere," I say. "But it's also me kinda running out of hope that something like this can be undone."

Danny whirls, grabbing my arm and staring into my eyes. "I'm not going to give up. If there's any chance of getting Samantha back, I have to take it. Stop trying to trick me into giving up."

"I'm not trying to trick you. If you can somehow 'fix' me, I'd be so damn happy there aren't words to express it. I just don't want you to drive yourself crazy and lose your sanity to an obsession with something that may not be possible. You're starting to worry me."

Some of the challenge melts out of his expression. Perhaps hearing me welcome being 'fixed' conflicted enough with his belief I'm a demon trying to steal his wife. He appears to be debating what to say next, but doesn't get anything out before Mary Lou practically drags us inside to the kitchen. She slides the glass door shut a little too hard, then whirls on him, pointing.

"Look, Danny, I know there's some really weird shit going on, but I'm not going to sit there watching you treat Sam like trash. I know my sister, and I trust her completely. This isn't easy for her, you know. She needs both of us to be in her corner, not pushing her away. Whatever chip you've got on your shoulder now needs to get dropped or it's only going to keep growing until it's too heavy to carry."

He starts to reply, stops himself. Thinks a moment, tries again, but still can't say a word. I never did understand how my lawyer husband could always crumple under my sister's stare. This time, however, I think somewhere inside his brain, he realizes she's right. I can't bring myself to look at him because I'm afraid of reading his mind without wanting to. Talk about a paradox. In order to stop feeling like a monster, I'll need to learn how to be a monster… at least enough to turn it off. Maybe I can forget about it entirely, like I pretend not to have fangs.

"I'm only trying to keep things as sane as possible," says Danny.

Mary Lou smirks. "Then you should stop treating Sam like she's some stranger who can't be left alone near children."

"Look in her eyes, Mary Lou. Don't pretend you don't see it." He lifts his gaze off the floor. "The little flame. That's the other… *thing*. That's not Sam."

My sister shakes her head. "If a tick burrows into your butt, do you stop being Danny? So, she's got a hitchhiker. Big deal. This is supposed to be a happy moment. She passed her private investigator's test. Can you at least *try* to be supportive?"

The entity—and, yeah, I'm pretty sure at this point that another consciousness does indeed share my skull—writhes in resentment at being compared to a parasitic insect, but I tamp it down until its presence becomes unnoticeable.

And... wow. I feel a blessed reprieve at the presence having been removed from my forethoughts, even if temporary.

Good to know.

"It's okay," I whisper. "He's having a difficult time coping. Hell, I am, too."

"No, it's not okay." Mary Lou hugs me. "He needs to support you."

"He is… in his own way." I explain in brief his attempt to find a cure that will put me back to normal, skipping mention of my near certainty it's a fool's errand for Danny's benefit. This I know... for my kids, for any chance of saving my relationship, for my own sanity, I have to deal with what happened to me and not hang my hopes on the impossible.

"What exactly are you asking me to do here?" Danny taps the tip of his shoe at the floor, looking down.

"Stop treating her like you've got a pet tiger in the house. And for God's sake, stop throwing off so much gloom today." She puts an arm around us both and pulls us into a hug. "This is a happy moment."

My sister's trying to celebrate that I'm an official PI now, but it lacks the same sense of victory as the night after I'd been sworn in as a federal agent. Wow, did we party that night. Most of it is *still* a blurry haze of memory. Being a private investigator does kinda feel like settling for the second place finish, but honestly, it has to count as first place since working for the government is now impossible.

Time to make the most of it.

Chapter Sixteen
Something Weird This Way Comes

Know what stinks more than having a PI license and no clients?

No, not Anthony's diaper. Working the grave-yard shift at a truck stop restaurant.

Welcome to late February. November, December, and January passed with little fanfare other than Ellie Mae's seventh birthday on the twenty-seventh of November and a relatively austere Christmas. Half the presents Mary Lou got for my kids, she labeled as being from 'Mom & Dad' so it looked like they came from me and Danny. I'm going to get misty-eyed thinking about that for the rest of my li—well, for a long time.

Danny's law practice hasn't exactly been kicking ass and taking names. He did, however, win that case defending the strip club owner. I now know the definition of conflicted emotions. Apparently, the guy had hired a couple dancing girls who'd fallen four or five months short of their eighteenth birthday and lied about their age. In the most awkward of awkward moments, one girl's uncle—father's brother—went to the club, recognized her, and freaked the hell out. In fact, the only good thing I think to come out of that whole affair is that the uncle swore off ever going to a strip club again. So, yeah, a slimeball who didn't exactly work too hard to make sure his dancers were legal got off on a technicality. And because of that technicality, the other stuff—drugs—that got found during the resulting investigation ended up being thrown out.

My husband had enabled a real paragon of society. Kinda makes me wonder which one of us is the real monster. Well, maybe me because I didn't say much while appreciating the money he earned doing it. Because of that case, we still have a house. Danny thought winning that one would give him a little fame and bring in more clients… but it wound up having the opposite effect: infamy.

We even had some protestors from a church show up at the house, and Tammy learned the phrase 'smut fixer.' Should I be happy she can read protest signs or horrified?

Anyway, the only clients Danny's been getting lately have been on the greyer side of the reputation curve. But income is income according to him. Watching him lose weight, stop being such a perfectionist with his hair and adopt a five-o'clock shadow, makes me feel like a background character in some neo-retro Franz Kafka *Metamorphosis* play. It's as though Danny's personality and moral compass are disintegrating in real time right before my eyes. He almost took a case defending a business owner accused of exposing himself to not one, but five of his employees but couldn't quite sink that far.

Honestly, it's good he passed on that one or I might've left him.

Things are getting tight with money. The mortgage is eating pretty much all of our income. Though, this isn't anything new to me... the money part, I mean. Most of my childhood felt like I'd grown up in the Great Depression, no shoes, only owned two dresses, sometimes having a slice of bread or two with homemade jam for dinner. No way am I going to allow things to get that bad for my kids.

Hence why I started waiting tables at Earl's Truck Stop. And no, the owner isn't named Earl. It's Jose. He figured a truck stop ought to be called Earl's. I picked it because the place stays open 24/7 and my shift starts after the kids are asleep. It's not exactly tons of money, but the schedule is right and it's something. Admittedly, it's a massive kick to the ego. After all the work I put into becoming a federal agent to end up waiting tables in a dive restaurant like the pothead girls in my high school who never did their homework is embarrassing. Every damn night is full of dread that I'll run into someone who knows me.

Christ... the idea of waitressing for anyone I used to work with at HUD is more mortifying than that time Anthony tore my bikini bottoms off at the beach and went running around trying to make me chase him. Something tells me Danny won't be in the restaurant to metaphorically wrap me up in a towel.

Someone once said that a person needs to hit rock bottom before they can climb. Not sure who did, but if I ever find them, they're getting a punch in the nose. Then again, we still have a house and my kids are healthy. Can't really call this *rock bottom*. Things could be far worse, and it's up to me not to let it get to that point. Hence waiting tables.

My life is a series of paradoxes.

I'm a vampire who tries to go out in the day, loathes the idea of drinking blood, and tries to forget entirely that she's really a monster. Another paradox is that in order to make money as a PI, people need to know I exist. That means advertising... which costs money I don't have. Mostly, it's been Danny telling people at the courthouse and law firm about me. We did run ads in some local papers and with this place that prints adverts on paper placemats. Fortunately, Jose, my new boss, doesn't use those placemats. It would be uncomfortable to have to stare at my name on the tables of people I'm bringing food to.

Gah. I can't believe I'm a damned waitress. Nothing against it really, it's an honest job. Just feels like a massive waste of a college degree and all that training. I could've goofed off for all those years if I'd have known this is where it would end up. Of course, without going to college, there'd be no Danny and consequently no Tammy or Anthony. Thus, the circumstances wouldn't have led to me being tempted to go out jogging at night and get attacked.

Then again, every time I think about that night, my inclination grows that it had been more than a random attack. No matter the location or circumstances of my life, it's likely the same thing would've happened to me. Even if I'd ended up like my brother Dusk, wandering Europe to find inspiration for his fine art career with nothing even close to a permanent home.

Damn, he turned thirty-five two months ago and I haven't heard from him. The cell number I had didn't even ring. Just beeped a few times and went dead. Hope he's okay. The last time I saw him face to face, he'd been twenty-four, right before he flew to England. If he showed up in front of me now, I might not even recognize him.

Nine years is too long. Then again, I had spent nine years building a life for me.

Damn waste of time. No, the kids came out of it. And Danny.

And I had been damn good at being a federal agent.

And working as a private eye could still possibly pan out.

Possibly.

Anyway, among many other things that stink about waiting tables at night, it's only a part-time gig. Tonight is an off night, so I'll have nothing to do later but sit at the dining room table at home, surrounded by bills. Danny has started wearing an amulet, a silver disc with a black opal set in it. He thinks it'll protect him if the entity inside me ever takes me over. At least he's accepted—or claims to have accepted—that some of me remains. He helped me set up the LLC stuff for my private investigation business. Even though he doesn't seem to trust me and I scare the crap out of him, he still wants me to make money. Losing the house affects him, too.

The biggest change, though, is that he's come around to the idea of me being home alone with the kids while he's at the office. Not sure if that means he trusts me more than I think or he's simply gambling because we can't afford day care.

The past few months haven't been a complete wasteland in regard to work on the PI front, but a handful of lost/stolen expensive dog cases and a background check or two aren't going to cut it. Money from HUD has dried up. I could've tried to get on Social Security Disability, but that would've required a whole bunch of jumping through hoops and doctor visits. While it's true I can't work a traditional day job, inviting the scrutiny of doctors to my present unreal existence would not have ended well. At best, I'd have needed to violate their thoughts. At worst, I'd have ended up caged some-where in a CIA lab.

The PI thing sounded good on paper, but it's falling way short of making enough money. Unless something changes soon for either me or Danny, we're on course to lose the house. No, I'm not going to ask Mary Lou or even Chad for money. That's not fair to them.

Now, while the kids amuse themselves with a mixture of television and toys in the living room, I go online in search of cheap or free ways to solicit clients. In the midst of begrudgingly admitting that I might need to spend more on my web-based ads, the phone rings.

I grab the cordless handset to answer. "Hello?"

Only breathing comes over the line for a few seconds, then a voice with a thick Eastern European accent asks, "Daniel Moon?"

"Umm, not exactly. I'm his wife. He's at the office right now. Who is this?"

Click.

Well, isn't that special? Grumbling, I set the phone down and return to my reading, wondering why some creepy sounding guy with a possibly Romanian accent would be calling for my husband. If it had been work related, wouldn't he call Danny's office number? No, that had the distinct feel of 'weird' to it. Doubt hits me. What if the reason his income has been dwindling is that he's allowing his pointless quest to 'save' me to cut into the time he should be working? His loss of clients can't *all* be due to his defending a major sleazeball.

Anthony wobbles over to me. "Potty."

"Okay." I smile, take his hand, and lead him to the bathroom.

At least my son's getting to be a pro at using a toilet—even a small one. We'll probably be safe weaning him off diapers real soon. He hasn't had an accident since early November. Soon after he's finished and plopped back in front of the TV, the phone rings again. It's tempting to answer with 'what the hell do you want?' but I don't.

"Hello?"

"Is this Samantha Moon?" asks a woman who sounds like she's been crying recently.

"Yes."

"You're a private investigator?"

"That's right." Ooh! I sit up straight. "What can I do for you?"

"I need to hire someone to... help me. The police don't believe me and they're not looking in the right places."

"Um, okay…" I open a notepad window on the laptop. "Can you tell me your name and what's going on?"

"My name's Brooke Olsen," says the woman, her voice starting to crack with grief. "My son Braxton is missing."

A chill washes over me and I can't help but look over at my two kids. "Oh, no… I'm so sorry. What happened?"

"Brax was playing out in the yard behind our

house. We're in Idyllwild, right up against the woods. I was in the kitchen cooking and watching him. The next thing I know, I look up and he's running off into the trees like he saw a rabbit or something and wanted to chase it. I rushed outside to go after him, but he disappeared." She breaks down in soft crying for a few minutes.

I can see where the police are probably taking this story. Kid runs off into the woods and the parent's right there to chase but somehow loses him? Right away, it sounds like a lie. Either this woman wasn't right there to chase him or she had something more directly to do with the boy going missing. However, the grief in her voice sounds pretty genuine, at least over the phone. Also, it's unlikely that she'd want to hire a PI to look for the boy if she'd hurt him and made up a lie about him running away. A killer would want to avoid scrutiny. No innocent person ever objects to an investigation, especially if the investigation could clear them.

"Can you walk me through what happened?" I ask.

Brooke sniffles and sighs. I picture her wiping tears from her face. "I realize how this must sound. That's what the police kinda think, that I did something to him. I swear that's not true. I was standing in the kitchen by the sink, washing asparagus for dinner, keeping an eye on Brax out the window. Except when I looked up again—no more than twenty seconds from the last time I looked up—I see him run into the woods. He knows not to do that."

"How old is your son?"

"He's seven."

I type that into my notepad file. "Okay. How long after he ran into the woods did you go after him?"

"Immediately. Well, I first yelled for him out the window to come back, and when he didn't, I ran outside. I was no more than twenty or thirty seconds behind him."

That sounds reasonable except for how a boy could entirely disappear in half a minute. Sure that could happen at the mall or other large public place with an active abductor in play, but out in the woods behind their house? He could have gotten lost. Then again, no seven-year-old could cover so much ground so fast that he wouldn't hear his mother calling for him. It's possible he fell and got hurt and *couldn't* respond, but the police surely searched the area and would've found him.

"The police conducted a search, I'm guessing?"

"Yes. They didn't find him. A big search party went into the woods all week every day. Hundreds of volunteers. They even brought in a helicopter with that heat-sensing thing on it."

"Are you married?"

"Yes. Ken is a wreck. Ho doesn't blame me, at least outwardly. But I know he does. Of course he would. I was the one watching our son."

"And where was he at the time of the disappearance?"

"He was at work in town."

"What does he do?"

"He's a medical doctor. I'm a nurse." She lets out a shuddering sigh. "There's more…"

"Oh?" I ask.

"I'm convinced something weird happened to Brax. Something the cops don't want to believe and I can't really explain."

"Such as?" I type 'weird' into my note file, but delete it.

"This is going to sound crazy."

I stifle a chuckle. Not going to laugh at a woman with a missing boy. "I can handle crazy."

"That's good to hear, because... yeah, here goes..." She takes a deep breath as if searching for the courage to continue. When she does, her voice is whispery and hesitant. "Ever since his disappearance, I've been having odd dreams, seeing things I can't explain. When it's dark, I hear Braxton calling for me outside. Every time it happens, I run right out there and follow his voice, but I can never find him. Also, there's stuff happening in the house. Doors opening on their own. Chairs aren't where we left them. There are even footsteps in the attic some nights."

Oh, no. Either the kid's dead and haunting her or the woman's cracked. And if those are my only two choices, then I really effing hope she's cracked and the boy's still out there to be found. "And you're sure you're not dreaming this?"

"Positive. My feet have cuts and scrapes from running into the woods in the middle of the night straight out of bed. My husband is the only one I've told about it who doesn't think I'm crazy, but he doesn't hear Brax calling for his mommy. I've been contacting a bunch of investigators but as soon as I start mentioning the strange stuff they're all mysteriously booked solid." She lets out another shuddering breath. "I don't know what I'm going to do if you don't help me. I'd about given up on hiring someone, but your ad popped up and, I dunno. Felt like there was a chance. Samantha Moon, will you please help me figure out what's going on?"

My heart sinks in my chest under an anvil of worry… and a little guilt. I feel scummy taking money from the parent of a missing boy, but my kids have to eat and need a roof over their heads. In her position, I wouldn't care how much money it cost to get my child back, which means I absolutely cannot take advantage of her. Sonny usually charges people between fifty and a hundred bucks an hour depending on the situation. If it's some wealthy idiot doing something superficial and pointless, he quotes the upper end. Someone like Brooke Olsen, he'd help for fifty or even less if she couldn't afford that.

Truth was, I would help this mother search for her missing child for free, if I had to. Hell, I might even have insisted on it, if my back wasn't against the wall financially. Besides, this case has weird written all over it, and who better to handle weird than an undead detective?

"Okay. I'll help you find Braxton."

Having a woman sob thanks at me like I'd already found her kid merely for agreeing to help is more than a little uncomfortable. Equally awkward is answering her when she asks what my rate is. On autopilot, I quote her $50 an hour with an eight-hour deposit. If it takes less than that—I can only hope—she'll get back the difference.

She agrees without hesitation. Hopefully, that means my fee isn't a burden. Then again, paying $400 for a chance to help find your kid is a small price to pay. Undoubtedly, she would have paid more.

I may be a literal bloodsucker, but some things cross the line.

Chapter Seventeen
Unexplained Phenomena

Idyllwild, California is—in an ideal world—an hour and forty-five minute drive away from my house. In the real world populated by morons, it's closer to two-and-a-half hours. Oh, what I wouldn't give to be able to fly like the vampires in *The Lost Boys*. Admittedly, that *is* kind of silly to think about, but damn would it come in handy.

Then again, have I really tried to fly, ridiculous as that might sound?

No, I haven't. Nor do I ever expect to.

If ever there's a statement about how crappy California traffic can be, I used my ability to influence minds to make three different idiots move out of my lane and *didn't* feel like a horrible creature for doing so. It's not as though I'm trying to break the sound barrier. The Momvan isn't a sports car. I'm merely asking the universe to allow me to drive *at* the speed limit.

My sister is a legit superhero for watching the kids on short notice. My kids, too, have super-powers—tolerance. They don't mind going over to Mary Lou's place so Mommy can work. I sent Danny a text that a PI job came up and the kids were with her. So far, he hasn't replied with anything beyond 'K.'

I arrive at Brooke Olsen's house a little after six. It sits at the end of Shady View Drive, basically right on the side of a mountain. Miles of forest-covered hills stretch up to the east beyond the house. She's pretty much at the edge of Idyllwild here. From what I can see getting out of the van, it's not an easy hike to go into those woods. Lots of uphill walking, pale dirt, exposed rocks and roots. Without a trail to follow, it would be more climbing than hiking.

Brooke—or so I assume—runs out the front door of a two-story house with blue siding. The place, even in the daylight, gives off energy like Danny's figurines. It's not the same type though, almost 'colder' and darker. Kind of like how heavy metal and country are both considered music—regardless of what Danny thinks about country—but they're quite different. I find myself staring at an upstairs window until Brooke stops in front of me.

She looks younger than I expected from her voice, late twenties perhaps. Her shoulder-length auburn hair and hoop earrings say 'office manager,' but the flannel shirt and jeans make her look like a trail guide.

Instead of saying hi, she catches me looking into the upstairs window. "What's up there? Is something wrong?"

"I'm not sure, but I'm starting to believe you about strange things going on here."

She emits a nervous chuckle. "Already just from looking at the house? I thought you were a PI, not a psychic."

"Investigators have hunches." I smile.

The instant we make eye contact, I'm sure she had nothing to do with her son's disappearance. Again, I cringe internally at the reminder of becoming something other than human. But it's hard to argue that mind-reading isn't insanely helpful for a PI. For a missing child, I'll set aside my revulsion at being inhuman.

"Mrs. Moon?" asks Brooke.

"That's right." I shake hands. "Brooke Olsen?"

"Yes. Thank you for coming out here. I had no idea you were that far away." She fidgets at her sleeves. "Whatever happens, it means everything to me that you're helping."

"Got kids, too. Can't imagine what you're going through. Whatever I can do to help, I'm here."

"Please, come inside. What do you need me to do?" Brooke starts walking to the house, peering over her shoulder back at me.

"Let's start off with maybe you showing me where you were standing when he ran off?"

"Okay." She jogs up the small porch and goes

inside.

As soon as I'm past the foyer, I sense someone staring at me from my right... but there are only curtains, a sofa, and a television there. Still, an energy has collected in the corner that feels like a human presence. The room's a few degrees colder than outside, unusual for February. No whirring comes from the central air ducts, and it's unlikely they're running the AC at this time of year.

"Samantha?" asks Brooke from the hallway opening.

"Sorry. And please, call me Sam." I peel my gaze off the empty corner and hurry after her, thick grey plush carpet muting my footsteps. Hmm. She said she heard someone walking around, but this place looks fully carpeted. Even the stairs to the second floor are covered in it. Doubtful there's carpet in the attic, or maybe if there is a ghost here, it's an echo of the past? If a spirit remembers hardwood from its lifetime, would they still make footsteps?

And, for that matter... were ghosts a real thing? Truth was, over the months, I'd been seeing hints of static energy collecting here and there, though I didn't know what it meant. I see static energy all the time. In fact, it is this energy that illuminates the night for me. I see waves of it flowing from sources unknown. Well, some of this energy sort of... gathers in pockets, sometimes forming shapes. Sometimes even forming humanoid shapes. But were these ghosts? I don't know. They appeared more like... drive by bits of intelligence that came and went.

What I was sensing here... I dunno. A lot different than drive-by energy. Like real energy, attached to this place.

Meanwhile, the kitchen is surprisingly large for the house with an island counter in the middle. A table, chairs, and a couple of bookshelves take up the left side of the room. Countertop and cabinets wrap around the right side. The air's thick with the smell of dishwasher detergent.

Brooke stands by the sink, facing a rectangular window above it that looks out over the deck behind the house and their backyard, a relatively small area that's been made level, surrounded by a retaining wall that I estimate to be about waist high to an adult. Beyond that, the forested hill stretches upward.

She points. "See that smallish tree that's kinda split into a V like two trees grew out of the same spot of ground?"

"Yeah."

"Brax ran over there, climbed the wall, and scrambled up the hill. He seemed to be chasing something. I called to him from here, out the open window." She waits about ten seconds before hurrying to the patio door and opening it. "I called him again from here, and when he didn't answer..." She runs across the yard to stand near the same V-shaped tree sprouting from the hill.

I jog over to her.

"Probably yelled something like 'Braxton get back here!' but he didn't even say anything, so I climbed up and followed him into the woods, but I never even saw a trace of him." She clenches her jaw, fighting off tears.

The hillside at this point isn't *too* steep for a seven-year-old to run a ways off. A hundred-ish yards of trees has a lot of hiding places, but it doesn't make any sense for a boy his age to ignore his mother calling for him.

"How long has he been missing?" I ask.

"Eighteen days now." Brooke bows her head. "Yes, I know what they say about the odds, but I *know* he's still alive."

I look around up the hill. Motion in an upstairs window makes me whirl to stare at the house, but there's no one watching us. "Are you home alone right now?"

"Yes. Ken's out with another volunteer search party." She sniffles. "Why?"

"Thought I saw someone move in the upstairs window on the left." I suppress a shiver of dread at where my mind wants to go. "Is that your son's room?"

She shakes her head. "No, that's our room."

Okay, the kid's not haunting his bedroom, but it doesn't mean he's not here, either. Then again, I'm hardly a ghost expert... but damn if I didn't sense something in that window. I close my eyes and let a long breath out my nose, begging Fate to let this poor kid be alive somewhere. After eighteen days, it's highly unlikely that he's going to be found alive if he got lost in the hills. However, given the incline to the ground here, it's somewhat difficult to become lost. Even if he didn't emerge from the woods near his house, finding his way out of the forest should have been as easy as going downhill or following a stream. Maybe he did wander out some distance north or south of here and someone grabbed him? Possible, but unlikely. The average person finding a little boy on his own wouldn't abduct him. Odds of him stumbling across a creep are pretty low.

I'm sure the cops have asked around at all the neighbors' houses but it's not a bad idea for me to try. They might open up to someone without a badge… and I can read minds. If that poor kid's trapped in a basement around here, I'll find him.

And wow, it's time for me to stop watching 20/20.

Brooke steps up onto the wall and wanders into the woods. I follow her as she demonstrates the path she took searching for him. No surprise there aren't any tracks after more than two weeks. We weave around trees and rocks, marching a couple hundred feet before reaching a trail that runs mostly north-south. A dirt mound with exposed roots and stone stands in front of us, another V-shaped tree jutting from the top. The forest cover is pretty dense, enough not to be able to see too far in any direction.

Nothing pulls me anywhere or stands out— except for a pervasive sense of eeriness straight ahead.

"I stopped here on the trail and shouted for him," says Brooke. "Eventually, some hikers came by. They hadn't seen him, but when I explained my son bolted into the woods, they called 911, as I had left my cell in the house. The cops showed up pretty quick. One of the detectives thinks another hiker might've abducted him."

"That is one possibility, but kinda seems unlikely to me. Way out in the middle of nowhere, it's pretty darn difficult to abduct an unwilling child without anyone noticing. Would Braxton have gone with a stranger?"

Brooke shakes her head. "I don't think so. He's a friendly kid, but I don't think he'd let a strange person walk him away from home. It's so unlike him to just run off like that. We've been in this house for five years now, and that's the first time he's even gone past the wall behind the yard. He knows he's not supposed to go hiking without his father or me with him."

I'm about to ask what he'd been wearing, but I'm pretty sure I just heard a faint child's voice in the distance call out, "Mom?"

I freeze. Brooke's non-reaction to the voice means my grip on sanity is weaker than I thought or the call had been too faint for mortal ears to pick up. I raise a hand in a 'shh' gesture at her. After thirty seconds and hearing nothing else, I call out, "Braxton?"

This, of course, makes Brooke shout his name

even louder.

We both fall silent, listening.

"Mom?" replies a little kid. Sounds like he's yelling from a long way off.

Brooke's eyes well with tears, but she doesn't seem as excited/relieved as she should be.

"What?" I whisper.

"That's the same call I've been hearing for over a week. No matter how far I run into the woods, he never sounds any closer."

"Is that Braxton?"

"I... don't know. It could be. I can't hear it clear enough. Who else would it be? Thank God you can hear it. No one else can, especially not Ken. I'm sure he thinks I'm going crazy."

I grasp her shoulders. "Wait here. Let me give it a shot. I'm a pretty good tracker."

She nods, crying harder. And with that, I dash off into the woods.

Chapter Eighteen
Ghost of a Chance

I rush through the forest, pausing and listening often.

The next time the distant boy yells for his mother, I make my way up into the brush heading toward where the sound came from. I wasn't lying about the tracking. These days, I've got the ears and nose of a bloodhound plus I don't get tired... just hungry.

For the better part of an hour, my sense of hearing leads me deeper and deeper into the forest. Occasionally, I call out for Braxton. Unsettling thoughts drift up from the murky darkness in my mind like 'it's just a child' or 'this is a waste of time' or 'ugh, must you?' That's absolutely coming from the hitchhiker inside me. There's no such thing as *just* a child.

Unfortunately, the boy stops responding and the

last time he yelled 'Mom,' he didn't sound any closer than the first time. Feels like I trekked for a couple miles into the woods uphill, heading northeast along the mountain. Unless the kid's running away from me—which makes absolutely zero sense —something paranormal has to be going on.

I really want to trust Brooke's maternal instinct that her son is still alive. If I'm chasing the ghost of a seven-year-old boy, this is going to end with me sobbing on Danny's shoulder whether he wants to touch me or not.

Brooke is still standing on the hiking trail by the time I get back to her almost two hours later. Okay, now I know she's completely innocent of whatever happened. The poor woman just stood there outside at night in February with only a flannel shirt on, hoping to see her kid appear out of the trees.

"You're right. The voice kept drifting away. C'mon, you need to get inside before you freeze."

She's quiet as we head the 200 feet or so back down the hill to her yard. We enter the kitchen via the patio door. I stop short a few steps into the house, staring at the dark silhouette of a long-haired woman in the hallway that connects the kitchen to the living room. The figure is completely black except for two glowing white eye sockets locked on me.

It's enough to stop a heart, even one that beats twice a minute.

Brooke, oblivious to the apparition, crosses to the archway nearer that hall and flicks a switch. The figure vanishes the instant the lights come on.

"You saw her, didn't you?" Brooke turns toward me.

"I-I'm not sure what I saw," I say, my voice noticeably shaking. I mean, this was my first ghost after all. "Did you see it too?"

"Not right now, but I have seen her on and off. You literally look like you've seen a ghost." She gives me a 'I knew I wasn't crazy' sort of relieved smile. "What did you see, exactly, Sam?"

"A humanoid shadow," I say. "And two white spots where the eyes should have been."

"Long hair?"

"Yeah."

"Yup. That's the woman who's been manifesting ever since Brax went missing. I think she's trying to help somehow but can't communicate with us."

"How often do you see her?" I ask.

"Maybe three times total. She both freaks me out... and gives me hope. I mean, why else is she here other than to help us find our son?"

That I didn't know, but when the initial shock wears off, I set up my laptop on her kitchen table. Brooke gives me her WiFi password. While adding more to my notes file, asking her what the boy had on when he vanished and setting up a case record for this job, I do a preliminary search of Brooke's home address to see what hits I can get. I might need to ask a favor from Chad on this one.

The whole time I search, Brooke tearfully

rambles about her son, stuff he likes, his cute habits, and so on. Truth is, it's sounding like her brain's considering him dead but her heart refuses to accept that. Hearing her talking about him is heart-wrenching to the point I'm nearly crying right along with her.

A search result links to an eight-year-old article on a local paper's website. It doesn't have a ton of information beyond saying a local woman named Lily Peyton was found dead at her home (this house) under suspicious circumstances. Another—much shorter—article dated a month later mentions the police had closed their investigation and categorized the cause of death as undetermined.

Well, unsolved violent murder is usually a recipe for a haunting. Assuming, of course, ghosts exist. Call me gullible, but I'm leaning toward a hard yes. Anyway, the first article has a low-quality picture of a thirtyish, pale woman with dark hair, probably a driver's license shot given her bored-and-slightly-irritated expression. I imagine the face into a silhouette with pale eyes... and holy sweet mama if it doesn't look just like the apparition from the hallway.

Soft thumps pass overhead like someone walking around upstairs.

Brooke peers at the ceiling. "She's been getting more and more restless."

Okay, this is one freaky house. I note that my internal alarm has remained silent. Whatever is here doesn't mean any harm... at least, not to me.

We both jump at the sudden *thunk* of a door closing in the living room.

"Ken?" calls Brooke. "Is that you?"

No one answers.

She emits a nervous laugh. "Maybe I should be a lot more freaked out by all this stuff going on, but I just want my son back. I'm not going to let a ghost bother me. Besides, I think she's trying to help."

The phone rings.

I jump out of the chair. Brooke screams.

We exchange a glance of 'okay, I feel stupid.' Hand pressed to her chest, she gets up to answer.

"Mind if I look around?" I ask.

She waves at the hall in a 'go right ahead' sort of way, then picks up the phone. "Hello?"

"Hey, hon," says a man, his voice audible to my super sensitive ears. "No luck yet. The volunteers are exhausted. Calling it a night. I'll be home soon."

Figure that's the husband. I hurry down the hall to give her some privacy and go upstairs. A door near the end of the corridor creaks, but it could be drifting in a draft. Maybe a window is open? The second door on the right leads to the boy's bedroom. The scent of 'child' saturates it. Looks like a fairly typical room for a seven-year-old boy. Plenty of plastic dinosaurs, GI-Joe toys, and so on. All this stuff so full of warmth could easily turn painful if he never returns. It makes me wonder what Anthony's room will be like in four or five years. Probably kinda similar. Dinosaurs and toy military planes. Dammit! I need to find this kid.

I pluck the pillow off his bed and—after making sure Brooke isn't watching me—sniff it. Being able to detect human scents like a tracking dog is one of those things about me that makes me squirm. Every reminder that I've become inhuman comes with some degree of revulsion and wanting not to believe it's real. However, if it lets me do what the normal police can't do and find this kid alive, I'll deal with it. Though, I'm sure a search party—at least the one the cops ran—would've already used dogs.

I drop the pillow back on the bed and return to the hallway.

"Lily?" I ask. "Are you the one haunting this place?"

A clatter comes from the floor directly ahead. Whoa, what was that? I move toward the sound and soon come upon the bathroom. Ah, there's a hairbrush on the floor. I pick it up and drop it. Yup, the same sound. My gaze lands on a Superman toothpaste tube. Three brushes in a rack, one small. Damn, my heart is breaking.

"Are you trying to help find Brax?" I ask, turning slowly in place.

At a sense of someone running by the hall outside, I lean out the door. Soft footfalls continue away to the left toward the master bedroom.

"What happened to you? Did someone hurt you?" I creep down the hall to the bedroom and nudge the door open.

"Yes," says a woman—right behind me.

I jump forward and spin around.

A slim woman with dark hair, grey eyes, and pallid skin stands in the doorway, her nightgown wavering about her legs in a nonexistent breeze. Her posture has an unnatural lean like a broken doll, head tilted slightly to one side, fingers curled like claws. She stares at me with unbridled delight, a mood that thoroughly catches me off guard, even more so than her sudden appearance.

"Is Braxton still alive?" I whisper.

Lily raises her left arm, pointing at the wall. She nods once, and disappears. I turn and face the wall where she pointed. Pretty sure she's not telling me the kid's inside the walls, so I head to the bedroom window on that side. The direction she indicated is east, toward the woods. So do I tell this woman that a ghost said her child is okay? That sounds insane as well as possibly being a lie. Nothing requires spirits to be truthful. I'm going to need more than a possible hallucination before I get Brooke's hopes up.

And I probably shouldn't allow a ghost to get *my* hopes up, either.

Chapter Nineteen
Unlikely Explanations

I spend a while longer wandering around the house trying to get the ghost to give me more information, but succeed only in stirring up random bumps, creaks, or sounds like small objects being dropped.

Stupid ghost.

When I go downstairs, I find Brooke pacing in the kitchen. "What's going on up there, Sam? All those noises! It's way more intense than usual. Are we doing something wrong? Is she trying to tell us Brax is running out of time? Did you see her?"

Admittedly, this is an insane amount of activity in a short period of time, which gets me wondering how much of it is due to me being here. One of the conversations Danny doesn't know I overheard when he'd been on the phone with his Romanian buddy involved the man warning him that strange things might begin happening around our house. This guy believed me to be a paranormal magnet or energy source, and similar to how moths seek flames or bright lights, other entities weaker than me could be drawn closer.

"Briefly. I asked her if he was still alive and she pointed at the woods."

She bounces on her toes. "I knew it!"

"Brooke, we don't know who this ghost is or what her motivations might be. She might not even be a real spirit."

"Umm." The woman stares at me. "As opposed to what, a fake ghost?"

"More like a demon or dark entity trying to upset you when you're vulnerable."

A heavy *slam* hits the ceiling.

Brooke screams again. I reflexively duck.

"Or maybe not. Guess that pissed her off." I look up. "Hang tight. I'm going to go check around outside again."

She reluctantly sits at the table. "All right."

Having night vision does come in handy. I don't need a flashlight or one of those heavy sets of goggles to see perfectly in the dark. Unfortunately, there doesn't appear to be anything useful out here. I catch scraps of the boy's scent out behind the house, but the trail stops about six yards away from the retaining wall. Eighteen days might be too long for a person's scent to linger in the wild, so that doesn't necessarily mean he vanished into thin air so close to his backyard.

The only neighbor on the street, Terry Waters, lives on the opposite side about twenty yards down. He seems like an amicable sort of man, early forties, long grey hair back in a ponytail, Rush 2112 T-shirt. He's single, has a golden retriever, and happily talks with me once I explain that I'm a private investigator trying to help find a missing boy. He nods and seems saddened by the whole ordeal, and tells me about the police showing up, and the many search parties he's seen crossing his property. He'd joined in on a number of them.

"Probably something to do with that house," says Terry. "Last people to live there took off in six months. Surprised the Olsens have lasted this long."

"Have you lived in the area long?"

"Oh yeah. Been here my whole life."

"What do you do for a living?"

"Sound engineer in San Jacinto."

I nearly ask what exactly that entails and decide I don't care. I nod toward the Olsens' place. "Did you know Lily Peyton?"

He shrugs. "Depends on what you mean by 'know.' We didn't really talk or anything. The girl moved in there oh, about twelve years ago? Alone. No husband. Don't see that too often."

"You think it's odd for a woman to buy a house?" I raise an eyebrow.

"Not in the sense of her being a woman. Just don't see a lot of single people buying homes, men included."

I keep my eyebrow raised.

He chuckles at my obvious reference to him being a single homeowner. "I grew up here. Parents passed on." He gestures across the street. "Far as I know, Lily had a bit of money. Don't recall what she did for a living, but it paid well. She mostly kept to herself. Quiet. Seemed nice, though. Friendly if you talked to her but she wouldn't start the conversation."

"Okay. And she died in the house?"

"Yeah. Must be ten years or so now. Real shame. Figure she was about my age. Too young to die. Police never did catch anyone."

The article said she died eight years ago, but people often lose track of time. "What makes you believe she was killed?"

He waves around randomly. "Ehh, just stuff I heard the cops talking about. Position of her body and some such things. My parents were still here back when that happened, though Dad had been sick already. Never saw anyone come or go from her place. No strange cars. Snow Dog did go nuts barking that night, but we didn't see anything. Figure he heard something we didn't."

I peer around the guy at the golden retriever sitting there with this goofy dog smile. He doesn't seem to mind me. Most animals give me a wide berth these days. "He doesn't look that old."

"Oh, that's Rufus. Snow Dog was a husky. He went over the rainbow bridge two years ago."

"Sorry."

He bows his head. "Thanks."

"So your dog heard something that night. Maybe a scream?"

Terry shrugs. "Maybe. Then again, if she fell down the stairs, she would've screamed, too."

"Fell down the stairs?"

"The cops talking to each other again. Heard one of them say they'd found the body at the bottom of the stairs."

I look deep into his eyes, not really trying to do anything more than get a read of the guy as a whole. Doesn't strike me as being involved beyond eavesdropping on the police. For some reason, I get the feeling he has a parabolic microphone and a fascination with law enforcement.

"Did you overhear them say anything else that might be helpful?"

"Got the feeling they were frustrated. Like the detective knew someone killed her but had no way to prove it or even who did it. House sat empty for about a year after that. Bunch of guys showed up one day and took all the furniture out. Never did see any relatives or whatnot come to collect her stuff. Guess she didn't have any family, or at least any who cared about her. Couple months after the movers gutted the place, this real high-strung couple moved in. Think they came from LA or some such place and wanted the quiet life."

"I'm guessing they got the opposite."

Terry laughs. "Yeah. Heard a woman scream every so often. Not in pain or anything, more like startled. Anyway, they took off right quick."

"Did the Olsens have similar experiences?"

"I think so. The guy, Ken, stopped by once or twice to ask about the house. Rufus sometimes gets to barking at the place, staring at the street like there's someone out front. Oh, ya know, now that you mention it… one time I was out walking Rufus, I spotted that kid of theirs sitting on the front porch steps talking to no one."

"Imaginary friend?"

"Maybe. I didn't bother to ask. Rufus seemed to want to run inside right quick though."

Apparently, 'right quick' was the hick phrase of the day. "You wouldn't happen to know if anyone has a particular grudge against the Olsens, would you?"

"Not that I know of. Quiet family, for the most part."

"Great. I appreciate your time."

"Not a problem." He smiles, waves, and backs inside.

Rufus whimpers at me from the front porch, with a 'please don't eat me' look in his eyes.

"You're safe," I whisper, grinning.

He wags his tail, seeming relieved.

With nothing whatsoever to show for my time, I head back to Brooke's house. A dark Land Rover sits in the driveway that hadn't been there before. A man with perfect hair and a chiseled jaw answers. Between his looks, flannel shirt, jeans, and Timberlands, he's stepped straight off the pages of an L.L. Bean catalog.

"Can I help—?"

"That's Sam," says Brooke, behind him.

"Oh. Sorry. Come in. I'm Ken." He steps aside, letting me by, then shuts the door. "So I hear you've become acquainted with our house ghost."

"Yeah." I head to the kitchen where I'd left the laptop.

Ken follows. "You get used to her. Lots of noise, but I think she just doesn't want to be alone."

"Did you find anything?" asks Brooke, hovering behind him.

A child that age surviving for eighteen days on his own in the woods around here is pretty unbelievable. That, plus his scent trail simply vanishing points toward an implausible explanation of the supernatural kind. Could another vampire have made a snack of him? Or could aliens have abducted him?

Holy cow, Sam. Aliens? Really?

"I'm still looking. I know it seems implausible, but my instincts are telling me he's out in the woods somewhere. He might have found a campsite with provisions and shelter."

Ken paces, frustration oozing from his pores. "We've been all over the hills. I've been out there every day since he ran out of the yard. How is it possible that Braxton is out in the woods and no one's found him yet?"

"There's a lot of land out there, Mr. Olsen. The growth is dense, the terrain is steep and treacherous in spots. My best guess is he's fallen into some place that the search parties have missed. It's also possible he's found shelter somewhere, maybe in something abandoned."

Ken shakes his head. "Only thing abandoned in ten square miles was that cabin, and there was nothing there."

"Cabin?" I look up from my laptop screen. "What cabin?"

"The sheriff's team located a small cabin about half a mile into the woods and a bit northeast."

Brooke lifts her head off his shoulder. "The one detective, Holt, said he thought Brax had been there. He didn't say what made him think that."

"Hon." Ken squeezes her. "They turned the place upside down. It's just a shack out in the woods that's been there for decades. If Brax had been there, he didn't stay."

A strong *thud* shakes the house. The Olsens both peer up at the ceiling.

"Does that mean Lily thinks the cabin's important?" asks Brooke.

Thud.

"Gotta be coincidence," whispers Ken.

"Lily's part of the family, basically," says Brooke. "She wants to help us find Brax."

I pull up a map of the area on the laptop. "Can you show me where that cabin is?"

He leans over my shoulder and points to a small spot of terrain in the crook of a valley between peaks. "About there. Why? You're not seriously considering going out there alone are you?"

"I am."

"Wait. You're not going now? At night?"

I wink. "I do my best work after dark. Besides, I'm a lot tougher than I look."

Chapter Twenty
Dead End

Ken Olsen isn't too happy with the idea of me going into the forest alone at night, but he's also exhausted from hiking it all day. Still, he starts putting his coat back on. I'll be much faster without —as much as I hate to think this—a mortal slowing me down. It takes both his wife and I to convince him not to exhaust himself and to get some rest, and that I'm a highly trained federal agent who's fleet of foot.

"Fleet of foot?" he asks.

"I'm like a fox out there," I say.

"Oh, brother. I'm too tired to argue any more. Just be safe."

Searching the woods for a missing boy isn't what I expected to end up doing as a private investigator, but I couldn't care less about what matches the job description when there's a kid involved. All my experience as a fed is telling me we're trying to find a body. Ghost or not, the most likely explanation for no one finding him and his not answering anyone calling his name is that he fell into some pit somewhere and broke his neck. Cases like this are heartbreaking because a family can go decades never knowing what happened.

Time to get some answers, good or bad.

It's really foolish of me to even entertain hope that I'm going to find this boy alive. That's only going to make it hurt all that much worse when or if I locate the remains. And hearing the kid's voice, distant and ghostly, a few hours ago didn't do much to reinforce the idea he's still alive.

It also didn't do much for my sanity. Luckily, Brooke had heard it too.

Given what happened to me, vampires clearly exist. Lily's haunting the house, so ghosts clearly exist, too. Weird as it sounds, we probably heard Braxton's spirit wandering around lost, unable to find his way home. Eighteen days on his own... cripes. And a cabin out in the woods. Yeah... that's not sketchy at all.

Nope.

A few minutes into the hike, my phone buzzes with a text.

Mary Lou: *What's Up?*

I text and walk at the same. *Still at client site looking for a missing 7-year-old.*

The phone rings. My sister isn't the biggest fan of typing with her thumbs.

"Hey," I say by way of answering.

"Oh my God, a missing kid? What happened?"

I give her the thirty-second version. "I'm honestly astounded I have signal here. Heading into the woods to check on this abandoned cabin business. Police already dismissed it, but maybe I can pick up something they missed."

"Hope so. Tammy and Anthony are finally asleep."

"Tammy and Anthony? You still have them?" I check the time on the phone. It's after 9:30.

"Yeah. Danny called and asked if they could sleep over here. I told him sure."

"You are a life saver, Mary Lou. I'm gonna head back home after I check this cabin out. Kinda hard to walk away when there's a kid missing."

"Understandable. I'll get Tammy to school tomorrow and I'll keep Anthony with me. What time do you want me to bring them home?"

I step over a big rock. "Three or so. Not sure exactly what's going to happen with this case. I might end up having to be down here again tomorrow."

"Oh, that's fine. I don't mind looking after the little ones. Did Danny call you?"

"No. Not a peep."

"What is *wrong* with that man? I have half a mind—"

The call drops.

I sigh at the phone. No signal. I backpedal a few feet but it doesn't help. Drat. I stuff the phone in my pocket and continue deeper into the woods.

A near-cloudless sky lets the moon bathe the woods in an eerie blue. The pale dirt catches the light, glowing to my eyes like radioactive cesium powder. I'm still not used to being able to see in the dark as easily as a normal person in broad daylight. Well, that is if daylight consisted of millions of squiggly flashes of light that touched on everything, illuminated everything. Anyway, the trees and vegetation obviously present a physical barrier to sight, but at least I don't have to worry about someone ambushing me out of the shadows.

"Mom?" whispers a small voice somewhere up ahead, off to the left.

I'm not terribly hopeful of catching up to the apparition, but it still seems like a good idea to follow it. And I do, picking my way over the mountainside, scaring up critters that scurry through the underbrush in glowing balls of energy. Every so often, the child's distant ephemeral call comes from the left or right, leading me deeper and deeper into the woods.

A sudden flash of motion comes at me from the side.

I spring away to my left and drop into a fighting stance, ready for the creep—but it's not a guy. My rapid motion startles a charging mountain lion to an abrupt halt. Ears back, bright yellow eyes wide, the big cat stares at me. For once, the way I tend to scare animals *doesn't* bother me. I neither want to become cat food nor hurt this creature.

However… if there are mountain lions in this area, that doesn't fill me with hope for Braxton's safety. A kitty this big would carry a small boy off with ease. Fortunately, this cat doesn't smell like blood. I stand to my full height and take a step toward it, giving off as much 'alpha' as I can. The critter's hackles rise, tail fluffing up. Yeah, that's right. You don't want to tangle with me.

"Go on," I say in a low voice. "Get outta here."

Our staredown lasts another twenty seconds before the big cat bolts and runs off into the trees. Rustling and scratching tell me it's decided to climb out of my reach. I almost feel bad for scaring it, but that beats having to hurt an animal.

Once I'm sure kitty wants no further part of me, I resume trekking along the mountainside, sniffing at the air, but picking up nothing but the scent of vegetation… and possibly big cat pee. No, I didn't scare him that bad. Probably old territorial marking or some such thing.

The faint child voice says, "I'm here," and sounds fairly close this time.

I pick up my pace to a jog, calling, "Braxton?"

The boy doesn't answer me, but I do stumble across a roughly fifty-foot oval space of flattish ground—at the far end of which is a small, squarish shack with one door and one window.

Bingo.

A thick cluster of underbrush has sprung up to fill the area behind the shack with a nest of brambles. Here, I pick up a handful of human scents, but none of them are familiar, as well as a charred smell, suggesting the fire pit a short distance in front of the shack has been used recently.

I cross the clearing to the cabin and take in a deep breath. Braxton's scent is faint, but present.

Okay, that just sent a chill down my back. Remote cabin out in the woods plus missing boy makes me jump to the horrified assumption that some creep lives here and he's got the kid locked up underground. Whoever uses this cabin must've spotted the boy in his yard, somehow lured him into the woods, and whisked him away to here.

Instinctively, I reach under my left arm... but my gun's gone. Dammit. Well, technically, it had been the government's gun. And, honestly, I don't need a firearm to deal with mortals. As a PI, I could jump through hoops and get a permit to carry one, but I'm not sure it would be worth it. How many cheating husbands or bail jumpers are going to be carrying silver daggers? Damn few, if any. So yeah, not too much to worry about since there isn't too much a mortal can do to me that won't go away in a few days. Speaking of healing, that cut on my arm from the silver knife? Yeah, it took three weeks to disappear. For a while, I thought it would be a permanent scar, but it eventually faded entirely.

Mental note: silver sucks.

Bonus: my alarm sense isn't going off.

The rickety door covered in peeling red paint doesn't appear capable of locking. The knob is tiny, more for a cabinet than a front door to a house.

Perhaps with too much confidence due to the lack of any ringing in my head, I push the door open like I own the place. There's a slide lock on the inner face, but it's so dinky even a kid could probably bash it in.

Inside, the cabin stinks of wet dog and moldy fabric. A rusty folding card table occupies the near left corner, only one chair tucked under it. Shelves hold an array of old coffee cans in varying sizes, though I doubt any of them hold actual coffee. Most of the wet-cloth smell comes from a steel-framed cot against the far wall opposite the door. The wall to my right consists mostly of a brick fireplace. Hmm. It doesn't *look* like it's been used within the past twenty years.

Braxton's scent is all over the place in here. My mom-senses tingle with worry in response to me remembering that guy on the East Coast who kidnapped a girl and kept her in a bunker under his house. Cops had been in and out of his place and never found her until he finally cracked under the pressure of constant surveillance and—miraculously —surrendered her alive.

Damn, I hope this isn't another case like that.

A few minutes of rummaging around leads me to a section of floor by the cot. It's subtle, but stepping on that spot creates an echo that human ears would likely not pick up. Yeah, there's definitely a hollow under the floor. I crouch, searching the debris under the cot, pushing papers, bottles, and cans out of my way until I find a rusty puncture-type can opener that doesn't move when I try to brush it out of my way.

Turns out, the can opener is bolted to a short metal post, kinda like a lever-style door handle, but on the floor. Could be camouflaged on purpose, could be simply made out of whatever junk had been here. Still, I think the cops dismissed it as a simple old can opener on the floor or just didn't bother searching the junk crammed under the cot that well. I grab it and pull, opening a three-foot-square wooden trapdoor. The entire cot folds up against the wall, part of the same mechanism.

I peer over the edge down a rough-hewn shaft. Looks like someone dug this out over a hundred years with a damn teaspoon. And this is mountain dirt and rock. Someone had some *real* determination. This doesn't appear to be recent though. Could be the lair of an old prospector from the 1800s, maybe a miner, someone with the knowledge and tools to excavate rock... and a need to hide gold.

A standard aluminum ladder leans against the right side. Okay, that's definitely not from the 1800s. More like Home Depot. The stone/earth is solid for about six feet before opening into a chamber below the cabin. From here, all I can make out of the space are multiple scraps of carpet on the floor. It's dark down there, but not so dim that I can't see, which means it's pitch black to a normal person.

"Braxton?" I whisper.

No response.

Oh hell.

I sit on the edge, step on the ladder, and climb down.

Chapter Twenty-One
The Bunker

The chamber is roughly twice the size of the cabin's interior space—which isn't saying much. Fortunately, the underground room has only one human scent saturating it, and it's not Braxton. Whoever he is, he's in damn dire need of a freakin' bar of soap.

Wire rack shelving lines two walls of the bunker, loaded up with various long-shelf-life foods. Most of it is canned goods, but there are also several huge boxes of cereal and big bags of pasta like those you get from a wholesale outlet place. There are even family-sized bags of Doritos and Chips Ahoy. The second shelf holds a few sets of folded jeans, an Army coat that looks thirty years old, sweaters. Knives. Two huge footlocker style trunks with padlocks sit in the corner. No guns at least. I'm getting the distinct impression whoever lives here is on the antisocial side.

By scent, I can tell that someone's been here recently. The boy, however, didn't come down here. Well, that's both a relief and a frustration. We're not dealing with a kidnapper creep. Braxton most likely found the cabin while wandering around. Maybe the guy scared him off. Could be the man took him somewhere, but that doesn't feel likely either. Unless he's some kind of ex-special forces woodlands survival god, the search parties would've found him dragging an unwilling child around.

Unless of course, the kid wanted to go with him, which is equally strange. Seven-year-olds don't usually run away from a loving home. Randomly chasing a rabbit into the woods, sure. Deliberately avoiding searchers for days, fleeing into the deep woods to hook up with a hermit... yeah, something wrong with that story...

So what the hell *is* going on?

I look around the room again, checking everywhere that doesn't require breaking padlocks. There's no sign of any additional hidden rooms and zero indication that the boy had been down here. Hmm. Does going into an abandoned cabin technically count as breaking and entering? Hard to say. Either way, this is going nowhere. And some of this food down here looks recent. Those Doritos aren't expired yet, not until next year. This cabin doesn't really count as 'abandoned.'

Why did that ghostly voice lead me here if it's a

dead end?

Good question. I'm an investigator. Suppose I should start doing some of that investigation stuff, eh?

I climb back upstairs, close the trapdoor and arrange it to look as undisturbed as I can, then head outside and make my way back to the Olsen's house. They're both still awake but running on fumes. After an explanation of my findings, I urge them to get some sleep and promise to return tomorrow.

Ken brings up my fees, even though I intended to hold off on mentioning anything about it until finishing the case one way or the other. He gives me a check for $400 to cover the initial eight hours. I notice his name printed on it has an M.D. at the end, so most of my guilt at charging them subsides.

Still, I am going to feel like garbage taking their money if my efforts turn up a small corpse. Yeah... if that's where this road leads, I don't think I'll cash this check. Waiting tables sucks, but taking money from grieving parents is just evil.

Chapter Twenty-Two
Just Gone

Off the clock, I spend another few hours searching the woods after leaving their house.

That turns up nothing, so I head home with enough time to make it before sunrise without having to break any laws. At four in the morning, there's nil traffic, so the ride only takes me an hour and twenty-six minutes.

I realize my children are at my sister's, but seeing empty bedrooms after spending most of my day searching for a missing child kicks me in the feels and I end up crying for no good reason. Danny is at least home, if asleep. It's tempting to cuddle up to him, but he'd only freak out and push me away. It hurts to think about, but not many people enjoy spooning a dead woman.

***

When I wake up the next 'morning,' the first thing I do is call Chad.

"Helling."

"Chad? It's Sam. Wondering if you can help me out with something?"

"Hey, Sunshine. Good to hear your voice again. How's it going?"

"Ehh, it's going. Kinda rough actually but I'll manage." I give him a brief and somewhat factual account of becoming a private investigator. I do *not* mention waiting tables at Earl's. Knowing him, he'd drag the entire crew there to 'support' me with a huge tip. But, it would feel like mockery. And sadness. Okay, mostly sadness. "Working on a missing child case now. And yes, before you ask, the cops are on it, too."

"Oh crap. Any leads?"

"Nothing concrete yet. Any chance you might be able to look into the death of a former owner of the property. I think there might be a connection between that and the boy's disappearance."

"Sure. What's the address and timeframe?"

I give him the address. "The woman's name was Lily Peyton. She was found dead in the house eight years ago on June 13th. From what I picked up, the cops considered the death suspicious but didn't have any evidence or even a suspect."

"Okay. I'll see what I can find out."

"Thanks, Chad."

"Anytime, Sunshine."

We hang up.

Grr. Hearing him call me that is starting to feel like he's making fun of my nocturnal nature. I know he doesn't mean to, but still.

Meanwhile, I hit all the resources available to me online, looking for anything that might point to a kidnapping. Ken's a doctor, and Brooke is a nurse. She seems to be home a lot so maybe that's *former* nurse and she's become a stay-at-home-mom. More likely, she's on leave due to the disappearance. Still though, there isn't much I can think of for a nurse to do that would make enemies willing to grab her kid. Predictably, I strike out with the internet resources. And besides, if someone targeted the family on purpose, there would've been a ransom demand or some manner of contact by now.

With little else to do here, I hop in the shower, dry off, douse myself in sunblock, change into fresh clothes suitable for hiking, then head out to the garage for something to eat. How tasty is cow/pig blood? Imagine a bologna smoothie made from store-brand bologna. Then imagine having to eat *only* bologna smoothies for the rest of time. It's sorta morbid to think that all the half-gallon plastic bottles that come into the house with milk for my kids end up going to Jaroslaw the butcher to be refilled with blood. Well, technically, he's not a 'butcher.' I'd been thinking of him as this sweet old man who runs a little mom & pop store selling steaks and sausage. Actually, he works at a slaught-erhouse, which explains how he has access to so much animal blood.

When I open the mini-fridge, I notice a stack of plastic pouches, kind of like a super-morbid version of Capri-Suns. Capri-Moon? Looks like Danny's moved ahead with his pouch idea. At least they aren't IV bags. That would be far too morbid for me. I grab one and look it over, shrug, pop it open, and drink. The portion is just about perfect to satisfy me for one meal. Once finished, I stand there a moment holding the limp empty, trying to figure Danny out. He's sending such weird, sometimes even hostile, signals... but then he does something like stocking the fridge with blood packets to help me out.

What is going on?

The man is seriously confusing me. One minute, he seems ready to leap through a plate glass window to get away from the dangerous creature in his house, the next, he's caring again. I don't have the brain cells to burn trying to comprehend that.

Sated with a blood meal, I head over to Mary Lou's place to see my kids and beg their forgiveness for disappearing on them—and having to disappear again today. They're both remarkably cool about it. Of course, having my sister's kids to play with goes a long way to bribing their acceptance. They're all pretty small now. Wonder if they'll stay close when they hit the dreaded teenage years?

Far too soon for my liking, I touch up the sunblock and head out the door for the arduous drive out to Idyllwild. As horrible as it would feel to cash the Olsens' check and not find their kid alive and well, I may end up having no choice in the matter simply for gas money. If long-distance jobs become the norm, it might be worth it to refit the Momvan to a sun-proof box and just sleep remote.

I arrive at the Olsen place about quarter after six. Hey, if nothing else, I'm keeping a regular schedule.

A silvery-grey Crown Vic is parked on the street outside. It looks so much like the one I used to drive for work that a momentary sense of WTF comes over me, expecting to find Chad here. However, it doesn't have federal plates. Gotta be local cops.

Brooke answers the doorbell. She looks beyond exhausted with red-rimmed eyes. Seeing me seems to give her a small charge of hope and energy. She invites me in with a gesture, too worn out to speak. A pair of detectives on the couch, a lanky black guy and a stocky woman both in their early thirties are discussing with Ken their lack of progress. Bags under her husband's eyes and his formerly perfect hair disheveled say he's been up all night.

The cops look up at me as I walk in.

"Who's this?" asks the woman in a manner that suggests she's having a bad day.

"My wife's hired a private investigator to help out," says Ken in a tone like he's calling me a waste of money. Or maybe he's simply losing hope.

The detectives both regard me the way cops often look at mall security.

"Hi. I'm Samantha Moon." I approach and offer a handshake. "Used to work as a federal agent. Got two kids now. Couldn't turn down a request to help find a missing boy. What can I do to help?"

Both detectives shift from condescension to something approaching respect. With any luck, they'll assume I retired because of having kids. Not that I feel the need to lie about what happened, but it's probably not going to do much for their confidence in me if I start off talking about my medical issues or narcolepsy.

"I'm Detective Arvin Holt." He shakes my hand. "This is my partner, Detective Tanya Bartlett."

I shake her hand next. "Pleasure."

Both look down at their hands, no doubt wondering why mine is so damn cold. Note to self, avoid shaking hands if possible.

"Mrs. Moon believes Braxton is still out there," says Ken. He looks at me. "The detectives had been gently trying to introduce us to the greater probability that the worst has happened."

That explains their drained appearance.

"I've always tried to maintain a positive outlook as long as possible in cases like this."

"Have you worked many cases like this?" asks Detective Bartlett. He doesn't appear too thrilled that I might be giving the parents false hope.

I tell them about the guy who ran off with the twelve-year-old that ended up as a shootout in the woods where he'd been keeping her. The happy

ending there—getting the girl back in one piece—
appears to improve the Olsens' mood. Also, the
detectives have fully switched gears into thinking of
me as a competent equal. Go me.

We discuss the goings on with the present case.
They're remarkably open with details considering
I'm a civilian. That tells me they're getting desperate for anything that would help find Braxton.
Mostly, they've been searching the woods. At this
point, their leading theory is a wild animal might've
gotten him. Now on day nineteen, it seems they're
gearing up to put this in their cold case file. They
didn't find anything to suggest abduction by someone with a vendetta against the parents. When they
discuss clearing Brooke of any suspicion in the
disappearance of her son, the poor woman breaks
down sobbing. Detective Bartlett quickly soothes
her with something about it being standard proce-
dure to investigate the last known person to see a
missing child, and they never really suspected her.

Detective Holt looks at me. "Have you found
anything of note?"

"As far as concrete things go? That cabin out in
the woods has a hidden chamber underneath it. I
found recent signs of habitation, but no evidence
that Braxton had ever been down there." I exhale.
Probably would not go over well to say his scent
wasn't present.

"A hidden room?" asks Detective Bartlett.

"Yeah. The construction looked pretty old. I
don't think whoever is living there now made the

place."

"We spent a fair amount of time out there. Never saw anyone in the area." Detective Holt scratches his eyebrow. "Could be they saw us there and kept out of sight. I'm guessing you didn't have any better luck canvassing the woods up in the hills?"

"Unfortunately not. Though I did hear something that sounded like a child yelling for his mother."

The detectives eye Brooke.

Holt whistles, glances at me. "So you're buying into the spooky stuff, too?"

"Let's just say I've seen some things that leave me open minded."

"Well, no wonder we haven't found the boy. A ghost abducted him." Detective Bartlett shakes her head.

Ken picks at his sleeve. "Before moving into this place, I had the same opinion about that stuff. But too much strange stuff has gone on since we started living here for me to dismiss it now. Bet if you two spent a night or two here, you'd change your mind, detectives."

"Do the feds believe in that supernatural stuff?" asks Holt. "Next thing you'll tell me, the *X-Files* are real."

It feels wrong to laugh in front of the Olsens, so I merely smile. "If it's real, I didn't have enough security clearance to know about it."

The detectives give me a half smirk.

We talk for a little while more, mostly about the detectives' plan to try one last time to have a helicopter go overhead tonight with FLIR, looking for heat signatures. If that doesn't come up with anything, their next step involves 'sniffer dogs.' I understand they mean dogs trained to find bodies, but the parents appear to take it to mean tracking bloodhounds. I don't feel a need to correct them; neither do the detectives.

Eventually, they depart with a promise to return either as soon as the helicopter finds good news, or tomorrow with the dogs. Once the cops leave, the Olsens both look at me expectantly, as though I'm going to open a trenchcoat I'm not wearing and pluck their son out of a pocket inside.

"I've got a friend from the agency looking into what happened here before you moved in."

"What good will that do?" asks Ken, his tone brusque. "Look, I don't mean to come off like a dick here, but, my son's been missing for almost three weeks. I know the odds are crap. Can't say I'm altogether thrilled with Brooke wasting your time with this, but at this point, I'm happy to have any help possible. Be honest. Do you think we'll find him alive?"

Brooke emits this strangled squeal of grief.

I sit there gazing into space, hoping for some kind of otherworldly insight to hit me. Alas, I may have some telepathic abilities, but I'm not Miss Cleo psychic. Or at least the type of psychic she claims to be. I've got a Wi-Fi link to other brains, not a third eye.

"Yes," whispers a female voice behind me.

Considering I'm sitting on the couch which is up against a wall, no one could possibly be behind me. The others appear to not have heard it.

"How open are you to things scientists would laugh at?" I ask.

"If it means our son is alive, you could read all the tea leaves you want," says Ken.

I almost chuckle. "No, I'm afraid that's a bit outside my skill set. Perhaps I imagined it, but I think Lily answered your question with a yes."

"Yes, we will find him alive?"

"That's how I understood," I said. "Then again, she's just a ghost."

Brooke's eyes well with hopeful tears. "But... how does she know? Can she find him?"

"I'd like to believe that." Ken leans back and rubs his tired eyes. "I still think someone lured him into the woods, grabbed him, and ran off to a waiting car or something. Kids don't just vanish into thin air right out of their backyards."

True, the scent trail ended only a short distance into the trees, but after eighteen days, that could be explained as a simple act of nature. His scent migrating from the yard to that distance could simply be from his spending so much time in the yard. The trail stopping doesn't jibe with someone carrying him off. The CIA did various tests on the use of dogs and human scent tracking, trying to identify exactly what it is that the animals are smelling.

They found that a man in a rowboat left a detectable scent trail along the banks without setting foot on them. By virtue of that, it's easy to assume that a carried child would leave a scent trail on ground he didn't touch but passed close to.

Of course, I caught the boy's scent at the cabin, too... and that had been after the disembodied voice led me to it. Sadly, the scent had been faint. What that meant, I don't know.

"No, they don't simply vanish," says Brooke. "However, do you remember detective Holt saying the dogs lost the trail only a few yards into the woods? Even if someone carried him, there would've been a trail going straight to the point he got into a car. Or more likely an SUV or truck. Then again, wouldn't I have heard it drive off?"

"And there's no way anyone's driving a car around up there. Maybe a little quad thing." Ken scratches his head. "But those aren't quiet. You would've heard the engine."

Brooke fidgets at her sweater. "I didn't hear anything."

"If you don't mind me asking," I say, "is there something specific that makes you believe someone abducted him? Have there been any threats or demands?"

"No." Ken looks down. "It's just that the police and the sheriff's office have canvassed every square inch of ground and haven't found any sign of him. Not even a shoe or scrap of torn piece of clothing on a bush. It's literally like he disappeared into thin air. Someone had to have grabbed him, stuffed him in a car, and drove off. We've been searching the woods, and he's probably not even in the state anymore."

"Ken!" says Brooke in a raised voice, her whole body shivering from worry and dread.

"Sorry," he mutters.

"I don't believe your son was kidnapped. There's something going on here that defies a reasonable explanation." I look up at the ceiling.

Ken massages the bridge of his nose. "Paranormal stuff?"

"Mom!" calls a phantom child voice from the woods behind the house.

He lets his arm fall away, his mouth open in shock that suggests this is the first time he's heard the call. "That's my son's voice!"

Chapter Twenty-Three
Visitor

Sadly, it is for naught. Once again, the voice eludes us.

Still, I burn another few hours fruitlessly searching the woods before giving up and going home in time to beat sunrise. Aside from the ever-distant ghostly child voice calling for his mother, I did notice the same filthy scent from the bunker scattered here and there around the hills—including close to the Olsen's house. I'm convinced someone's living out there, probably off the grid. Why he's roaming around near civilization, who knows, but it's probably not good. Maybe he's hungry. Or maybe he's a psycho.

One thing for sure... I'm about to find out.

Sadly, my sense of smell isn't quite as sharp as a dog's. Too bad I don't know any werewolves (like those things are real). Since I'm still learning this stuff, I'm curious to note that although I can detect human scents—and even differentiate individuals— they don't feel like 'trails' I can follow the same way a dog appears to follow an invisible painted line on the ground. I'll catch a whiff, move a little and sniff again, and the smell will either still be there or not. Braxton's scent doesn't exist beyond six meters from the yard... although I am certain I caught it in the cabin.

The whole ride home, I argue with myself over what sounds like the most logical explanation here: there's a man living in a remote cabin, and he probably abducted Braxton. Evidence points to that. Man's scent near the Olsen house. Braxton's scent at the cabin, even if he didn't go down to the secret chamber. But that still doesn't explain how the boy's scent could simply stop. Even if he'd been carried off, he would've left a trail. Also, Brooke didn't see anyone grab the boy. Certainly, if a rough-looking woodland hermit ran out of the trees to grab a seven-year-old, the kid would have started screaming. The guy could've chloroformed him and stuffed him in a bag, maybe that would block his scent—but Brooke would've caught up to him in the timeframe described.

Physically, it doesn't make sense. Logically, it doesn't make sense.

Dammit. Am I allowing my weird life to cloud my thinking by giving serious consideration to a supernatural explanation here when the probable truth is far more mundane? Maybe there's a mentally unstable guy out there who lured the kid away from his home. Could be, he had no malicious intent, but an accident happened. Unlikely. About as unlikely as a ghost helping me find a missing boy.

Damn.

I arrive home a little after four in the morning and park the Momvan in the driveway next to Danny's old Beemer. That car looks much nicer than its age. He got it on the cheap, fixed it up, and now looks like he's worth a lot more than he is. Something about appearances, he said. A lawyer who looks successful becomes successful. No one trusts a litigator getting out of a beat up Honda Civic.

The kids are sound asleep in their beds.

For a little while, I drape myself over Tammy's bed, kiss the top of her head and whisper apologies for being away so much today and the previous day. She doesn't react, but even lightly hugging her while she sleeps makes me feel better. After spending some time cuddling Anthony the same way—he babbles in his sleep in response to me apologizing —I slip into my bedroom.

Danny's curled up on his side with his back to the mattress. Sure, he's giving me three-quarters of the bed, but it still feels like he's calling me names, insinuating he shares his bed with a feral creature that could shred him on a whim. I gaze down at my pointy fingernails. Perhaps I *am* capable in a purely physical sense of doing something like that, but me wanting to hurt Danny is about as likely as me sprouting wings.

In another lifetime, I might have crawled into bed naked, woke him up early, and tried to get cute. Now? I just flop face-down after taking only my shoes off. There probably is enough time for a shower, but between Danny's rejection and my heartsick feelings about Braxton, it's a miracle I had the motivation to even walk far enough across the bedroom to fall on the bed instead of the floor.

I *hate* being so powerless to do anything about this. What am I missing here?

My mind fills with an imagined scenario of being Brooke standing at her sink, watching a small boy play in the yard, then suddenly up and run off into the woods. She described him as reacting to something he saw. She thought he had been chasing a rabbit. I picture him making an 'ooh!' face and running the same eager way Tammy does if she sees a puppy or kitten somewhere.

That's not the reaction a boy would have to a man who's been living in the wild.

And speaking of living in the wild, where did he get all those canned goods, Doritos, and wholesale boxes? Does this guy walk all the way into town to go shopping? Maybe that's my next move. I'll canvass the downtown area and start asking around if anyone knows this guy. Someone who looks like they live alone in the woods making regular trips into town would surely stick out and get folks talking—especially given how badly in need of a bath he smells.

My heart wants so badly for Braxton to be okay, but my brain's standing there with its arms folded, tapping its foot, and shaking its head. Yeah, I know my brain doesn't have a head. Leave me alone. I'm seeing them as little cartoon characters to distract myself from breaking down into sobs over what's really happened. No seven-year-old lasts twenty days alone in the woods. If he'd wandered back to civilization or been found by hikers, someone would've figured out where he belongs by now. The boy's not mute.

Heartbroken, frustrated, and just plain sick and tired, I close my eyes and wait for sunrise. It'll be a while yet, but at least it will knock me senseless when it comes up. If there's anything good about what happened to me, it's that sleepless nights full of worry are a thing of the past. No matter how emotionally twisted up I am, the instant that sun peeks over the horizon, it's night-night time.

Or should I say 'day-day' time now? Nah, that sounds stupid.

My door creaks. At first, I don't really pay much attention to it. Being at the Olsens' house has somewhat desensitized me to random noises. That place is legit haunted and not in a small way. However, our house isn't.

The sense that I'm being stared at needles at me until I open my eyes—and find Anthony standing beside the bed in his pajamas, his face inches from mine, staring at me.

Gah!

I jump hard in a flailing fit then scramble around to sit, clutching the edge of the mattress, gasping. Danny falls to the floor with a *thump* from me jostling the bed. All I can do is stare at my son. What is it about small children sneaking up on sleeping parents that's so damn creepy? Wait… it's more than that. The look on the boy's face *is* absolutely wrong. Anthony's not wearing the expression of a two-year-old who had a bad dream or even woke up having to potty. That's definitely a glower of irritation.

You know that movie where the poor kid gets hit by a truck and comes back from the dead? Yeah… *that* kid is staring at me right now. What the hell?

"A-Anthony?" I whisper. "What's wrong?"

He climbs up onto the bed, standing on the mattress, eye-level with me. After a few seconds of staring, he speaks in a polyphonic voice part little boy, part whisper of an adult woman. "Saman-tha…"

I'm about to scold him for calling me by name, but… that voice.

"Anthony?"

"Not right now," says my son, shaking his head.

"Lily?" I reach toward Anthony, but catch myself hesitating, afraid to touch him. Wait, a second. That's my son, dammit. Nothing is going to stop me from—

"Braxton," says Not-Anthony.

I blink, confused, certain it was a female voice

coming through my son. "Wait. You're... Braxton?"

My son shakes his head. "No. But the boy is alive. He will return as soon as you find my killer."

This is too damn freaky. For a moment, we stare at each other, the room silent except for Danny snoring from the floor. "Lily."

He nods.

"Who killed you?"

Anthony turns to the side, tossing his head like a woman with long hair. "You already know." He peers back at me, his annoyed expression fading to one of pity. "Shame about your son. That's far too young to die."

Growling, I jump to my feet, scooping Anthony into my arms and yelling, "Leave him alone!"

My boy blinks in confusion. All traces of unnatural adulthood melt out of him. "Mommy?"

"Anthony," I mutter, shaking with worry that this ghost just threatened my son's life. I cling to him, trying not to cry in front of him.

He hugs me back, yawns, and rests his head on my shoulder, already on the way back to sleep.

"What are you doing?" barks Danny.

I glance left. He's started to pick himself up off the floor, paused grasping the top of the mattress and glaring at me as though he caught me seconds before I could do something ghastly. Oh, no way. The warning scowl I fire back at my husband slaps the attitude right out of him; he goes from ready to jump on me and tear Anthony out of my arms to pale and wide-eyed—probably how I'd have looked facing down that mountain lion if I'd been normal. Except I'd stared down a freakin' mountain lion and won. Danny's not going to intimidate me.

"Something woke Ant up in the middle of the night and he needed comforting."

Anthony lifts his head, looks at Danny, looks at me, then gets fidgety and starts crying. I bounce him and whisper comforting things, but it's pretty obvious he knows Mommy and Daddy are having some issues. At the sight of Anthony becoming upset, my husband swallows hard and stands, walking around the bed to stand beside us and doing a fairly good impression of his old self.

That seems to calm the boy.

"What do you mean 'something'?" whispers Danny.

"Later." I bounce Anthony in my arm as if to say 'not in front of him.'

Danny nods.

A few minutes later, after we've gotten the boy back to sleep and in his bed, we retreat to our room and I explain what happened.

"You're serious?" Danny rests his hands on his hips looking at me much the way I'd have looked at anyone who claimed a ghost possessed their kid back before my life went off the rails.

I gesture at the perhaps 120 figurines all over our room. "Are you going to stand there and give me that after what happened to me, after you've been dabbling with voodoo or whatever these things are? You're trying to find a 'fix' for *this*"—I pantomime fangs with my fingers—"but a ghost is somehow too much of a stretch for you to believe?"

He turns away, raking a hand up over his hair. For a few seconds, he mutters to himself, shaking his head, then lets his arm fall and looks at me again. "No. You're right. I'm just... angry that it happened to Anthony. I don't like having my son's life threatened by something I can't do anything about."

At hearing him say 'my' son instead of 'our' son, I narrow my eyes. However, for the kids' sake, I bite back my annoyance. Going down that argument path feels like a short trip to divorce court, especially when he's in one of his moods like this. He's pissed, but not really at me. Can't say I like seeing this darker, douchebag side of my husband that's come out over the past few months, but at least his anger is based on a threat to Anthony's life.

"We can do something about it. I just need to figure out who killed that woman." I blink. "Son of a bitch."

"What?" He quirks an eyebrow.

"The tone. Her tone... Braxton *was* kidnapped, but not by a person. Lily Peyton took him."

He blinks. "The dead woman kidnapped the little boy?"

"Yeah."

"Do you realize how crazy that sounds, Sam?"

"I'm a vampire."

He scratches his head. "Yeah, so?"

"Do you realize how crazy *that* sounds?"

Danny smirks. "Touché. But still. A ghost? How the frig can a ghost do anything except move objects around a house, if that?"

"I dunno. This is all new to me too."

He rushes closer, grasping me by the arms. "Sam. You've gotta figure this out before she hurts Ant."

"Yeah." I nod. "Trust me, there's nothing I wouldn't do to protect *our* children. Nothing. Annihilate myself, kill anyone threatening them, even find a way to destroy a ghost. Our kids are off limits."

My words are only partially meant as a warning to Danny. Mostly, I'm directing that inward at the thing in my head. When it tempted me with how 'yummy' my daughter's blood smelled, I made it clear in no uncertain terms what would happen if my kids ended up hurt: my butt straight into the sun. Death to me... and whatever was inside me. Amazingly, I think it understood.

Danny steps back, pale and small. It's probably the moonlight, but at the moment, he looks like someone with late stage cancer and little desire to keep fighting. "What happened to our life, Sam?"

He called me Sam. And said 'our life.' Wow. I try not to get emotional when I answer. "We're still trying to figure that out. Look, Danny... I realize this is way beyond anything you ever imagined possible. It's obvious that you're afraid of me, worrying how long it'll be before I lose control.

But, I swear to you. I got this. Somehow, some way, I am beating this. I'll never hurt you or the kids, or anyone I love. And on that note, I'll never hurt another human being. We have a good system in place with Jaroslaw. I don't know who or what is inside me, or why. But they picked the wrong woman. The wrong mama."

"Heh." He cups my cheek in his hand, but can't quite hide the tightening of his jaw at how cold I am. "That's for damn sure. So what are we going to do now?"

Wow. Human contact. His hand is so damn warm. God, how I craved his touch. I'm sure there are tears in my eyes. "Make it work as much as we can? Even if things are a little weird between us, Tammy and Anthony deserve as normal and stable a life as we can give them. Whatever you've come to believe about me, know that I could never harm you or the kids... or anyone."

"You said you'd do anything to protect them. Does that include keeping your distance if you ever start to doubt that you can control yourself?"

His words cut me like a silver knife. At least he didn't twist the blade by sounding like he *wanted* me to go away. I may be many things, but a hypocrite is not one of them. "If ever I have the slightest bit of doubt in that regard, yes. I'll go far enough away that they'll be safe."

"You sound pretty confident that you can control it."

I stare into his eyes. "That's because I am."

Seconds pass.

He flinches first. "Okay. Look, I'm sorry for being a little funny lately. Just… some of the things that I've been reading are freaky. No idea how much of it is true, but your kind are beyond scary."

"Really?"

"Yeah. But, honestly, those stories are talking about ones who've been around for centuries. Their humanity fell away and they became something else. Something truly horrifying."

"Assuming the stories are true. I'm guessing you didn't find this stuff at the public library or on Yahoo."

He chuckles. "Not exactly. Hard to say what's true and what isn't anymore. What's myth, what's reality. I mean, my wife now has fangs."

"Ugh. Don't remind me. I'm trying to pretend they aren't real."

Hearing that appears to relax him. "Well, if you think you can hold off on going insane until the kids are elderly, I'll try to keep it together for their sake."

"Deal. And I'm not planning on going insane at all."

"Say that again in 250 years."

I roll my eyes. "As if…" Seconds later, it hits me that's not impossible and my jaw hangs open.

"Yeah, you're probably *going* to be around that long, or longer." He sighs, then ends up laughing. "That's so ridiculous I can't even process it."

I grin. "Right. So, whatever we are now: husband and wife, roommates, friends, co-parents... we keep things sane for the kids."

He offers a handshake.

Gee. I guess it's not 'husband and wife' then. Still, whatever. For the kids. I accept.

We return to bed. He's not cowering all the way to one side anymore, but intimacy is gone.

No time to worry about that now, though. A damned ghost just threatened my son.

Chapter Twenty-Four
Sign

Waking up before sunset is a bit like playing a puzzle game.

Despite my repose being dreamless, it's not without fitfulness. My body reacts to things going on in the environment around me like alarm clocks, voices, motion, or touch. Even my desire to wake as early as possible can puncture the veil of sleep a little. The puzzle thing comes into play once I become aware of my consciousness floating around in a void. Comparable to mentally hopping from stone to stone across a rushing stream, it requires navigating a treacherous, slippery path from 'the other side.'

If I slip, I lapse back into unconsciousness and have to try again minutes or hours later.

This afternoon, my angst over Anthony and Braxton pokes a hole in the black curtain across my mind earlier than the alarm clock. A brief not-quite-dream goes by of me crossing a river, stepping barefoot on slick stones, a visual metaphor for my desire to drag myself out of vampiric rest. The instant my toes plunge into the dry sand on the far bank, my eyes open.

Murmuring male voices drift down the hall from the front of the house, one being Danny, the other deeper, with a thick Romanian—I'm guessing—accent. Sounds like the same guy who hung up on me the other day. He's incredibly difficult to understand with Barney on in the background, but I get the feeling they're attempting to find some way to protect Anthony from a ghostly attack. Or should I say *another* ghostly attack?

It's Saturday, so my husband is probably going to be home all day unless he runs off somewhere with this dude, chasing the occult. I have bigger problems at the moment, like Lily threatening my son. That, and finding Braxton.

A shower plus a change of clothes later, I'm covered in an epic amount of sunblock and make my way down the hall, pausing in the front room to take in the scene. To my right past the couch, Tammy and Anthony are both engrossed in the television. On the left, Danny sits at the dining room table with a man who appears in his later forties, still wearing a dark wool coat inside. Short but thick semi-curly brown hair atop his head is the same color as the two-foot beard hanging from his face. An array of small bottles and books are arranged in an arc in front of the stranger, reminding me of Dolores and her Tarot cards.

Danny and his guest pause in their conversation to look at me. The moment I make eye contact with the guy, I get a weird feeling in the pit of my stomach. He doesn't *scare* me per se as much as he gives off a real sense of the supernatural. Kinda like Indigo Murillo, something tells me this guy knows I'm more than a garden variety suburban housewife. Wait, I'm technically more than a housewife now. I'm a private eye... and a waitress, too, I suppose. Then again, I only work part time at Earl's. Luckily, Jose the owner was willing to work around my PI schedule this week. Honestly, for eighteen-ish hours a week, if he fires me, I'm not losing much, anyway. In fact, if he fires me for being unavailable too often, it would mean my PI business is eating up all my time—which is a good thing.

Anyway, the man at the table looks at me in such a strange way it leaves me standing there bewildered. It's almost as if he's *worshipful* toward me to the point he'd think nothing of pulling out a knife and killing someone if I made the slightest gesture of discontent in their direction. He says something in a language I can't identify. The presence lurking deep in my mind reacts to his words with amusement and a haughty laugh, but the meaning of what he said eludes me.

Surprisingly, Danny gives me a reasonably warm nod of 'good morning.'

"Who's this?" I ask.

"Mr. Ionescu. A client."

"Please. Call me Marius." The man bows his head at me.

A client. Right. With potion bottles and tiny books straight from Ye Olde Magick Shoppe on the table. Or, maybe Danny means *he's* Marius' client. Whatever. Not worth calling him out directly.

"Well, you two have fun. I need to head back to the Olsens' place today."

Ever since we moved into this place, having a detached garage has annoyed me. Right now, it makes me irrationally angry to the point of wanting to hunt down the contractor who built the house and throw him off the Golden Gate.

Grumbling under my breath, I storm into the garage, whip open the little black mini-fridge, and grab the nearest baggie of blood. Like something out of a twisted beer commercial, I toss it back while standing in the open refrigerator door. It's not the fridge's fault I'm a monster, but it has the misfortune of being near me, so I kick the door shut. Not hard enough to damage anything, but the whole fridge does slide back a little.

For a moment, I stand there in silence, with the only sound reaching my awareness being the inane singing of a purple dinosaur coming from the house.

Dammit.

An intense, overwhelming feeling of being an unwanted stranger in my own home comes over me. I'm such a failure. Couldn't cut it at HUD. Not cutting anything as a private investigator. Barely cutting it as a wife and mother. Danny's income has been on a downturn. My family is going to collapse around me at any moment, and here I am standing in my goddamned garage drinking blood.

I stare at the empty baggie dangling from my fingertips, thoroughly unable to understand how my life has gone so crazy. Maybe the kids really would be better off without Monster Mom around. They're so little, if I died that night while jogging, they wouldn't even really remember what having a mother felt like. Their lives would eventually return to normal. Danny would probably re-marry. He's not a bad looking man, and up until his mind shattered when he started considering me 'dead,' I'd have called him kind and loving.

Would it have broken him the same way to simply lose me from a random attack at night? How much of his current mental state is due to the unbelievable circumstance of vampires being real. For a man who completely rejected his parents' views on religion—and anything lacking a hard scientific explanation—he's leapt headfirst into this weird shit. Now, he seems to believe in everything.

And what if he really did leave me? There's no way for me to support a house and family. It'd be a chore to do with an ordinary job. Even the salary HUD once paid me wouldn't really handle the house and kids alone. What do monsters like me do? Live in scary, remote castles and prowl villages at night preying on the unwary. How on earth did folkloric vampires afford their mortgages?

I'm such a failure, I can't even be a proper vampire. Who ever heard of a poor bloodsucker? They're always upper class, wealthy, elite. And why the hell am I so convinced Danny is going to leave? His focus on making me human again is well past obsession into something else. When he realizes it's pointless, how much worse is he going to crack?

I really should've died that night in Hillcrest Park. It would've been so much easier for everyone involved.

When this case is over, maybe I'll walk off into the sunset and just keep going. Better I get it over with now when Tammy and Anthony are so small. I can't remember anything from that age. My earliest memories are from like six or seven. Disappearing now will do more to protect my children than anything I could do in person. They deserve normal. Without me to worry about, Danny could go back to getting clients and earning enough to keep the house and support them.

I don't belong here anymore.

He's right. I'm not Samantha Moon anymore. Not the real Sam Moon.

The idea of never seeing my kids again plunges me into a pit of grief so deep I can't even cry. All I can do is stand there staring into nowhere until finally, the bag slips out of my fingers and drifts to the floor. Not even a bit of trash wants to be around me. It's bright out today. A shower to get rid of the sunblock, a bikini, our backyard… that would solve everyone's problems.

Well, except maybe the Olsens' problems. Bah. Ken's right. I'm a waste of money.

A faint creak comes from behind, the small door on the side of the garage.

Maybe my memory wipe on Indigo Murillo failed, and she's sneaking up behind me with a silver dagger.

I hold completely still, head bowed. Go on. Do it. Get it over with.

A tiny bare foot with pink-painted toenails steps into view. Small arms encircle my waist.

"Don't be sad, Mommy," says Tammy, peering up at me, her hazel eyes as wide as can be. "Barney's over. You can come back inside now."

I sink to kneel and cling to her.

Maybe there really is someone up there watching us. I'm not even sure where this overwhelming sense of being a failure came from in the first place, but my daughter showing up out of nowhere, looking for me. If that's not a sign, I don't know what is.

"Okay, Tam Tam." I stand, picking her up. "Let's go back inside."

Chapter Twenty-Five
Dead Set

Since I'm now sure that Lily Peyton is respon-sible for Braxton's disappearance, I afford myself some much-needed sanity time with my kids, and sprawl on the rug with them for about an hour. As soon as I start explaining to them why I need to leave the house—to help a scared little boy—my cell phone rings.

It's Chad.

"Got some information for you, but I'm not sure how useful it is."

I lean back against the sofa with Anthony crawling all over me. "It's more than I've got. Let's hear it."

"According to the police report, Lily Peyton's body was found fully dressed at the bottom of the stairs. Cause of death is listed as an internal decap-itation due to a broken cervical vertebra. The ME's report describes some finger bruising on her throat, but it's not pronounced enough to indicate attempted strangulation. The rest of the bruises on her appeared to match a hard fall down stairs. No other marks on her body or defensive wounds. She didn't have anyone else's DNA under her fingernails. Also, there's no sign of a break-in. The woman had been single, no relatives. Didn't look like the cops found anything to explain any motive. I'm getting the feeling they figured they would never solve the case and wrote it off."

I sigh. "No wonder she's pissed."

"Who?"

"You're going to think I'm crazy, but there's a chance that woman's haunting the place."

Chad's quiet for a moment. "Sam, have you considered talking to a professional?"

I grin. "Are you teasing me or being serious?"

"Ehh, somewhere in between. Ghosts? Seriously?"

"Come out to the property with me if you're curious. Bet you'll not be a skeptic when you leave."

He laughs. "Sounds fun, but I'm a bit busy dealing with the new guy. Boy's so damn green he still smells like the plastic wrap Quantico shipped him in."

I chuckle, though it's tinged with sorrow and possessiveness. Despite knowing I have no right to feel this way, it makes me angry to think someone else is sitting at *my* desk. "Sounds like you have your work cut out for you. And... I'm sorry for leaving."

"I understand. You are clearly having some medical issues. Gotta do what you gotta do, right?"

Yeah. I have to do what I have to do... just like Lily. If a damn ghost can keep on fighting after death, so can I. "Something like that. So, the cops had no suspects at all?"

"Not that they wrote down anywhere, no."

"Okay. Thanks for looking into that. So who's the new guy?"

"Dominic Ferraro. Has a rulebook surgically implanted in his posterior region." He spends a few minutes telling me how nervous the poor guy was on their first property inspection. Chad feels all kinds of strange at having enough seniority now to mentor the new guy.

I chuckle, but stop myself from reminiscing too much about my first few months as a federal agent. Too soon. It will only make me maudlin. "Hopefully he mellows out like I did."

"When, exactly, did that happen?"

"Oh, very funny." I sigh. Despite his teasing, it does cheer me up a bit.

He peppers me with a few questions about how I'm doing, hinting that he could loan me money if needed.

"Thanks. I appreciate that. Things aren't quite that desperate yet, but I'll keep the offer in mind."

"You do that. Take care, Sunshine. I mean it. PI work can be risky sometimes."

I smirk. Barring another Indigo-with-a-silver-knife situation, there isn't much out there that scares me. "Will do. A little more income would be nice, but I'm dealing."

"But there *is* money in it. If you're half the investigator you were here, you'll be okay."

"You're too kind."

"I mean it, Sweet Cheeks. You'll do okay."

"Sweet Cheeks?"

"I miss that face of yours."

"Aww. I miss you, too."

We hang up.

Before my brain can start dwelling on the job I loved so much and had to give up, the need to protect Anthony and find Braxton drags me to my feet. Danny and I get into a brief not-quite-argument about how much money I'm spending on gas, but he relents when he sees the check from Ken Olsen. This leads to another argument about why it isn't in our bank account yet. The 'you gotta be kidding me' look he gives me upon hearing how it would bother me to cash it if we found the boy dead tells me that this man is no longer the same Danny I married.

Maybe I'm being too sentimental. People with terminally ill children still owe tons of money after the worst day of their lives occurs. Though, maybe that's a bad comparison. Making money off people suffering is evil no matter if it's me doing it or giant insurance companies.

Can't dwell on that now.

I hug the kids and head out to the Momvan for the long drive ahead.

Maybe someday I'll be successful enough not to take clients who live so darn far away.

***

Once again, I arrive at the Olsen house a bit after six at night. Traffic was annoying but not *too* bad on a Saturday.

Brooke answers the doorbell. "Oh, Sam. I thought it might be the police again. Come in, please. Ken got called to the hospital on an emergency." She leads me to the kitchen where an Ouija board is set up. The fragrance of a micro-waved chicken-and-rice dinner hangs in the air. "I've been trying to ask Lily to help, but it's not working."

"About that... I think I might've figured out what's going on, but it defies rational explanation."

"If it brings my son home, I'll believe anything."

"It's not really a matter of belief. My conclusions are either right or wrong. So... I think that Lily might have taken Brax."

"What?" She stares at me. "But she's like... part of the family. Braxton talks to her sometimes."

I snap my fingers. That's right, the neighbor, Terry, said he saw the boy talking to no one. "Aha!"

"What, Sam?"

"Your son didn't run off into the woods chasing

a rabbit. I'm pretty sure he saw Lily calling him. That's why he didn't yell or anything. He thought he was going with a friend."

"But..." Brooke looks around at the kitchen, worry fading to fear. "Is she dangerous?"

"I'm not sure one way or the other about that." My suspicions say yes since the ghost threatened my son, but I'm not going to make Brooke panic. "It's anyone's guess what happens to the mind after death... and becoming a ghost. What I do know is this: she was murdered in this very house and she's angry that the killer got away with it. After eight years, her frustration at being ignored built up to the point she did whatever she could to be noticed."

"Sam, I feel for her. But I need to know... did she hurt Braxton or not?"

"At this point, I don't think so. She's... put him somewhere." I sit and tell her about what happened with Anthony last night—except for the threat. "She wants me to find her killer and then she'll bring Braxton home."

"You're right. That does sound insane." She exhales, walks over to the kitchen sink. "But, it does kinda make sense. What do we do now?"

"Good question."

"This is too much to think about without more coffee. Want some?"

"I wish. Can't have it anymore for medical reasons."

"Oh, that stinks." She opens the cabinet door. "Oh, seriously? That man. You'd think a doctor would know better."

"What?"

"A whole bag of cookies disappeared. Again. Geez. What's gotten into him lately?"

I twist around in the chair to glance at her. "A bag of cookies?"

"Yes."

"Chips Ahoy?"

"Wow." Brooke whistles. "You're good. Yeah. Braxton adores them. But I guess my husband does too these days. Maybe the cookies remind him of our son or something."

Oh, crap. "Umm, Brooke?"

She runs water into the carafe. "Yeah?"

"Has anything else gone missing from your pantry? Do you and your husband shop at one of those bulk grocery stores? Like a Costco or something?"

"Yeah, we get some things at a wholesale outlet. Did you ask if anything else was missing?"

"Yes."

Umm. Hold on a sec." She sets the carafe down and goes into a giant walk-in pantry closet. "I can't put my finger on anything specific, but it does kinda feel like we're going through canned stuff way too fast. Oh, dammit. I thought we had cereal."

"A giant box of Fruit Loops and strawberry Special K?" I offer.

Brooke emerges from the closet and stares at me. "Are you a PI or a psychic?"

"It's complicated. But, no. The food you're

missing is walking out into the woods and ending up in a little bunker under that cabin."

She gasps, leaning back against the kitchen counter, her face as pale as mine. "Someone's breaking into our house? Oh, God. I think that's been happening for years. It always feels like there's less in the pantry than should be there."

"That explains how the guy's surviving out there. He's probably breaking into every house in this area, stealing food, maybe clothes, who knows what else."

"So damn scary. Holy crap." She paces, muttering about demanding her husband buy cameras to monitor the property. "He could've done anything to us."

"Considering he's probably been at it for years, it's probable that he avoids contact with people. He most likely waits for the house to be empty, and breaks in when you're both at work. You're still working, right?"

She nods. "Yeah. Nurse. Been on an extended leave of absence."

"Doctor and a nurse, huh?" I wink.

"Aww, not like that. We met at a conference. I used to live in Tennessee. We actually don't even work in the same hospital. Why do you ask?"

"Just curious. Guess I'm a romantic at heart. Anyway, yeah. The guy's unlikely to enter the house while you're here. He doesn't want to risk being seen or caught. And a security camera would do wonders."

"Gah. It's why we moved up here... to get away from the bullshit." She runs her fingers through her hair. Bet she doesn't have to worry about inadvertently clawing her scalp. "Still, it's terrifying to think that someone's walking right into our house whenever he wants. How is he even getting in?"

"It's not all that difficult to pick locks. But whatever this guy's doing, it's unrelated to your son."

A heavy *thud* hits the ceiling.

We both look up.

"Sounds like someone disagrees." Brooke gazes around for a few seconds. "Lily, are you saying that man in the woods *does* have something to do with Braxton?"

The carafe flies off the counter. Instinctively, I leap out of the chair in an attempt to catch it, and manage to get my hands on it before it shatters on the tiles. The maneuver leaves me flat on the floor, both arms stretched out in front of me holding the water-filled glass pot.

Brooke yelps, then stares at me in awe. "Holy shit. I've never seen anyone move that fast."

I roll around to sit and hand her the carafe. "Having two kids is exponentially crazier than one. Usually, I only dive like that to catch a falling baby."

She emits a nervous chuckle. "Well, I think Lily's mad. She doesn't usually break things."

"Probably wants me to get moving and find her killer." I jump to my feet. "She said I know who it is, but… Crap."

"What?" Brooke backs up against the sink, staring at the archway out of the kitchen with a fearful expression. "Crap what?"

"That has to mean I've seen the person who killed her but just don't realize they're the one who did it."

My thoughts drift to Terry Waters, the neighbor. He admitted to being in that house his entire life and knowing Lily. This little spur of a street only has two houses on it with lots of woods around to block view. If he'd been on friendly terms with her, she might've invited him in, explaining the lack of evidence indicating forced entry. Heck, he might not have even meant to kill her. Lonely single guy, single woman across the street. What if he made a move and she wasn't interested? Could've started an argument that ended with her falling or being pushed down the stairs. He panics, leaves, maybe calls the police himself a day or two later to say he hasn't seen her around.

Dammit. I need to call Chad again and ask him if the police report mentions how they came to find the woman dead in the first place. Who reported it? The guy seemed friendly and honest, and even with my mental abilities, didn't give me a feeling of guilt. Then again, I have been trying to forget such abilities exist. But if he's a true sociopath, he wouldn't feel any guilt about what happened, and so I might have missed something.

"I've got a lead."

"You do? Where'd that come from? More psychic stuff?" Brooke bites her lip.

"No. Just thinking. Have you met the guy across the street? Terry?"

"A couple times. Seems like a nice man. What? You think he killed Lily?"

"It's a possibility I need to look into."

"Mom!" shouts a child outside. "Where are you?"

Brooke and I lock stares. That boy sounds like he's *right* in the backyard, not way off in the woods.

She bolts for the door, and I run after her.

Chapter Twenty-Six
Fleeting

We burst out onto the deck to find the yard empty.

Brooke runs to the end, grabs the railing and shouts, "Braxton!"

Her voice echoes back from the trees.

"Mom?" replies a distant child's voice, once again sounding miles away.

"Oh my God. What's happening?" whispers Brooke, visibly shaking. "Lily, please let him come home. I swear we'll find whoever killed you. Just please let me have my son back."

Hearing her voice crack in grief is almost enough to send me racing home to hold my kids. "Come on, Lily. The boy's got nothing to do with this. Neither does Anthony. You want help, fine. I'm here to help. Leave them out of it."

A scrap of white catches my eye, so bright it's

almost glowing. The smear of light darts out from behind a tree and races up the hill away from the house.

"I see something," I whisper, then sprint off the deck, cross the yard in six strides, and leap the retaining wall, chasing the too-fast-to-be-human blur of white into the forest. Fortunately, I'm also too fast to be human—but this thing is still getting away from me.

I feel like a fighter pilot trying to tail a UFO.

Brooke follows, crashing and scuffing behind me. I don't look back, too focused on whatever it is leading me along. It keeps calling for 'Mom' in a child's voice, but never gets closer or reacts when Brooke shouts 'I'm here' or 'where are you' or 'please stop running.'

The scrap of light weaves around the trees, gliding without a sound up the hill. Sadly, the glowing streak doesn't have the decency to follow the many trails out here; instead, it zips over brush and root and even *through* the tree trunks themselves. I spend more time jumping or climbing than running, at a pace that would exhaust a living person in mere minutes. Even straight up leaping to clear eight-foot-tall hills and dashing over flat spots fails to get me any closer to the floating apparition.

Glimpses of it are so brief, I can't tell what exactly I'm trying to catch. My brain fills in nonsense like a girl in a nightgown, or a spirit, or even a faerie. It's probably just a blob of ecto-plasm... which in and of itself is damn weird.

So says the vampire.

After several minutes of hard climbing and running, I no longer hear Brooke struggling to keep up with me. Not long after I realize she's fallen far behind, the light source disappears. I keep going toward where it last manifested, until a small boy's cry of 'Mom' pulls me to the right.

The sound of a child's weeping leads me forward for a little while more, until it occurs to me that I'm heading toward the cabin again.

Okay, Lily. Message received. Good chance I'm not actually hearing Braxton, but that ghost mimicking him.

I slow to a more cautious stride since the area around me is familiar, and continue up the hill toward the oval clearing around the hermit's cabin.

No lights are on inside, but if the dude who lives here is home, he'd likely be underground.

As quiet as I can make myself be, I cross the clearing to the little shack and pull the door open. The interior looks the same as before; nothing significant enough for me to notice has changed other than the smell of chocolate chip cookies this time. My alarm sense is quiet. Pretty unlikely that a recluse is going to have a silver knife on him anyway. Plus, if this dude's MO is to avoid contact at all costs, he'll probably run away from me. Hence, the sense of safety.

But why would Lily lead me straight back here?

Is she trying to give us Braxton?

I pull the trapdoor open, pushing it—and the

folding cot—up against the wall before climbing down to the bunker, not particularly concerned if the guy is here. The newish-looking groceries on the wire shelves make sense now. This guy has been 'shopping' in people's homes. The Chips Ahoy bag is open, half gone—but there's no sign that a boy had ever been here. Also, Braxton's scent still isn't down here.

"What the heck, Lily?"

Hands on my hips, I stand there looking around. Gotta be missing something. The ghost wanted me here for a reason.

My gaze settles on one of the large footlocker-style trunks. Its padlock hangs open, unlike the last time I'd been here. Hmm. Okay. For an instant, I dread finding a small body stuffed in the box, but that isn't possible. His scent would've been all over this chamber. I take a knee, pull the lock out of the hasp, and open the lid.

Numerous brass screw-hooks stick out from the underside of the lid, most with keys dangling from them. The box contains an assortment of clothing as well as stuff like a military mess kit, collapsible shovel, socks, and some jewelry. One set of keys twitches despite there being no moving air in here.

Curious, I gingerly reach out and cradle them, not quite lifting them off the hook.

Within a second of my skin touching the metal, my mind fills with an image of Brooke's house, viewed from the woods behind it.

Okay, whoa. Where did that come from?

I blink, shake my head, and paw at the layer of clothes at the top of the box, revealing several wristwatches, rings, multiple wallets, a Sony Discman, a couple Mp3 players, even earrings.

Oh, shit.

This is a box of trophies.

Terry Waters didn't kill Lily... this freakin' hermit did.

Why would I think of the house as soon as I touched those keys? Unless... oh crap. The cops didn't find any sense of forced entry because the killer *had keys!*

I grab one of the wallets and open it. Nothing remains inside with any information. No license or credit cards. Wallet two is the same way, as are the next five. The more I rummage, the more I get the hunch that these things all probably came from hikers. Dead hikers? Wow, I need to bring the two detectives in on this. None of these trophies are clearly identifiable as to who they came from. It would be a tall sell to a prosecutor just from this, but it has to be enough to at least open an investigation.

Would Lily let Braxton go home if the cops at least begin to look into her case again? It's either that or go after the guy myself. But... I'm just a PI now. I can't pounce on some dude and drag him to jail because of suspicion.

I need to get out of here before he realizes someone found his secret room. Not that I'm afraid of him personally, but spooking him might cause him to flee the area and make the case truly unsolvable. After closing the trunk, I climb out of the bunker and reposition the trapdoor to look undisturbed.

Footsteps approach outside.

Still crouched by the hatch, I perk up like a rabbit hearing a predator, listening to the rustle of boots approaching the cabin. Heavy footsteps. A man, definitely a man.

Well, crap. There's nowhere for me to go that won't end with me being seen. Maybe he'll believe me a lost hiker who happened to stumble across this shack? Depends on how thoroughly he's been watching the Olsen house.

Even if he's seen me before, there's no way he could know I'm aware of Lily, or of his stash of trophies, right?

Only one way to find out.

After all, he's about to open the front door...

Chapter Twenty-Seven
Voices in the Woods

Nope. Not quite.

The footsteps stop before reaching the door, and a soft *thump* precedes a man grunting in a way that makes me picture an older guy easing himself down to sit.

The smell of recent death fills my senses, mostly blood. I ease myself to my feet and creep up to the door, peering out the small, grimy window. A man with wild, stringy hair sits on a tree stump a short distance in front of the cabin with his back to me. Glint flashes from the edge of a ten-inch knife that he's using to skin a small furry critter. Guess man cannot live on Chips Ahoy and Lucky Charms alone.

How do I want to play this? There is a quite real chance this guy is a serial killer. It's also possible that he merely finds things people drop, but why would he keep empty wallets in that case? And the amount of watches and jewelry in that box kinda defies logic to be unlucky hikers misplacing stuff.

He's taking food out of houses, so maybe he's stealing that stuff too. What made me go straight to serial killer? Hunch? Paranormal insight? I don't know, but it's time to find out.

Okay, one innocent lost hiker coming up.

I push the door open and step outside.

The man jumps to his feet and scrambles back a few steps like a startled chihuahua. He's gotta be well past sixty. Bushy pewter-colored eyebrows go up, then down, narrowing in suspicion. Initial shock gives way to an appraising look… and my alarm sense goes off, but not too loud.

"Sorry," I say, trying to sound innocent. "I slipped on a trail and got separated from my group. Been walking around for hours trying to find the way out of here. Figured I'd wait until daytime. Didn't realize anyone lived here. I thought it was abandoned."

Seconds pass in silence, the man looking at me with an unsettling stare. Blood dribbles down the pelt of the half-decapitated rabbit hanging by its ears from his left fist. It's oddly mesmerizing. The scent of a fresh kill calls to something dark within me that I've been trying my damndest to deny.

Surprisingly, this man isn't giving off anything even remotely sexual. Never thought having a man *not* size me up for a grope would unsettle me so much, but that stare… it's 'do I kill it or talk to it?'

Joke's on him. I'm already dead.

"You don't look like no hiker," says the man, part wheeze, part croak, as if he had to summon a voice up from a long forgotten place. Probably been awhile since the guy spoke to anyone but himself.

"I'm not a hiker. Came out here with a search party looking for a missing boy. Rock shifted under my foot and threw me down a hill. Have you seen a lost child around here?"

He shakes his head. "No one belongs out here."

"And why's that?" I take two steps closer.

"These woods are sacred. You shouldn't be here. And no boy should be here either."

My alarm sense rings slightly louder. "The boy lives near the edge of the woods in a house that used to belong to a woman named Lily."

His teeth emit a creaking sound as his jaw clenches tight. The fingers clutching the knife tense and relax repetitively. It's more than a little disturbing that I can hear the noises the tendons make. He flicks his gaze to the left. "So?"

I've seen this body language before, many times. Every time Chad and I started asking a tenant about why we smelled drugs in their place they had the same guilty, twitchy presence. This guy definitely killed her. There's no way in heck I'll be able to prove it, though.

"You've been living here a long time. Did you know Lily?"

The man stares at me, shaking his head ever so slightly. The scent from the dead rabbit is intoxicating. Fresh. Not in a bottle. Not sitting around in a fridge for hours or days.

Fresh, fresh, fresh...

I shake my head, searching for calm. If I could still salivate, I'd be drooling right now.

I hate myself. That poor rabbit... I simultaneously want to comfort and savage it.

"Hungry?" asks the man, noting where my stare's gone.

"Not for rabbit," I say. I peel my gaze off the critter, and decide I'd better change the subject. "You watch people. Steal from them. A man like you sees things. Someone killed that woman a few years ago. Tell me, what did you see?"

"I keep to myself. Don't like people much. Never spoke to Miss Peyton."

"Are you sure? I don't remember mentioning her last name."

His attempt to not scowl results in an odd sort of facial tic. "People talk about it a lot. All sorts of cops around back then. Even got word out here. The trees whisper secrets."

Yeah, this guy has been alone way too long. "I've talked to people, too. One of them said a guy with long, grey hair was in the area around the time she was killed."

"Nah." He takes a slow step closer. "She didn't get killed. Fell down the stairs."

I circle as he advances, keeping us the same distance apart.

The smell of rabbit blood gnaws at me, demanding to be consumed. The critter's dead black eyes keep staring at me, pleading. "How did you know that if you didn't know Lily?"

"Like I said, people talk." He flashes a twitchy smile. "You shouldn't have come here."

"Because it's sacred? I didn't realize this is sacred ground. Not exactly any signs posted. I'll get out of your way then."

The man takes a step toward me. "Can't make you wander off now. At least wait until daybreak."

A glint of moonlight from the knife in his hand catches my eye. Again, I back up, keeping us the same distance apart.

He twitches. "Couple times, I hear a voice out there that sounds like a little kid, but ain't see nothin'. Tried goin' after it once or twice, but it keeps getting' farther away like." He relaxes, ambles past me, and rests the rabbit on a tree stump. "Mostly sounds like it's coming from over there." He raises his left arm, pointing at the northwest edge of the clearing.

I look toward that spot... and nearly let out a scream of anguished rage.

Two small jean-covered legs stick out from the undergrowth, the ankles bound by thick rope, not moving. The small figure slumps to one side, clearly no longer alive.

Oh no...

Stunned by the horrific sight, I stand there shaking from grief and fury. How the hell did I not see him there—or smell him? My inner alarm rages, but I'm too overwhelmed to notice or care.

An instant before I run to the boy's remains, the hermit pounces on me from behind, dragging his blade across my throat. The pain barely registers as more than a nagging pull at my skin. I grab his arm and shove him off before he can slice all the way to my spine. Instant lightheadedness sends me stumbling down to all fours. Air blowing *into* my throat feels too damn much like the night I lay in the park, neither dead nor alive.

Tammy's voice shouts 'Off with her head!' in my imagination.

Note to self: stop reading violent stories to my kids.

The hermit walks back and forth behind me, hesitant to approach, watching me bleed out… though I'm not losing blood as fast as a living person would be. In fact, it's not bleeding much at all. An instinct much like what yanks a hand back from a burning pot causes the blood to recoil from the air, retreating into my body.

"Damn woman, see what you did!" yells the hermit. "Made me do the purification at the shrine. This ground is sacred. Not s'posed ta do the purification here. All your fault! You're not supposed to be here."

I wheeze, trying to tell him what he can do with himself, but the knife did a number on my vocal cords. Too dizzy to stand, I sway there on my hands and knees, waiting for the artery to close. Is my brain seriously going hazy due to lack of blood flow or is this psychosomatic?

"Because of you, I'm gonna need to re-sanctify the whole grove. That's gonna take me a month. Hope you're happy."

Blood and air mix in my mouth; I swallow both and lift my head toward where Braxton's body—isn't. What the hell?

The hermit walks up behind me and grabs a fistful of my hair, pulling my head up to expose my throat. "Make peace with your spirits."

With a grunt, I ram my elbow back into his chest. He barks a grunt, then collapses on top of me as dead weight, unable to breathe. As soon as I stand, he snaps out of the daze and grabs on to me, attempting to pin my arms. Trees whirl around me in a disorienting blur as we struggle. The guy's surprisingly strong for being older, though he is more than a little on the burly side. This dude could probably give Chad pause. Still, he's only mortal. Again, he goes for my throat with the blade, but he can't keep me immobilized using only one arm.

I reach up past my head and grab his coat, yanking him forward while bending into an angry jiu-jitsu throw and hurling him as hard as I can. Screaming, the murderous hermit goes flying upside down, smashing into a tree easily twenty feet away. A loud *crack* accompanies the impact. My amplified reflexes make time appear to slow. He hangs inverted against the tree for a half-second that feels like ten before falling straight down on his head and flopping over on his chest.

Everything's still a bit hazy. My hand pressed to the slice across my neck, I stand there watching the hermit do nothing at all for at a few minutes. He's not moving. Can't tell if he's still breathing. The tree cracked, so maybe I didn't break his neck. Still, it doesn't look good for him.

"Well, crap," I croak, my wound well on the way to healing. Probably be gone in another ten minutes, or at least the skin will have closed. Cut muscles underneath might take a while more. "Dammit."

Chapter Twenty-Eight
The Perfect Weapon

Another couple of minutes later, the skin on my neck doesn't feel damaged and my voice sounds normal. Wow, maybe it's good to be me. I think.

I stare at the guy, gripped by a strange revulsion and urge to stay away from him. His head lolls to the side like a ragdoll's. I'm no doctor, but it kinda looks like his neck broke.

Never in my life has terror gripped me so hard. Not 'monster in the woods' terror. No, this is 'I'm going to jail and never seeing my family again' terror. I freakin' just killed a guy. So what if I didn't intend to. Just wanted to get him the hell off me. Except, of course, throwing a man twenty feet into a tree hard enough to shatter his spine isn't normal. How the hell would I explain that?

Wait, Sam. Calm down.

Not normal.

Exactly. No one would believe I could have even done that. Self-defense, right? Except, I'm not hurt. Shit. What am I going to do? Pacing doesn't give me any answers, though it does help burn off some excess energy. I catch a whiff of rabbit blood and the next thing I know, I've got the poor critter in both hands, sucking at the wound in its throat.

There's not much blood left in him, but by all the powers of the universe, it tastes amazing.

And yeah, I hate myself. Cute little innocent rabbit, and I want to eat them all.

Once the poor fluffy critter's dried up, he goes back on the tree stump. The spot where I thought Braxton's body had been tied to a tree is empty. No child, no blood, no trace that anything or anyone had been there. I squat low, sniffing. The boy's scent isn't even there.

Dammit, Lily. She did that. Distracted me with an image so horrifying I'd let my guard down, gave the bastard an opening. No damned wonder she looked at me like she'd found treasure. She knows what I am. Knows I'm a killer, a higher-order predator. Maybe she didn't realize how much it horrifies me being this creature, but a vampire still had to offer her a much more powerful tool of revenge than any cop.

That ghost didn't want justice... she wanted vengeance.

And a creature like me is the perfect weapon.

"Okay, think, Sam," I say, and begin to pace.

In seconds, I know what I have to do. It's

obvious.

obvious.

It's also highly illegal.

I pause, shaking my head. How effed up is it that I'm using my investigative skills to fake a crime scene? Part of me wants to just bring the cops here and tell them what happened. Obviously, 'cut my throat' would have to be explained as 'tried to cut my throat.' But my blood is on that knife. No, there are too many inconsistencies. How do I tell the truth when the truth is unbelievable and looks like a lie?

It would be too difficult to make it look like an animal attack—no I am most certainly *not* going to rip out his throat with my fangs. Suppose I could stick his knife into him, but then the cops will be looking for a killer, and why stab a guy with a broken neck? No, this needs to look like an accident somehow, but what? Hmm. The guy broke his neck... how could he possibly do that? Aha! He fell into his bunker.

It is a bit of a stretch as the hole isn't *that* deep, but the guy is older, right? And kinda beefy. Good amount of body weight behind that fall.

I head into the cabin, crouch beside the mildewed cot, and open the trapdoor to study the scene. Maybe I should've taken a few more forensics classes, but never imagined I'd be needing to stage the scene of someone's death at all, much less to cover *my* involvement. My hands shake from that thought. I killed a guy. How the hell am I ever going to tell my kids that someday? Or Danny? No.

I can't. What if he thinks I liked it? Even if I don't seem to be happy about it, he's going to wonder if the *other thing* in my head is slowly gaining control. Grr. I hate having to lie to him, but it's the only option for now.

Focus, Sam. Keep it together.

Hmm. The shaft is potentially deep enough to result in a broken neck, but it kinda defies belief that an accidental fall off this ladder could result in an injury that severe. Dammit. This is not going to work. How the heck am I going to explain the guy slumped dead against a tree with his neck snapped? Only one real option left: try to keep a straight face and claim to have found the guy dead already. No one would possibly believe I could've done that. He's so much bigger than me. Of course, I'll need to clean my blood off the knife first.

A little ringing starts up in my ears.

What the…?

The hermit rushes in the cabin door, eyes wild with rage. He's clearly not dead and probably more than a little upset with me. As soon as we make eye contact and he realizes he's not being stealthy at all, he erupts in a shouting ramble of bizarre nonsense about 'the ones who watch' and what he has to do and how awful a person I am for making him spill blood right here on the sacred place.

Yeah, umm… no.

He lunges at me while giving off this keening war cry. Between my supernatural strength and speed, I don't have too much difficulty catching his knife arm by the wrist, deflecting the attack aside. In an instant, I've got him flipped around with the offending hand chicken-winged up behind his back.

Out of reflex, I open my mouth to identify myself as a federal agent and tell him he's under arrest, but stop myself. Those words will almost certainly never leave my lips again.

Before I can even think 'dammit,' he rams his left elbow into the side of my head. He's a big guy, so it's like getting clubbed with a tree branch. The hit throws me stumbling into the rickety cabin wall. I land half-seated on an old metal desk covered in spiral notebooks, loose papers, and an old manual typewriter. Does every crazy hermit in the woods write a manifesto?

He rushes in to attack again. I grab the edge of the desk for support and rock back while kicking at his arm. My boot nails him in the wrist with a faint *snap*, launching the knife across the room. Unfortunately, his body doesn't stop going forward and crashes over me atop the desk. Papers, books, and some random trinkets fall off the side. The wall behind me wobbles like it's about to break. This dude is easily strong enough to rip down the cabin without tools.

"Desecration!" screams the guy before grabbing my throat in both hands.

It's tempting to just sit there and let him strangle me fruitlessly since I don't need to breathe, but there's just something about having a big man trying to choke me to death in a cabin straight out of a horror movie that my brain refuses to accept with calmness. Grabbing at his wrists, I struggle, gasping for breath I don't need, while stomping at him in an attempt to knock him away.

He shrieks in pain as I squeeze his likely broken right wrist. His grip weakens, allowing me to pull that hand away from my throat, but the fingers of his other hand dig into my neck, slick with blood still seeping out from the slash that hasn't quite sealed yet. Gurgling, I keep fighting, but he's big, strong, and has all the leverage at the moment since I'm sitting on a desk that's collapsing out from under me.

"The watchers take you!" roars the guy.

I snarl, putting my pointy fingernails to use on the guy's left forearm. He's so incensed with whatever pseudo-mystic crap has taken over his mind, he doesn't even notice he's bleeding as he forces me down, crushing my neck into the desk. We're too close for me to kick at him. No room to get my legs up. The guy's manic eyes widen even more. Maybe he's noticed I'm not passing out even though I probably should have by now. Still rambling about what his watchers will do to me, he rapidly searches the area for anything to use as a weapon. His knife's across the room, way out of reach unless he lets go of me.

A spark of inspiration lights up his face.

My warning bells go off as bad as they did in Indigo's cabin.

Shit!

When he grabs something on the desk behind my head, I twist and ram my knee into his side, knocking him almost off his feet. He stumbles, falling on top of me but keeping himself mostly upright by his grip on my neck. Still screaming—no longer even in English, or actual words I'm sure—he raises a thin letter opener over his head.

The instant I see it, panic explodes in my brain. *Silver.*

His face tints red from the light glowing in my eyes. An inhuman growling hiss comes out of my throat of its own accord along with my fangs extending.

Screaming, the hermit jumps back, losing his grip on my throat as well as the letter opener. Blind with terror, he bolts directly away from me, trips over something in the junk all over the floor, and spills forward head first down the shaft.

The man's terrified shrieks abruptly stop with a fleshy *smack* and the rattle of an aluminum ladder.

I lay there for a while listening to my heart racing... or trying to race. It's definitely picked up a few beats per minute. Fear recedes, as do my fangs and the glow from my eyes. Unlike Indigo, this guy had the strength to hold me down. I'd been seconds from having a silver pointy thing stuck into my heart. The reality of a near-death experience washes over me, lessening the revulsion I feel at myself for not being entirely human anymore.

Something tells me I no longer need to fake a crime scene.

In the few minutes that pass while I lay draped over the desk trying to calm down, not a single noise comes up from the bunker below. Not a groan, rustling, or even whispered prayers to whatever imaginary forest spirits this guy thinks watch him.

Finally able to gather my wits, I push up to stand and creep over to look into the hole.

Sure enough, the guy went into the floor like a dart, headfirst. His legs stick upward, one foot resting on a ladder rung, the other off to the side. Blood trails out from the corner of his mouth. Admittedly, I misjudged before, but *now* it's pretty damn obvious his neck is smashed. Hopefully, the medical examiner will see the scratches on his arm and think they came from a mountain lion. Pretty good chance of that, right?

I mean they thought a coyote tore my throat out.

One small problem—he's got my blood on his hands from trying to strangle me.

With great care not to disturb him too much, I lower myself into the bunker and take a moment to force him to smear his hand all over his slashed-up forearm, then rub the palms together. The ME will hopefully find only his blood, and possibly 'inconclusive' other DNA. The marks my nails left on him aren't anything a doctor would link to human fingernails, so I feel pretty safe there. After all, this area does have the occasional mountain lion. I was witness to that earlier.

Yeah, that's it. He probably saw a big cat

coming for him and ran, tripped, and went headfirst into the stone floor. Sure as heck, he looks like something scared the complete hell out of him. The mortician is going to have fun trying to make that face look sedate for a viewing.

I point at him. "Don't you even think about haunting me, you piece of shit. That was totally self-defense."

With nothing else left to do here, and not wanting to disturb the body or ladder, I crouch deep and jump at the hole in the ceiling. For a second, it feels like I'm legit flying as strength far in excess of human normal catapults my 107-pound self straight up high enough that I can grab the edge of the floor of the shack up top. I should be like 128, but death kinda caused me to drop a few pounds. Probably water. Or my organs have started to atrophy.

Ick. Whatever.

Pulling myself out of the hole is equally simple. Once above ground, I leave the trapdoor open. It's tempting to close it and cover up the dead guy even more, but that wouldn't work with the 'running away from a mountain lion' story. A dead guy couldn't close the trapdoor behind himself. Besides, I'm not going to tell the police anything more than I found the guy like this. As for the knife, a wipe-down with a bit of scrap cloth gets rid of my blood. Without a medium in the way (like ink or blood) my body no longer leaves fingerprints, so that's not an issue. The bloody fabric, however, has to come with me for now. Into a pocket it goes.

I head outside and survey the area, shaking my head. Shrine… yeah right. I put my hands on my hips. "Okay, now what, Lily?"

She doesn't answer.

"Lily?"

Nothing.

Chapter Twenty-Nine
Lost

Maybe she's already led the boy home. Damn. Sure hope this guy's the one who killed her and I didn't just straight up murder some crazy man. No, not murder, I tell myself over and over while walking back toward the Olsens' house. He attacked me and ran away before falling to his death. A legit accident. I'm still freaked out that I threw such a big dude like that.

The fiend who attacked me the night I ceased being a mortal had also hurled me against a tree hard enough to break my spine. So, yeah, I know the feeling. The 'like master like daughter' aspect of that is a wee bit uncomfortable to think about and gets me contemplating whether or not the one who tore my throat out intended for me to ever get back up.

No, he wanted me to get up. He wanted to turn

me, too. He was just having fun at my spine's expense, like the killer whale who toys with the seal before eating it. Maybe he'd had a bad day and took it out on me. And yet...

The moment I turned, the moment I felt the blood dribble into my mouth, had been oddly... tender. Like my attacker had a change of heart.

Or had been two different people. One who had attacked me, and the other who turned me.

Naw. That sounded ridiculous. *Two* vampires that night?

My swirling thoughts turn to the events of the past few minutes, mostly whether or not to feel guilty about that man's death. I'm not supposed to be a damn executioner, even if I didn't actually kill the guy. I didn't come out here to end his life. A weird tangent thought redirects my spiral of dread. Hematophages—those that feed on blood, of which I now fall into that category (and yes, I looked it up) —don't kill the creatures they feed from. In a purely biological sense, a vampire *isn't* a killer. Every other animal or insect in nature that feeds on blood uses stealth, takes a little blood, and goes off on its way. Instead of being too small to notice, vampires have the ability to force people to forget. The amount of blood it takes to sate me wouldn't be enough to kill a person unless I fed multiple times too soon together from the same victim.

So, no. I'm not *supposed to be* a killer.

And yes, it's quite obvious to me that vampires are *not* part of nature. Undeath isn't natural.

But then again, what *is* natural? Could it be said that by existing, I am part of the natural world? Something created vampires, and it for damn sure wasn't humans. With this and other basic thoughts circling my brain, I trudge down the hill in the general direction of Brooke's place.

A flash of white light off to my left makes me stop short, grabbing a tree to keep from slipping down a steep section. Rather than run away, the weird glow drifts straight toward me. Paranormal things like this shouldn't freak me out considering I'm technically one of them now. But, I can't help but feel the hairs on the back of my neck stand up and a strong urge to run like hell.

However, I remain still.

The glowing patch glides up to about ten feet away, then stretches out, elongating vertically into the shape of a woman in a simple white sundress. Other than mildly translucent and luminous, she looks quite close to an ordinary living person at least in terms of presence. Her skin is pallid and her eyes grey, clearly dead.

"Lily," I say, more as an acknowledgment than a question.

"Thank you," says a diaphanous voice that seems to come from much further away than where she's standing. Or hovering.

"Not exactly how I'd been hoping this would go, but you knew he'd die tonight."

A hint of a smile forms on her grey lips.

"You didn't have to threaten my son's life."

She frowns. "I didn't."

"But you said…"

Lily half turns away, gesturing at the woods. "Follow."

She drifts off in that direction, a floating life-sized chess piece, her legs not moving, no sound issuing forth from where her feet pass through the underbrush.

I tromp after her. "What about Anthony? What did you mean he's too young to die? If that wasn't a threat, what was it?"

Lily ignores me, gliding at a speed that forces me to scramble in order to keep up with her. We move mostly laterally across the mountainside, neither climbing nor descending. After a few minutes of rushing among the woods, the sniffles of a crying child break the silence up ahead. Lily disappears seconds before I spot a small figure huddled under a tree, concealed beneath low-lying branches.

"Braxton?" I call out.

The boy stops crying and looks up. He's shivering somewhat, but has a dark blue winter coat on and doesn't appear to be too frozen. Upon seeing me approach, he jumps to his feet and presses himself back against the tree, wide-eyed in fear.

"Hey, Braxton. It's okay. I'm here to help you. Your parents sent me to find you."

"W-what are you?" he asks in a wavering voice.

"I'm Samantha, but you can call me Sam." I stop a few feet away, trying not to freak him out even more. This boy does *not* look like he spent twenty-one days lost in the forest. He's not even dehydrated. It hits me that he asked 'what' I am, not who. Ashamed of myself for existing, I try to radiate non-threat. "I'm here to bring you back to your parents."

"Why do you have candles in your eyes?" Interesting. Not just anyone can see the light behind my pupils. Danny can see them, but only after looking intensely into my eyes. Must mean the kid is especially sensitive to the supernatural. No surprise there, since he's made friends with a ghost.

"It's so I can see Lily. You know Lily, right?"

He relaxes a little. "Yeah. She wanted to show me something, but I got lost and then it got dark. I tried to go home but I can't find it. I walked forever and ever and it's always the same tree I pass."

Had Lily tricked him into walking circles? Wait, no. Something stranger than simple misdirection happened here. Almost as if he'd been taken entirely out of this world. He should be starved, dehydrated, in much worse shape. Wow... she was willing to pull out all the stops to catch her killer.

"C'mon." I hold out a hand. "Your parents are very worried about you. Time to go home."

"What's the password? If my parents wanted you to find me, they'll give you the password."

Drat. It's probably evil of me to tweak a little kid with mental influence, so I don't. Instead, I smile at him, wanting him to trust me... and give him what I am sure is the truth. "They didn't give me one because you've been missing in the woods. A lot of people, including the police have been looking for you."

"Oh." He pushes off the tree and walks up to me. "Okay. You're gonna take me home?"

"I promise." I trace an X over my chest.

"Am I gonna get in trouble for being out so late?"

"No. Your parents will be way too happy that you're home safe to ground you."

Braxton takes my hand, peering up at me in confusion. "Really?"

"How long have you been wandering around lost?"

"Since this afternoon. Then it got dark."

"So, a couple hours?"

He nods.

I whistle and crouch down closer to his eye level. "Brax, Lily played a little bit of a mean trick on you. You've been gone for almost three weeks."

"What?" He gawks. "No way. Why would she do that?"

"You know how she's a ghost, right?"

He nods.

"And you know what it means when someone's a ghost."

"Yeah. It means she died. A long time ago."

I smile. I guess to a seven-year-old, eight years is a really long time ago. Relativity, right? "Yeah. Someone hurt her. And the police couldn't find the person who made her a ghost. She really wanted help, but no one paid any attention to her."

"Yeah. She talked about that. Asked me to tell my Mom and Dad about her. I did, but they didn't really believe me."

"I believe you."

"Did you find the bad person who hurt her?"

"Yes."

"Good. He was a bad man."

"Braxton... it's possible you won't see Lily again."

"Aww." He stares down. "I like her. Why not?"

He looks tired, so I pick him up and carry him. "Ghosts don't usually stick around unless something's wrong. Like for Lily, the man who hurt her didn't get in trouble for it. Now that he did, she might go wherever people go when they don't turn into ghosts. Maybe she'll stick around, too. I have no idea really."

"Oh. Okay. If that's better for her, it's okay, but I'm going to miss her." Braxton gets quiet, looking around at the woods, no doubt pitch dark to him. Maybe twenty minutes later, he asks, "Can you see at night 'cause you got candles in your eyes?"

"They help." I wink at him.

Eventually, the lights of civilization break through the trees from up ahead. I'm a bit off course to the north, so I veer left, making my way along the hillside to the Olsens' yard. It can't be *too* late yet, at a guess between ten and eleven. The voices of Brooke, Ken, and the two detectives murmur from inside. Good, at least she went home and isn't wandering around lost.

As soon as I jump down off the retaining wall, Braxton starts wriggling, so I set him on his feet. He zooms across the yard, scrambles up onto the deck, and attacks the patio door, slapping it with both hands while yelling, "Mom! Dad!" over and over.

The Olsens run into the kitchen, pulling the sliding glass door aside right as I reach the deck steps. Detectives Holt and Bartlett stop in the archway between kitchen and hall, both gawking in sheer astonishment. Bartlett whispers 'holy shit,' too low for human ears to pick up. It's impossible to watch the boy's parents scoop him up and smother him with love without choking up. Brooke, tears streaming down her face, manages to give me the most adoring smile of thanks I've ever seen. Ken's also a mess of tears, squeezing Brax so hard the kid gurgles. The way the two of them look at me feels as though I've literally resurrected their kid from the dead.

Watching absolute grief explode into elation is enough to make a vampire weep.

Chapter Thirty
Trophies

Emotions run high for a while.

I get drawn into the hugging, have both Ken *and* Brooke sob on my shoulder for a few minutes, then end up comforting the parents while the detectives delicately ask Braxton questions about what happened to him.

Not sure what they think when he says he followed a ghost into the forest and got lost. Probably credit it to a child's imagination. His impossible story frustrates them to the point they start to sound close to 'grilling' him over where he obtained food and water, but the boy continues to insist he'd only been gone for a few hours. He points at me and explains that I said the ghost did something that made three weeks feel like six hours.

Brooke cuts in at that point. "Why the hell did Lily do this to us?"

"You guys weren't listening," says Braxton, flailing his arms. "She needed help. Lily didn't do it to be mean."

"So if I understand what you're saying here…" Detective Holt makes a kind of 'knife-hand' gesture at me. "The boy was alone out there the whole time, no food or water, and yet he looks completely fine?"

"Basically." I wag my eyebrows, then nod to the side before retreating to the kitchen.

The detectives leave the boy with his parents and follow me out of small earshot.

"I found him fairly close to that cabin the search teams discovered. I suppose it's possible he could've gotten food and water there, but it's pretty unlikely."

"What makes you say that?" asks Detective Bartlett.

Oh well. Here goes nothing. I try to look a bit rattled. "Because if he'd gone inside that place, he'd probably have been attacked by this crazy old man who lived there. The first time I went out searching, I checked the cabin and found a hidden bunker underneath."

"Yes, you mentioned that." Holt nods.

"There's more to it. The guy's got a bunch of food and stuff that he's stolen from, I'm assuming, houses all around here. Brooke told me that her pantry has been suspiciously light. A bag of cookies and two huge boxes of cereal went missing recently… and they're both at the bunker. I got a theory in my head that maybe Braxton had caught the guy trying to break into the house and been taken to keep him quiet, so I went back to the cabin. The hermit was there this time, only I think he fell and broke his neck or something. Looked dead. On my way back here to call it in, I found Brax hiding under a tree."

"Broke his neck, you say?" asks Detective Holt.

"Looks like it to me. I checked for vitals, and found none."

Holt whistles, and Bartlett says, "Okay, show us what you found, if you can find your way again at night."

"I can."

"Then lead the way."

***

A touch past midnight, I emerge from the woods onto the flat clearing around the cabin. Detectives Holt and Bartlett follow, two uniformed officers behind them continue scrambling up the hillside, holding their flashlights high to check out the area. After entering the clearing, one of them spots the dead rabbit.

"Ick," says the guy.

Detective Arvin Holt starts toward the cabin. "So where is he?"

I follow, gesturing at the little building. "In there. Careful. Big hole in the floor on the right, under a folding cot."

He pats my shoulder in a 'stand outside and let us handle it' sort of way. Rising indignation stalls. I'm not an agent anymore. My days of gearing up in Kevlar and M4 carbines are past. Nodding, I take a step back.

The two uniformed officers go in first. I'd say they sweep the place for threats, but it's one room.

"Yeah, got a body down here, detective," says the younger guy, his voice hollow, as if he's talking down into a hole, which he probably is.

Holt and Bartlett go inside.

Alone, I meander around the clearing while they search the cabin, fingers crossed that the detectives accept my story of finding the guy like that and all goes smoothly. Which it should, since the truth is unbelievable. But if I have to, I'll prompt them to accept my story and close this case quickly. The presence in my head finds it amusing that 'goody-goody Sam' might do something illegal. But, covering up being a vampire isn't immoral—it's good policy.

When I get close to the hill behind the house on the left, I catch a whiff of rot. Uh oh. I know that smell. Dead human. Anyone who has ever encountered it will tell you—that is a stink that *never* leaves your memory. Even three years later, smelling it takes me right back to that day in early August when Chad and I found a couple of squatters dead inside a place during a property inspection. No one officially lived there, so the power hadn't been turned on. No power means no air conditioning. They'd been there for at least a week like that. So many damn flies. Only good thing about that day was not being responsible for the murder investigation *or* the cleanup.

I climb the hill, grasping branches and trees to pull myself up into the woods behind the house. After about a thirty-yard section of steep dirt, the ground somewhat flattens again for a bit. My nose leads me to what I'm certain is a shallow grave. Crouching, I rake my fingers over the ground, pawing at the dry dirt until a chance swipe reveals the distinct curve of a skull.

"Aww, damn."

A sudden, strong sense of being watched makes me freeze in place. The forest is so quiet that the activity inside the cabin a good ways behind me seems loud. Nothing nearby moves, but the weight of eyes settles on me. Gradually, I lift my head to look around. At least twenty glowing orbs have appeared, each hovering a foot or so off the ground.

I'm surrounded by ghosts.

They're not radiating malice or even eeriness beyond what comes with spirits in general. No, the mood in the air is one of gratitude.

"That man…" I begin, searching for something to say. "He killed... all of you?"

No words break the stillness, but I can't help but feel them responding with a collective yes.

"I'll make sure they find all of you."

The presence in the area fades, and the balls of light wink out of existence.

"My God..."

I carefully step around, working by memory of where the entities had been hovering as well as going by smell. The graves are fairly difficult to pick out from the forest visually, but once my nose confirms each spot, they become obvious as slight depressions in the ground or unusually thick patches of duff, deliberate attempts to conceal. I manage to mark eighteen graves by jamming broken sticks into the earth by the time Detective Holt calls for me.

"I'm here," I yell. "Up back behind the cabin."

Crunching from below and behind precedes a bunch of flashlights pointing up the hill. I move to the edge of the rock 'shelf,' and wave. "Up here."

The taller Holt walks into view first, followed by his female partner. He points his flashlight at my chest to avoid blinding me. "What the heck are you doing all the way up there?"

"You two need to see this." I beckon them with a wave. "Come on up."

The detectives grumble, but drag themselves up the hill.

I lead them to the exposed skull. "There are gravesites all over this area. I've found well over a dozen and I think there's still more."

Holt whistles. "How the hell did you find that? You don't even have a flashlight."

"The way the ground is slightly sunken in forms an oval the approximate size of a person. And, there's a faint odor of death." I point to the ground. "The spots where I suspect you'll find bodies, I've placed sticks as markers."

"I still wanna know how you saw all this in the dark," says Bartlett.

"Trick I learned at Quantico. Human vision is much more sensitive at night in the peripheral. Stand still in a slow turn, things can come into focus at the edge of vision when it's dark. And there's a fair bit of moonlight here."

"Damn." Bartlett pats me on the shoulder. "With eyes like that, why'd you quit the FBI?"

"I worked for HUD primarily, but the FBI borrowed us all the time. Didn't leave by choice. If I had my way, I'd still be there. But, medical crap happened."

"That's too bad. Mind if I ask what?" Detective Holt tilts his head.

"Months ago, I had a sleepless night and like a moron, went for a jog after dark to burn off energy. Got attacked and left for dead. Some kind of neurological damage made my eyes hypersensitive to light. Can't really see much of anything in broad daylight when outside except for a blinding glare. Not exactly helpful in dangerous situations."

"Oh, wow. That's funky. Sorry." Detective Bartlett shakes her head, exhaling. "Rough break. Did they ever get the person who attacked you?"

"Nope. He hit me hard and fast, then took off. Shortly before the attack, I'd been involved in a major drug bust, so the brass thought it might've been retaliation. Still an open case."

"Damn. Sorry." Detective Holt squats over the

grave, shining his flashlight on the half-exposed skull. "Hopefully, these victims can tell us a bit more about what happened—and I mean via forensics, not spirit voices."

I chuckle. "Yeah. Ran into a hiker the other day who said the man chased him off, rambling something about this clearing being sacred, some sort of ancient watcher spirt nonsense." This was, of course, not true. No such hiker exists. But I need to get this story on the record... mostly to help the detectives make sense of what they were about to uncover.

"Probably thought he had some duty to kill anyone who strayed into his domain," offers Bartlett, an observation that is shockingly on point. I wonder... did I somehow plant that seed of thought?

"Sick son of a bitch," mutters Holt.

"Go figure," says Bartlett. "They got Al Capone for tax evasion, and this guy dies to a slip and fall. The world's got a strange sense of humor."

I idly rub the front of my throat. "Yeah... it sure does."

Chapter Thirty-One
Still Here

Sunday, my plan is simple. I'm going to overdose on my kids.

Considering the Olsens are far from hurting for money and Braxton made it home safe with not even a scratch on him, I had zero guilt invoicing them for the time I spent on the case. Yeah, I fudged it a little downward compared to the time I actually spent roaming the woods, but $1,200 is still $1,200.

I am a bit clingy with Anthony, though. Over and over, Lily's words replay in my mind. What did she mean when she said 'that's far too young to die'? It struck me as a threat that she'd hurt him if I didn't find her killer, but she denied meaning that. Did she try to warn me something is going to happen to my son? Could it mean *I'm* going to do something to him? And how young is too young?

To me, too young for my kids to die is anything short of ninety. But it could mean any minute now up to... who knows. Lily died at thirty. Would she consider that 'too young' to die?

Or perhaps when she said she didn't threaten him, she meant it in the cheesy sort of 'it's not a threat, it's a promise' way. My mother always says that whenever someone accuses her of threatening them. I could drive myself crazy with worry over what might happen to Anthony. Do I dare risk paying another visit to Dolores with him along and flat out ask her if I am a threat to my son?

I can't decide if knowing the future is as much a curse as a blessing. If someone had told me about the attack that did this to me on my first day of college, and I believed them, you damn well bet the past ten years would've been spent living life to the absolute fullest, not worrying about school, career, or anything. No marriage, no kids. Can't be in anguish over losing something I never had, right? Knowing I would die at thirty-one would have rearranged so many priorities.

But, without that life, there would've been no reason for me to go jogging at night. Nor would we have lived in this neighborhood. Wouldn't knowing about a future event allow someone to alter that future?

Whether or not it's true, that idea lets me cling to hope—and cling to Anthony. He doesn't seem to mind the squishing. In an uncharacteristically *not* creepy moment, the hitchhiker in my head gives off a sense of confidence that should anything happen to Anthony, it absolutely will not be by my out-of-control hand. Or by her. Or it. Or whatever is in me.

It wants to stay inside me for some reason. How I know this, I don't know.

But know it I do. The thing within me doesn't want to jeopardize this opportunity. Yeah, that's the word I keep hearing: opportunity.

Really? Like riding along with me is so great.

Apparently, it is to her... or whoever is in me.

As much as this entity is the exact opposite of trustworthy, something about all this feels genuine.

But it doesn't erase *all* my worry. For the next few years, my picture is going to appear in the dictionary under 'hypervigilant mom.'

We get a super rare dusting of snow. In fact, I can't remember the last time it snowed here. A quarter inch of the white stuff happens here and it's like Armageddon times ten. The kids want to go play in it, even though it's barely as deep as our living room carpet. Tammy and I have a pathetic little snowball contest, since it's so powdery and doesn't want to stick. She doesn't want to have a 'fight,' so we compete to see who can make the best snowball. It's a close call, but of course, the child wins.

Danny returns home from his 'client meeting' around half-past five. Getting a lawyer to work on a weekend requires either vast sums of money or the intercession of powers beyond mortal comprehension. He probably went to see Marius again—the

Romanian mystic—or ran off to see someone else on his 'Fix Sam' quest. The pleasant smile he gives me on the way into the house fills me with unease.

It's the way you smile at someone before surprising them with a knife, though at least he's not giving off anger or malice. And my internal alarm remains silent. So, yeah. Whatever.

Anthony squeals and takes a spill in the snow, sliding on his front while screeching in glee. He proceeds to get up and do it again.

Tammy walks up to me. "Mommy, can we get a swing set?"

"I'll think about it."

She smiles. "I know you don't got lotta monies. Whens you got 'nuff monies, we can get a swing set. Don't gotta be now."

Aww. I hug her. "That's very mature of you, sweetie."

"You found the little boy. You gotta be the best pi-vate vestimator ever. Bester than everyone."

Okay, that makes me cry. "Thank you, sweetie. I'm doing the best I can."

***

That night, after the kids are asleep, I flop on the couch and stare at the blank television screen.

The fragrance of Danny's spaghetti sauce still hangs in the air. My nose will be picking that up for at least two more days. I hate not being able to have it anymore. Even chewing and spitting it out isn't the same, like my tongue lost its affection for real food. Why couldn't this cruel transformation at least let me enjoy the *taste* of food?

In the quiet stillness of a house with sleeping children, my thoughts once more return to worry about Anthony. Tammy as well, even though Lily didn't threaten her. I wish there existed some way for me to know for sure if it would be better for me to go away forever. Am I being selfish refusing to shield my children from what I've become, or is it the natural instinct of a mother to stay close to her children? My change has advantages as well as disadvantages. Like, in the unlikely event of a home invasion, whoever breaks in here is in for a *major* surprise. It's difficult to think of a more dangerous creature than a vampire mama willing to do anything to protect her children.

A weird herbal fragrance rolls over me a few seconds before Danny walks up behind the sofa carrying a steaming teacup. It's not wholly unpleasant, though it does smell mostly of water-rotted wood. Nothing anyone would ever want to drink for the flavor.

"Hey, hon." He leans on the sofa back and offers me the cup. "Made this for you."

I glance at it. "Why? You know I can't drink that."

"It might help."

"Help what?" I peer up at him.

"Cure you."

I shift my gaze to the brownish-red tea, a sachet

bobbing in the center that appears to contain crushed twigs, tiny black berries, some seeds, and ground leaves. When I look back up at him, the thoughts at the tip of his brain leap into my head. He thinks the tea will either make me not a vampire anymore—or destroy me. And the odds are about seventy percent in favor of destruction.

"Your 'client' helped you make this, didn't he?"

"Marius? Perhaps."

The steam wafting up from the cup doesn't bother me, and my alarm sense isn't ringing. "You believe this could kill me."

"You're already dead. Nothing can kill you."

I peer at his chest, possessed by a sudden shame over reading his mind that makes me unable to look him in the eye. "Is that what you think?"

Danny stares not quite into my eyes, then looks down.

An overwhelming feeling of being an abomination crashes over me, piling on top of the worry and guilt I've been feeling all day over what might happen to Anthony.

"Fine," I mutter, and gulp down the near boiling tea almost in one shot before giving him the kind of defiant stare someone might fire off before pulling the trigger when playing Russian roulette. The heat slides down into my gut, simmering.

A little guilt appears in his expression.

The simmering in my stomach twists to nausea. I sit there, fixing my husband with a cold stare that says 'you wanted to kill me, well you get to watch me die.' Nausea builds, but I keep it off my face. Danny opens and closes his mouth twice, searching for words.

When the discontent grows too much to contain, I lurch upward, projectile vomiting the tea all over him. He jumps back with a gasp of pain, though the liquid isn't hot enough to leave a burn. He stands there dripping, gawking down at himself.

I set the teacup back on the saucer he's holding. "Well, guess that didn't work."

Danny frowns. "Sam, I don't want to destroy you. I want my wife back."

"And I want my *life* back, but I don't think it's going to happen."

We stare at each other.

"I'm still me inside, Danny. The wrapper's changed a bit, but the inside's the same."

He sighs at the carpet, holds up a 'wait a sec' hand, then retreats to the kitchen. A minute later, he returns sans cup, patting himself down with a wad of paper towels. "Not exactly."

"Not exactly what?" I ask.

"You're not the same. Not entirely. Darker. There's a cruelty in your eyes that doesn't belong there. Even when you're just looking at... well, anything... you have this expression all the time like you want to hurt someone. That's not Sam."

Shame hits me again. I turn away, staring down-cast at my too-pale bare feet on the carpet. At least those nails aren't pointed. "You want to leave, don't you?"

"No. I don't want to leave."

I twitch when his startlingly warm hand rests on my shoulder.

"You don't?" I ask.

"Nope. I'm not going to give up on fighting for Sam, fighting whatever's stolen her body."

Two tears roll down my face, one from each eye. "I'm still here."

Danny stands there in silence for a while. His reflection in the blank television screen gazes at the hollow clothes occupying the reflected sofa. He frowns again at the sopping wad of paper towels, then walks off down the hall to the bedroom.

I reach up and wipe the tears from my cheek.

The bedroom door closes with a soft *click*.

My voice comes as but a whisper…

"I'm still here."

The End

Samantha Moon Origins continues in:
Sacred Moon
by J.R. Rain &
Matthew S. Cox
Coming soon!

About the Authors:

J.R. Rain is the international bestselling author of over seventy novels, including his popular Samantha Moon and Jim Knighthorse series. His books are published in five languages in twelve countries, and he has sold more than 3 million copies worldwide.

Please find him at: www.jrrain.com.

~~~~~

Originally from South Amboy NJ, **Matthew S. Cox** has been creating science fiction and fantasy worlds for most of his reasoning life. Since 1996, he has developed the "Divergent Fates" world, in which Division Zero, Virtual Immortality, The Awakened Series, The Harmony Paradox, and the Daughter of Mars series take place.

Matthew is an avid gamer, a recovered WoW addict, Gamemaster for two custom systems, and a fan of anime, British humour, and intellectual science fiction that questions the nature of reality, life, and what happens after it.

He is also fond of cats.

Please find him at www.matthewcoxbooks.com.

CPSIA information can be obtained
at www.ICGtesting.com
Printed in the USA
LVHW080138070819
626793LV00030B/501/P

9 781080 807727